NEVADA

MCPHERSON

CRACKER

BOOK 2

(e-book) ASIN: B0BXNQJVVN

(print) ISBN-13: 978-1-960882-00-4

For my dad

PRAISE FOR POSER

BOOK ONE IN THE EUCALYPTUS LANE SERIES

"*Poser* is what you would get if Quentin Tarantino ever made a *Lifetime* movie."

--Whiskey Leavins, author of *The Devil's Own Piss and Other Stories*, as well as *Murder in Greasepaint*

"A skeet taste of JAMES ELLROY and JAMES PATTERSON. Even WALTER MOSLEY bumps off these pages. NEVADA MCPHERSON is a new voice of choice (in mah book) that needs 2 B heard word for word, ya digg??"

---Duvay Knox, author of *The Pussy Detective*

"The writing is superb, the characters are engaging, and the interconnected stories are unpredictable. I'm looking forward to more from McPherson. Highly recommended!"

--Brian Bowyer, author of *Autumn Gothic* and *Road Harvest*

"A wholly original drama with crime elements, coming in like the long-lost child of Jackie Collins, Jacqueline Susann. and a touch of Elmore Leonard. This refreshing new novel is destined to become a classic among readers of loose melodrama and gritty realism."

--Manny Torres, author of *Dead Dogs* and *Perras Malas*.

"Kissed with romance and taut with threat, *Poser* is a smartly plotted debut novel in what is sure to be a memorable noir series."

--Patrick Whitehurst, author of *Murder & Mayhem in Tucson*

"When this book ends, you realize that it's the opening act for what promises to be a twisted saga of self-indulgence, self-discovery, survival, hope, and disappointment."

--Douglas Lumsden, author of *A Troll Walks Into A Bar* and *A Witch Steps Into My Office*

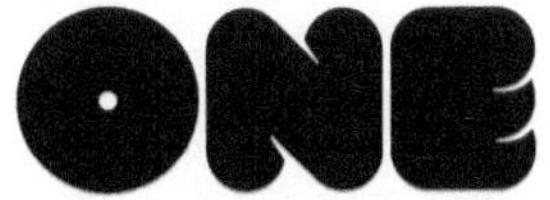

Ambrose goes to his early class at the community college, then rides his motorcycle into the city, to the S&M dungeon he works, to sit at Miss Dover's desk for a while. While she's in Europe, he's been cleaning out and straightening files, trying to get a handle on all things Dover, Inc.. He wants to prove he can do this, that she can trust him, and he'll be ready to take on a much bigger role in what promises to be one hell of a fashion/BDSM equipment/event empire. It would show Jessica that he's capable of more than she ever thought possible. And, by the time they hear about it, show his redneck parents and everybody in that hick hometown that he's come a long way since that night he fled in terror but found the courage to survive. Thrive, even. At least his brother Butch who's sitting in prison would be glad to know that.

Just as Ambrose is about to wrap things up, he gets lost in some papers from the back of the filing cabinet, copies of paid invoices from events held here several years ago. Most say "Company Party," with typical items charged, including ballroom and suite rentals, smoke and bubble machines, ocelot rental, a dozen extra cases of champagne, professional dancers, costumes, bartenders. . . *This place sure used to rock.* Maybe armed with new ideas and meeting with high-rolling European investors, Miss Dover can get it going like it used to be. Only this time it'll be sleek and sophisticated, with wild fashion shows and God knows what else. And for once, Ambrose is in the right place at the right time to get in on it. He stuffs the papers back into the drawer and closes it.

He offered to stay home with Beau today, but Beau has a play date scheduled at 3:30 with the Carson twins, and the babysitter, Caitlin, agreed to supervise them. Jessica had a meeting with some charity committee, so she'd left early, but he wondered if she just wanted to avoid him since today is Jessica's Tea-with-Mignon day, an afternoon outing planned with the new domme who'd flirted with Jessica at her recent art show. At first, Jessica thought Mignon was just being nice, trying to get to know her over tea, but Ambrose had to clue Jessica in that Mignon was hitting on her. Maybe deep-down Jessica knew that, but this had gotten her thinking and things haven't been the same since.

And he's got no one to blame but himself, which he hates.

Jessica's sister, Bennie, the receptionist, took the day off, since there were no sessions scheduled for today. One of the guest-dommes

Miss Dover had brought in to take care of select clients in her absence, has a couple of club appearances tonight. And their new tech genius, Rajit, is back in town but crashed out at home with jet lag, and maybe something else, too. Says he's not feeling so well. Meanwhile, domme Momo's been visiting family in Japan and, even before that, had taken time off to spend with her new daughter. That just leaves Ambrose here alone. *It's kind of a creepy place when it's so empty.*

He walks out into the hallway, through shadows that seem to have shifted now that a couple security lights are on. His heart quickens as he nears the dark area just beyond the next corner. No one's going to jump out and grab him, he tells himself. This place is a vault. Still. Something about walking through the darkness dredges up memories of getting robbed that night he got kicked out of his place. The same night he had to unload enough molly to try to appease his old boss, Lang. Amid other things. . .

He peers into the Tyrolean Suite, just to see if the room is in order for Thursday's clients. Sure enough, the sex swing is over by the bed, chains glinting in the low light, leather straps swinging ever so slightly. His opening the door must've stirred the air. Or the A/C just shut off. He unlocks the brakes on the elaborate contraption and rolls it into the closet. Some people say this room is eerie, and many actually want that, but gazing up at the collection of fake antlers, all sizes, on the wall opposite the bed, he realizes he'd never want to sleep in this room alone. Just being in here all by himself is weird enough. The antlers cast such jagged shapes on the walls, pointed shadows that would give him nightmares. Miss Dover said she'd seen a huge display of antlers at a ski lodge she visited in Austria, that she thought the Austrian references gave it a real *Venus in Furs* vibe from the book by Von Sacher-Masoch. She told Ambrose to be sure to add that to his reading list. As well as Marquis de Sade. Turns out the Charenton Suite, the one with the more rustic décor, distressed wood, wrought-iron fixtures, and candle holders was named for the French asylum where the Marquis was held for years before he died. Apparently, he directed the other inmates there in plays. The door to the hallway closes, causing Ambrose to jump. But that door usually closes by itself. *Crazy stuff all right, but insane?* Ambrose thinks about everything. *Nope.*

Before he heads back to Palo Alto, he stops to get a coffee-to-go and finds himself walking the streets again, same ones he used to skulk, sleepless and scared. He thinks of the night he got jumped behind Galaxy, close to the nightclub where he met Jessica's soon-to-be ex-husband, Mike. Is "met" the right word?

Good as any. It wasn't so long ago, but some places on this street have shut down since then, and the homeless are camped out in the entrance to one of them, lasting as long as they can until they're told to move along.

So many more homeless people now and so many places they're not supposed to be. More **FOR LEASE** signs, and shop windows papered over from the inside. Catching a glimpse of himself in a window, he pauses to look at his reflection. For a moment, he'd thought he was back in his old clothes: ragged jeans, nearly worn-out motorcycle boots, plaid flannel shirt, and a weathered leather jacket. He barely recognizes the young man staring back now. Is he still young? Maybe they're right: It's not the years, it's the mileage. He feels older than he looks. He stops at the next intersection to light a cigarette, mind wandering, and then realizes he's been standing there through two **WALK** signals. He finally crosses, going nowhere in particular.

Miss Dover had asked him that night in the ballroom what would happen if he found himself left to his own devices and he'd promised not to go back to his old ways. He doesn't quite know what the "new way" would look like if he didn't have Jessica and Beau to come home to. If Jessica decides she's over it, over him. He pauses, still smoking, peering through the diamond-shaped window of a wooden door to an abandoned bar. Inside, the bar itself is still there but the shelves behind it are empty. There's a small stage at the far end of the room, beyond a tangle of folding chairs. He remembers walking here not long after he'd arrived in the city, on his way over to Lang's to make a pick-up.

It was packed that night, with a small band and people drinking, dancing, having a good time. He ducked in for a quick beer as the song—a very jazzed-up, hyper-improvised version of "Minnie the Moocher"—rose to a crescendo. The trumpeter, a guy in his 40s, wearing a white suit, dark tie, and wine-colored alligator shoes, stepped onto the bar and walked the length of it, blowing his horn and stepping gingerly around any beer bottles parked there, to the delight of the buzzed crowd. That was one of the better memories from Ambrose's early days here, a few minutes of pretending he was just stopping in for a drink and real bargain show—not seeking refuge from the whole world because he felt so completely unwanted in the world. He used to think a place like this would go over well, but here it is: dead.

He glances at his watch and walks back to the motorcycle parked on a side street. Down in Palo Alto, Caitlyn will be bringing Beau back soon and Ambrose needs to be there. He tosses the cigarette. Time to go home.

At least it's still home for now.

✳✳✳

This never happens, falling down so hard, headlong off those towering heels onto the floor of that mysterious Parisian apartment, with its cracked crown molding and crooked chandelier. Miss Dover prides herself on her ability to navigate the steepest steps and most polished tiles in high heels with poise and grace, but to get up too fast, only to fall down, knocking over a bottle of Dom Perignon, no less: *Quel malheur!*

She was still woozy, and the side of her face ached as hands reached down to help her up: those of the younger man from earlier who'd seemed to be asking if she wanted breakfast, and the other one who wheeled in the cart. Still in a state of complete confusion, she paused to gather herself. One of the men, the younger one, said something to her but his voice echoed as if she were in a tunnel. She was still terrified about what all this meant. After meeting old friends for dinner and drinks the night before, she'd started walking toward the Sacre Coeur, enjoying the night air, planning to stop for an espresso before heading to the Metro or calling for a ride, and that's the last thing she remembered before ending up here with strangers who hadn't harmed her so far. . . But still, she had a feeling of total dread. Earlier in the day, she'd had the unpleasant and insistent feeling she was being followed by two men. She managed to ditch them outside the perfumery, having tucked a lovely bottle of that rare and exquisite scent into her purse and slipping out the back door of the place. And where was her pocketbook anyway? She thought, panicked. She remembered demanding these two men tell her "What the fuck's going on here?" just before the collapse. That spark seemed to have died and she lost the strength to try, sinking back down to the floor, those voices in their strange accents swirling above her.

The energy shifted as she heard someone else enter the room. She couldn't even turn to look but then heard a voice with a deeper, somewhat familiar tone. Whoever belonged to that voice stepped closer into her downcast line of sight. A pair of limited-edition Adidas sneakers. Velour track suit, navy blue with a white stripe. As her gaze traveled upward, her expectations of what could be transpiring here were radically altered, much to her relief. "Oh," she breathed, tears stinging her eyes, joy filling her heart. "It's you."

✳✳✳

It started out innocently enough: beautiful afternoon in the city with an exciting new acquaintance, but now it is nearly rush-hour and Jessica's texting Ambrose that she'll be home soon, and can he please be there when Caitlyn brings Beau? Ambrose must wonder why she's running so late. Or may think he knows why, which is worse.

Tea at the Fairmont was lovely and she felt an undercurrent of tension the whole time based on what Ambrose had said, joking that Mignon would have a room there for them to scurry up to, but he'd been wrong. No room reserved there. Afterwards, they'd walked around out in the sunlight together, stopped into a couple of shops and then for a drink at the bar of a boutique hotel. That's where Mignon got the room. Jessica had one cosmopolitan, but maybe it was sheer nerves that made her feel so dizzy.

She'd gone to the ladies' room to freshen up and, when she came back to the bar, Mignon flashed a key card, said she'd always wanted to see this place and she'd gotten a suite where they could relax for a while. Jessica had glanced at her watch, thinking *Maybe just for a few minutes* and then she'd go back to the Fairmont to get her car. Mignon had ordered up a couple more drinks and, the next thing Jessica realized, Mignon was helping her slip out of her dress so it wouldn't get wrinkled when they laid on the bed. "You have a long drive home, and a short nap will do you good. Besides, it isn't so very late, *chère* . . ." It wasn't then, but still.

Ambrose was right. And she'd gone into it with eyes wide open, so why was she surprised when Mignon started kissing her? She'd never kissed a woman but the more times it happened, the more natural it felt, and things went on from there. A surge goes through her whole body when she remembers some of the things they did. And then the things she did to Mignon in the shower. The shower, for God's sake! She bites her lip, gripping the steering wheel harder, just thinking about it.

The sun is much lower in the sky by the time she gets back to Palo Alto. *Beau's home by now, wondering where Mommy is, and Ambrose knows—or thinks he does.* She has the urge to stop somewhere, get something to drink and just pull herself together. There's no way to explain away all this. She can either tell the truth or lie and hope he believes her. But he predicted it.

Mignon had kissed her breasts, which she'd never experienced with a woman before, and there was oral sex, which she'd never, *ever* experienced with a woman. Ambrose is wonderful in bed, doing *that* especially, but it was just different this time and felt so new—because it was. Then Mignon joined her in the shower, offering to wash her back, and Jessica turned to Mignon, kissed her, rubbed her all over with luxury body wash and time just melted away. . .

She hears the text notification on her phone and glances at it sitting in its holder on the dashboard. It's Ambrose. Just checking to make sure she's okay. He's there waiting for her, along with her little boy, and here she is slinking back from as an innocent-tea-date-turned-illicit-romp in a high-priced hotel. Is she becoming wholly unfaithful and secretly gay like Mike? She panics at the thought. Can't be. Maybe it's even partly because of Mike's neglect and indifference that she's going out of her mind now.

She has a feeling that what happens at the dungeon where Ambrose, Bennie, and Mignon work, stays there. So Mignon won't kiss and tell. It's like some otherworldly place, where people go to escape reality. She'll always be an outsider looking in on that strange, little world. So why not do what she wants? After all, isn't that what people do at Dover, Inc.: whatever they want? She wants Ambrose for many different reasons, and today she'd wanted Mignon—for one reason.

When she gets home and walks into the kitchen, Ambrose is standing at the sink, holding Beau on his hip, rinsing a colander full of cherries. He looks beautiful standing there like a young dad, and Beau looks beautiful, too. "Hi," she says, placing her purse on a chair near the door. "What're you guys up to?"

Ambrose turns, smiles. "Just getting a snack."

She approaches, takes Beau in her arms. "Hey, honey." She kisses Beau, then kisses Ambrose.

He looks her in the eyes then turns back to the sink. "How was the tea party?"

"Good. Sorry I'm late. Traffic was a mess."

"We're just glad you're home." He places the cherries in a bowl and sets them on the counter. "Hungry?" he asks, watching her hold Beau.

She grasps Beau's little fist in hers, kisses it.

He looks sleepy but glad to see her and have her attention. He puts his arms around her neck. "Mommy. . ."

"Let's just order a pizza," she says.

"Okay."

She takes Beau as she heads toward the bedroom. She doesn't look back. The way he was looking at her. . . It seems to indicate he knows everything.

***

Jessica's sister, Bennie, takes the day off to go to the museum's mid-century modern décor & clothing exhibit and then shopping for lingerie. After a nice lunch at a new Thai place, she'd come home for a nap before smoking half a joint, soaking in a patchouli-scented bath and trying on the sari Rajit brought her from Mumbai before she'd gut-punched him with the news there's a new man in her life. He had every right to explore all his options, jetting off to his brother's wedding to meet his own potential bride that his parents had selected for him, but while he was gone, things happened, that's all. Wonderful things.

Bennie smokes the rest of the joint in the bedroom, admiring her reflection in the full-length mirror. The sari's vibrant pink, orange, and gold match her mood. She walks over to the closet to find the pink-beaded, pointy-toed, kitten-heeled Carlos Santana mules she'd scored about a year ago. She'd mostly been wearing them around the house like slippers, but with this, they look perfect for a night out. She takes a sip of jasmine tea, also a gift from Rajit's travels. She steps out of the mules, slips off the sari, then stands before the mirror in just her underwear, taking another hit, the smoke blending with the sandalwood incense on the nightstand.

Usually, getting high puts her in an introverted mood, but not this evening. After all, she's been feeling buzzy all day. So ridiculously happy. Something Jessica said to her that fateful day in the coffee shop comes to mind, the day she found out Jessica and Ambrose had sex the night before, after that splashy country club fundraiser. Before Bennie knew why Jessica was in such a good mood that day, she commented as much. To which Jessica had more or less replied, "What of it? You live half your life in a state of giddiness."

It hadn't been true that day, and Jessica may have meant it as a back-handed observation, but it's true now. She takes a hit from the joint before gently flicking some ash on the miniature Chinatown souvenir plate on her dresser. She smiles at herself in the mirror.

All too true.

***

Randy has just gotten out of the shower, slipped on a T-shirt and some underwear, and parked himself on the sofa with a beer when his phone rings. *It's her!* He picks up. "Hey, I was just about to call you."

"Were you really, or you just saying that?"

He answers honestly. "I was, really. What're you doing?"

"Oh, nothing," Bennie says. She sounds buoyant, like maybe she's had a drink or two.

"Must be doing something."

"Mm. Just relaxing a little. Getting high."

Bingo.

"What're you doing?"

"Not a goddamn thing." He takes a sip of the beer, wanting to ask her out again but he doesn't want her to think he's taking her somewhere cheap from necessity; she should think it's because it's quaint or kitsch. "Want to go out tomorrow night?"

"Sure." There's a smile in her voice. "Where we going?"

"It's a surprise."

"Ooh, I like surprises. Don't you?"

"Sometimes." He takes another swallow, sets the bottle on the end table, and settles back on the sofa. "Would you think I'm a pervert if I ask you what you're wearing right now?"

"I'm in bed, not wearing anything. What're you wearing?"

He looks down at his faded but clean Giants shirt and discount plaid boxers. "What if I told you I'm not wearing anything either?"

"Good. I love picturing you naked."

"You don't want to picture me in a police uniform?"

"All I want is pure, unadulterated *you*," she says. "Guess I could've texted you but then I'd miss hearing your voice. You have a sexy voice."

"Well, thanks." He's getting a hard-on and a skittery stomach in anticipation of what she might say. He reaches for the beer. All those hours of watching porn and now he can't think of a goddamn thing that would make for good, X-rated conversation. It's got to sound unforced: glib and easy. Just picture her naked in bed, he tells himself.

"So. . ." she says. "Why don't you tell me a bedtime story?"

"I will." Another sip of beer. "But first, I have a confession."

"What's that, pray tell?"

"I've never had phone sex before."

"You're a phone sex virgin? I don't believe it."

"So, be gentle, okay?"

She laughs that sparkling laugh. The kind that cuts through awkwardness and makes him want to tell secrets. "I'll be gentle all right."

"You have a sexy voice yourself," he says, catching a breathy note in her last few words that could mean she's getting turned on. If only she were sitting on his lap right now. If only he were there in bed with her. "What're you in the mood for tonight?" he asks.

"Truth or fiction?"

"Whatever you want to share."

That *voice*. Relaxed, semi-sleepy, like rolling over in bed and pressing against him, like she did the other night.

He slides his hand under the loose elastic of the boxers, getting turned on at the thought of sharing one particular story with her, without her knowing it's about her own sister and Ambrose. *Have to be careful not to get the wires crossed, though. The actual circumstances might creep her out. Anyway, if it were a movie, it'd be "based on a true story." So here goes.* "Well, one night when I was still on the force, I was keeping an eye on this rich couple's house while they were away. And I'd ride by a time or two a night, you know? Just checking things out."

"Go on."

"And one night I saw this—cat, run behind the house. I knew a lady down the street had lost a cat, 'cause I'd seen posters around the neighborhood, and this one was wearing a collar, so I went after it—to see if it was indeed the lost cat." Utter bullshit, but not a bad set-up.

"Right."

"And I didn't know this couple had gotten home already. They'd come back early and, when I went in the back yard, the curtains were open at the back window."

"Oh, really?"

He gets harder just thinking about it. Grabs hold of himself but has to keep his mind on the task at hand. The other task. "And the cat ran into the bushes below the window, and I went after it, and when I looked up, I saw them in there. . ."

"What were they doing?"

"They were undressing each other. The woman was wearing this wild red jumpsuit. I'd never seen anything like it before. It tied with ribbons in the back and the man was untying it and kissing her neck. Must've been made out of silk or satin or something smooth and slick because it just slid off her and fell to the floor."

"Wow."

"And she wasn't wearing any bra and I could see her breasts and they were all perfect and round and just the right size. I thought so anyway. Just like yours. And she stepped out of the jumpsuit and she was wearing these strappy high-heeled shoes. . ."

"Mm. Go on."

"And he just picked her up and laid her down on the bed and slipped her panties off her."

"Nice. And then what?"

He slowly strokes himself, getting harder still. Articulating what he saw just for her gives the whole scenario new life. The video of it he took may have gotten deleted, but he can still see it in his mind's eye. "Then he got between her legs and went down on her."

"Did she like it?"

"I couldn't hear everything, but, from where I was standing, it looked like she was going crazy. What're you doing right now?"

"What do you think?"

"Are you touching yourself?" he asks in a near whisper.

"Maybe. . . What're you doing? Besides telling me a story?"

"What do *you* think?"

He can hear her laugh. "Did he make her come?" she asks.

"I think he stopped just short of that. He got up and finished getting undressed."

"And then?"

"Then she went down on him, while he was standing right by the bed and, before he got back in bed with her, I took it out and started—you know. Pretty much what I'm doing now. I couldn't help it; I had this goddamn *raging* hard-on and I just couldn't resist."

"I'm not judging," she says, still with that naughty smile in her voice. "But I am curious about something."

"What's that?"

"Well. . . First of all, weren't you afraid they'd see you?"

"Sure, I was. That was an incredibly unprofessional thing I was doing. Don't you think?"

"It was, actually," but still no judgement in her voice. "What if they'd caught you out there, watching them and—"

"I know, right? They could've called the department and that would've been just another item on my rap sheet."

"Or they could've asked you to join in."

"*Jesus,* Bennie!" No judgement *and* she kicked it up a notch. "You bad girl."

"Know something, Randy?" she asks, voice still semi-dreamy.

He loves hearing her say his name. "What's that, Miss Jenkins?"

"There are those of a certain type who might've recorded that couple having hot sex. . ." The back of his neck starts burning. "You'd never do such a thing, would you?" she asks.

He stops, each second that ticks by another reason for her to think he would, so with every ounce of denial in him: "Hell, *no.*"

She giggles lightly, and he wonders if she believes him, or if she really doesn't give a damn.

"Would you?" he asks.

"Hmm. . . I don't think so. I'd be afraid I'd get caught."

"You don't *think* so?"

"Like you said, it'd be very risky. And, of course, wrong."

"Of course." He reaches over for the beer, takes a swig. "*So* wrong. 'Specially when they started fucking."

"How'd they do it? Him on top?"

"At first. Then she got on her hands and knees on the bed and he came at her from behind. God, he was fucking her *so hard*. Then she got on top of him."

"That must've been *wild*. And what were you doing all this time?" she asks, like she doesn't know.

"Just what I'm doing now."

"And did you come while you were watching them?"

"I did. It even got on their window. Crazy, huh?"

"Think she stayed fucked after that?"

Why does that sound somehow familiar? Henry Miller, maybe? Somewhere deep in the *Tropic of Cancer*. "Oh, she *had* to stay fucked. For at least a week. I want to do that to you, Bennie."

"Do what?"

"Fuck you just that good." Quieter: "What're you doing right this second?"

"Give you three guesses."

"How does it feel?"

"*Good*. . . Keep talking."

Whatever it is that turns her on about his voice he wants to make sure he does but he's not sure what that is, so *Better not overthink it*. "Just know how much I want you, and how much I wish I were there with you." He strokes himself at a steady pace, closes his eyes and thinks about her lying in that goddamn big, brass bed all alone, wanting to get fucked again by him of all people.

He hears her laugh. Hot, little sexy laugh. "Wish I could kiss you right now. . ."

"Like the first night we met?"

"You liked that?"

"Best. Kiss. Ever."

"What else would you do if you were here?"

"I'd go down on you 'til you came or couldn't take it anymore and then I'd fuck you all the ways I saw him fuck her and then some."

"I want you to."

"Think I'm 'bout to come, Bennie."

"Me, too." He can hear a break in her voice, like she's trying to catch her breath and talk at the same time.

"Now?"

"*Right* now." Same sparkling voice, but in the middle of an orgasm, somewhere between wanting something and getting it, and as he shoots off, he can feel it, too. And if they can't be in the same room right now, at least they're on the same phone line, and if any eavesdropping motherfuckers have been listening in on their conversation out there in hacker-land, they can just eat their goddamn, fucking hearts out.

✱✱✱

Alexei Rusovich looks out the passenger window, gazing at the impressive glass-and-metal structure at the edge of a cliff, the Pacific glittering beyond. He turns to his bodyguard, Dimitri, at the wheel. "What do you think?" Alexei asks.

"Very nice."

Maxim Rusovich, sitting in the middle of the back seat, is still sweating, albeit not as profusely as when he didn't know if the two in front were really taking him to see a coastal property, or if that was a euphemism for dumping his body where it would never be found. The bruising from the sock in the ribs Dimitri had given him a couple days ago for speaking with their old boss Sergei about what Alexi's been up to lately, still aches. If Alexei knew he had tried to call the boy at the dungeon, what would he do? What wouldn't he do? Yes, it had been precipitous, perhaps out of a misplaced sense of panic. Maxim hadn't even really known what he would say to the Dover, Inc. dungeon boy, and when there was no answer, he'd lost his nerve. He had considered at least a quick warning, even if only "Watch your back" mumbled through a silk handkerchief. Alas. . .

"You will check on it for me, won't you, Maxim?" Alexi asks.

"Of course," Maxim says. "However, you are aware that a property such as this one is bound to be quite exorbitant."

"You say that as though I cannot afford it," Alexei observes, gazing at the house. The ocean can be seen through the entire end of the glass living room.

"I meant no such thing." Maxim catches a glimpse of himself in the rearview mirror, looking weary, older than he'd looked a couple days ago. "Simply that this, right on the heels of the last acquisition. . . And before profits are realized—and, eh, processed—"

"I've waited long enough, Maxim."

Dimitri shifts slightly in the driver's seat, eyes forward, jaw set.

"As your good friend Sergei used to say, 'I want my candy now.' Besides, I anticipate all my income streams improving vastly in the coming year." Then, to Dimitri, "Back to the tearoom."

Maxim leans forward. "I would like to be taken home, please. My work here is done for now, yes?"

"No," Alexei responds. "You will have dinner with me this evening. I want to discuss with you some details concerning our other upcoming plans."

Subdued Russian pop music plays on the car stereo, a woman's crystal-clear voice rising above the brisk tempo. Maxim slumps back into the seat for the ride back, anticipating at least the very fine vodka that'll be served before dinner.

And the kitchen *does* turn out excellent weeknight specials.

Ambrose sits on the edge of Miss Dover's desk chair, too keyed up to sit back and relax. Going on several days now with no response to his texts or calls. It's an uncomfortable place to be, wondering if Miss Dover might take Maxim's mysterious client up on that offer to buy this building. He'd thought that whole idea was DOA from the get-go, that she'd dismiss it as soon as she got word of it, but so far—nothing. If no news means she's decided to sell but dreads telling them because Ambrose and the others won't like it, she's absolutely right. They won't.

But then, he tells himself, she is busy: halfway around the world with a lot on her plate, talking up investors for her BDSM clothing line and equipment. That offer someone made to buy this property using Maxim as an intermediary came so out of left field, she probably just laughed, forgot about it, and went on about her business, knowing that the dungeon is in good hands with Ambrose and Bennie. Miss Dover hasn't even met Mignon, who, in spite of his personal issues with her, is bringing in new clients. She hasn't met Rajit either but trusts their judgement in bringing him into the fold. Though, as Rajit now paces in front of the desk, his complaints intrude on Ambrose's uneasy thoughts.

"I cannot believe Bennie fell for that sex-starved maniac— whose crapulent apartment we just broke into, of all people!" he says, still chafed about what happened during the short time he was back in India. "I hadn't been up in the air for one hour before she met this guy, and he took her home at the end of the evening?"

"He didn't take her home with him, just drove her home," Ambrose clarifies.

"That makes little difference now." Rajit turns to him. "And you allowed this to happen."

"'Allowed' it? I didn't want it to happen."

"But you're the one who hired him for the night!"

"I had to get him out of his place long enough to get rid of that video. What're the fucking odds I knew she'd even talk to him?"

"True but when you saw this, why didn't you stop it?"

"I didn't know they were hitting it off 'til it was too late. When I asked her to leave with Jessica and me, she told me to back off and quit being so bossy."

"Apparently you were not bossy enough."

Ambrose stands, walks around to the front of the desk. "I knew she liked you, but I didn't know you had it this bad for her. Didn't you ever get a chance to let her know you were interested?" A question he'd asked himself, then he met Jessica and now finds that question returning, which isn't right but doesn't stop it from coming back.

Rajit sits on the sofa, frustrated. "Yes, but my parents were pressuring me to come home and I didn't know what I would ultimately decide."

"About moving home or the arranged marriage?"

"Both," he admits. "I'd been very confused for the past several weeks and then there was a morning, walking in Mumbai, I had a realization that I should return to the States and that Bennie and I could have a future together if I just follow my heart." He looks at Ambrose. "Then I came back as soon as possible, and she told me in no uncertain terms that she likes this—'person'—very much. I believe if I were to ask her out now, she would turn me down flat."

"So, what do you want to do?"

Rajit takes a deep breath. "Forget all this and throw myself into my work. I will help you and your associates build this business into the greatest S&M enterprise the world has ever seen." He stands. "What new project shall I tackle first?"

Ambrose wants to feel the same exhilaration Rajit is radiating, determined to plow forward in spite of profound missed opportunities, but since there are several things nagging at him today, he just hands Rajit a slip of paper. "Find out who this number belongs to."

"*Wonderful.* Another phone number. . ." Deflated, Rajit takes the paper and looks at it. "Is this for Dover, Inc., or you personally?"

"Dover, Inc.."

"Can you give me more information?"

"They called the phone in this office late last night, then hung up and called back right away but didn't leave a message. Then they called again. Don't you think that's odd?"

Rajit bobbles his head side-to-side in that way Ambrose is starting to get used to. "Maybe it was a wrong number. Perhaps they were drunk."

"Maybe, but there's something familiar about this number."

"Familiar?"

"I feel like I've seen it, but I can't think where. It's just got me curious, that's all. I tried looking for it online and can't find it."

Rajit sighs, starts for the door. "I will see what I can do."

"And finish installing that new cybersecurity software and test it out. When I talk to Miss Dover, I can tell her it's done."

"I'll get on it. When will you speak with her again?"

Soon," Ambrose says. Rajit starts out. Ambrose remembers one last thing. "Hey, Rajit?"

Rajit turns to him.

"Sorry 'bout what happened with Bennie. Maybe she'll come to her senses about that guy."

"One can only hope." He smiles, goes out, closing the door behind him.

When Ambrose is alone again, he realizes someone could say the same about Jessica and himself.

✳✳✳

Sergei is older, that's all, but dashing as ever with that mane of white hair and wearing Wayfarers. Reminds her of old pictures of Aristotle Onassis, the famous Greek shipping tycoon with a flair for dramatic and glamorous women. It's sometimes easy to forget Sergei has lived most of his 70-plus years as an underworld Russian "businessman," and not a film director, big-time producer, or garden-variety mogul whose life is tabloid fodder. She feels like an international movie star even as he now tries to make up for all she's been through with the confused fall in the room with two strange men. He spirits her away to his mansion in Monaco to dine on lobster and caviar within view of the patio and Mediterranean beyond. He didn't want to dine outside, however, because, as he explains, he wants no one to know her whereabouts.

He refills her champagne flute with Dom Perignon (he says that's the only real champagne) but doesn't partake of it, says he's had enough champagne to last a lifetime and anyway—his ulcer. He sips a skim latte as one of the servants, a diminutive young man with delicate features, pince-nez glasses, black tie and white jacket, removes the used plates, making no eye contact. She sips the champagne. It's starting to get to her, even after that fabulous brunch.

"I hope you can forgive me," Sergei says, sunglasses set aside for the moment. "I realize my methods are extreme, but you were in extreme danger; there was no time to debate the issue in the street."

"I forgive you," she says. "I knew there were goons following me but I sure as hell didn't know they were yours."

"Ah, my people are trained not to be detected so easily. Those were some sloppy hoodlums hired by Alexei."

She leans back in her chair. "For what?"

"To get rid of you."

"You really think he'd go that far?"

"He'll always believe your property is rightly his. I offered it to Ivan after Alexei's precipitant power grab pissed me off. I couldn't stomach the thought of Alexei somehow at the helm of my organization, occupying the location where we first started. It was just a run-down warehouse then, nothing at all special."

"How come I didn't know that was where ya'll started? Do tell!"

"Those were different times. Bad things happened there you're better off not knowing. Anyway, I'm sure Alexei's interest is not rooted in nostalgia. Looking back only serves to feed his bitterness. If I didn't have resources to fight him off, he'd as soon bash in my skull." He sips latte. "Perhaps he'd dip toast points in my blood to eat with brie and a nice chardonnay."

"After you gave him the tearoom, the import-export biz, the trucking—"

"Mere trinkets to a man with delusions of grandeur."

"And yet you never squashed him like a bug?"

Sergei looks wistful, shrugs. "I grew up with his father, who was a decent man. I suppose even before Alexei went rogue, I'd begun to lose my taste for cold-blooded murder."

She notices the way he draws out the word *murr-derr* like it might taste good coming out of his mouth but, as with the champagne, could aggravate his ulcer.

"You wouldn't even have to get your hands dirty," she comments. "You got people for that." Right after she says it, she realizes the glibness with which that observation slipped out of her mouth. Strange, how hanging with these genteel criminal types normalizes such things.

"Quite true. He was once my protégée. I am just a sentimental old man."

"I know he hates me for cutting him out, but I still don't see why he wants that place so damn bad."

The wistfulness leaves Sergei's eyes. "That, is the two-and-a-half million-dollar question." Which is what the place could go for, if real estate prices hold.

"With anyone else it might be worth considering. But, like you say, I get sentimental. And it's my security, you know?"

"I grew up quite poor, so I understand the need for security. Especially, as the years pass."

She looks around at the sunny room with its baroque décor. There are pictures on the grand piano of Sergei and Ivan from younger days, along with ones of Sergei and his late wife, a fashion model who'd overdosed on heroin despite all the rehab she'd undergone at the world's finest facilities. Many of the photos taken before Ivan's untimely heart attack even include hers truly, Miss Dover. That already seems like a lifetime ago.

She's flattered to see photos of herself in this lavish room. Sergei has no children she's aware of, but these are the closest things to family photographs he likely has. It strikes her also, that after her family disowned her, this was the closest thing *she* had to a family. She turns to look out at the sparkling waters of the Côte d'Azur, and flashes on Ambrose, that sweet pretty-boy runaway from Riviera, Texas. He laughed but clearly thought it was a cruel joke when she showed him pictures of the real Riviera, compared to the piece of shit, dusty town he'd come from. That's her other family: that fucked-up bunch of misfits back at her dungeon in the city. Waiting for her to come back.

"Alexei is determined to gain possession of that property only because something there substantially increases its value in his estimation."

"But what?" she asks, jarred out of her buzzed reverie.

"I'm not sure." Another sip of latte. "For that, I would kill to find out."

✳✳✳

On Sunday mornings for the last few weeks, Ambrose has been getting up early to watch on TV the preacher with the biggest megachurch in Houston. Today, sitting on the floor next to the coffee table with Beau, Ambrose stares at the screen while Beau joyfully abandons the idea of coloring inside the lines and starts scribbling on the back of his old drawings.

There's something about this preacher's message that appeals, especially the ones where the preacher talks about getting out of your comfort zone, and how most of the people God chose to do great things in the Bible were really messed up. There's something comforting about the slight twang of this preacher's accent. His delivery is sincere and his voice cracks with emotion. Sometimes Ambrose feels like this preacher is speaking directly to him. No doubt millions of other people do, too.

Today's sermon is about "You Are Enough." Jessica walks through the room, pausing to see what Ambrose and Beau are doing.

She stands, listening for a moment, sipping coffee. "Why do you like to watch him?"

"I like the way he talks. And I find his sermons—relatable."

She sits on the edge of the sofa to look at Beau's proud scribbling on the papers spread out on the table.

"And he always wears the best-looking suits." Slim & trim. Neat.

She looks up. "Suits? That's not the only reason you like him, is it?"

He realizes she's not totally listening, which she'd accused him of not long ago. "That wasn't the only thing I said."

"Not many guys around here wear suits to work anymore."

"I never thought I'd have a job where I could wear a suit to work and now that I can, I want to wear ones like that."

"Well, find some and I'll buy them for you." She leans down, kisses him, then stands, taking her coffee with her.

"You don't have to do that. I'll get 'em on my own."

"Maybe you'll get one for your birthday, you never know. When is your birthday, by the way?"

"June 11th."

"Gemini." She smiles, starts out, toward the staircase in the hallway. "I'm going upstairs to do some work. Be thinking about what you want for lunch. And bring Beau up later." She disappears around the corner.

He turns back to the TV, sips coffee. He will find out where to get those suits.

And he'll pay for them himself.

✳✳✳

Up in the art studio she made upstairs into, Jessica straddles a chair, elbows propped on the back of it, staring at a freshly primed 4'x4' canvas. She wants to explore a different theme for the new collection but is not sure what that might be. She's already attempted one piece but it turned out a mess, so sits over in the corner: a mosaic of bright colors that mean nothing. No heart nor soul. Maybe only fit for a board room or generic hotel lobby.

She runs her fingers through her hair, trying to put the other day at the hotel out of her mind, when she hears footsteps on the stairs.

Ambrose appears, carrying Beau. "Mommy!" Beau calls out. Ambrose sets him on the floor and he holds out his new drawing. "Look."

"That's great!" she says, taking the piece of paper, unsure what the shapes on it represent exactly, but she has some idea. "I see a circle there," she says. "You did a good job on it!"

"The moon," he says, pointing at it.

Jessica glances at Ambrose. He smiles. There's a softness in his eyes when he looks at Beau that touches her. "The moon—of course! And what's that?"

"Bird," he answers.

"A bird flying to the moon. Is that it?"

"Uh-huh." He sees his toys over in the corner and makes a beeline for the tricycle Mike bought him on their last outing.

Ambrose approaches, stares at the canvas with her. "What's happening here?"

"Not much," she confesses. "Beau's doing way better than I am right now."

Ambrose glances over at the abandoned painting in the corner. "What about that one?"

"What *about* that one?" she repeats. Even though he hasn't said anything about her coming home late the other evening after tea with Mignon, there's been an awkwardness between them neither is willing to address. She felt it earlier and it still lingers.

"You don't like it?" he asks.

"No, I don't."

He eases behind her, placing his hands on her shoulders, squeezing gently, taking his time like testing the waters. "Why not?"

"Because it's awful."

"Not awful."

"What is it, then?"

He holds her close, looking at the new canvas. Something about the two of them staring at it like this reminds her of that night she'd come home and he'd untied the ribbons down the back of that red jumpsuit she was wearing, while they'd held each other's gaze in the mirror. . . No mirror now, just an opaque surface. Feels good to be held like this, though, she must admit.

He sighs.

She turns to glance at him, wonders if he's really been listening, or if his mind's someplace else.

"You've already explored the coast, the hills around here, right?"

"Right."

He holds her closer. "Maybe it's time to go into the woods."

"The woods. . ."

He kisses her neck. It feels nice, and a little of the earlier tension melts away.

✳✳✳

"Let's go up to the cabin at Tahoe," she says.

Randy's so near broke that he's trepidatious but Bennie says not to worry about it; he can hit the job hunt Monday. He's filled out some online applications but doesn't have a good feeling about any of them. When he's not with her, he's been feeling so far below average. And wishing he hadn't fucked things up so badly throughout the past year.

Bennie said to come get her up at her parents' place in Woodside. She put her car in the shop at a dealership near there and spent the night cooking dinner and visiting with her dad, since her mom was at a spa in Carmel for the weekend. Bennie told Randy there's some stuff at her folks' house she wants to bring to the cabin, and that she'll pay the gas for all his driving. He doesn't want to have to let her, but. . . He types the address into his phone's GPS.

What he finds at the address she gave him is a sprawling, rustic mansion. He pulls up by the steps—entrance, rather—and checks the address again to make sure. He already knew her family has plenty—*Forbes* List rich—but this is Big Tech money, the likes of which he's never witnessed this close-up, not to just walk right up to the front door like a guest.

He steps out of the Jeep, intimidated. Approaching Sternwood Mansion in *The Big Sleep*, Philip Marlowe was dressed a hell of a lot better than Randy. *Of all days to wear fucking cargo shorts and run-down sneakers.* He'd dressed for the drive to the lake, but how could he have put his comfort above the chance her old man might be here? She said she'd have the stuff she's taking up to the cabin by the front door, and that her dad had an early tee-time, so he's probably gone already.

Randy walks up the steps, to the massive, ornately-carved front door, takes a deep breath, and rings the doorbell. *They probably know I'm here already and can see what I'm wearing. No visible cameras but there has to be something; no way a place like this isn't hooked up to a system.*

A young, Hispanic woman answers the door. She's dressed in a black blouse, khakis, and a black apron smock over it all. "Yes?"

"Hi. My name's Randy Burke. I'm here to see Bennie—Miss Jenkins?"

"Of course," she smiles. "Come in." She closes the door behind him. "This way, sir." He follows her through the foyer, with its glossy parquet floor. He's usually never called "sir" unless he's in danger of getting thrown out of somewhere, as in "Calm down, sir," or "That's our policy, sir," or "Please mind your language, sir."

A couple pieces of luggage and a fancy cooler are sitting there, waiting. He sees a stone fireplace in a large room at the end of a wide hallway. He also catches a glimpse of an artisan metalwork chandelier hanging over massive leather furniture. When he glances in the other direction, he sees through a door a fraction of an *Architectural Digest*-worthy kitchen. They walk through a den, or more like a library, with book-lined shelves along the walls of a long room with polished, wooden floors covered in places with those almost-threadbare-but-priceless Turkish rugs like Bennie has at her place. Skylights, lots of plants, and a giant fireplace at each end. In front of each fireplace is a low, round hassock that could serve as a table, surrounded by leather easy chairs.

The young woman guides Randy through the next set of open doors that leads to an expansive patio, where a rectangular swimming pool glimmers in the sun. Beyond that is a stone fence and the rolling hills. He recognizes this scene from one of Jessica's paintings he'd seen that night at the gallery. She must've sat here to paint it. There's a cabana down at the far end, and a table near each corner of the pool, each with four chairs, in addition to other deluxe outdoor furniture that indicates these people entertain a lot. Or could, if they wanted to. There's a man sitting at the farthest table from the house with his back to the pool, looking out over the hills as he sips a drink, reading a newspaper—an actual newspaper. Then Bennie walks out of the cabana, carrying a basket tote. She grins when she sees him and hurries over. "Hey, you made it!" she says. Then, "Thanks for showing him in, Rosa."

Rosa goes back into the house as he walks to meet Bennie, wanting to scoop her up and give her a real kiss, but there'll be time for that later and he's keenly aware of the guy over there with the newspaper.

"Most everything's ready," she says. "I got us some sunscreen for when we go swimming."

"In the lake? Isn't it a little cold for that?"

She shrugs. "The cabin pool's heated," then quieter: "Maybe we'll go skinny dipping!" She sets down the tote. "Come on, I want you to meet my dad." She takes his hand, but he pulls back.

"I hate to bother him if he's busy."

"Does he look busy?" she asks.

"Well, do I look okay?" He reaches up to smooth his hair, wishing this were over already and he and Bennie were leaving with him knowing he made a good impression.

"You look just fine!" she assures, stepping back and giving him the once-over. She lightly kisses him before bringing him to the far table.

When the distinguished man catches sight of them, he puts down the newspaper and takes off his sunglasses. "Well, well," he says, standing. "You must be Randy. Bennie's told me so much about you."

"Yes, sir. Hello." *This guy's all handsome and tan and country club, unlike anybody in my family.* Everything about him screams rich—in the most tasteful, understated way.

"Randy, this is my dad, Parker Jenkins," then, jokingly: "And don't worry, everything I've told him about you is very good."

"Great," he says, feeling stiff as he reaches out to shake hands. "It's a real pleasure to meet you, sir." Now, there's a guy used to being called sir. "Bennie's told me a lot about you as well. All very good."

Mr. Jenkins smiles, firmly grasps his hand.

Randy can't help but notice the silver—more likely platinum—Rolex on his tan wrist. "This is a beautiful place."

"Thank you. My wife has her eye on some property up around Carmel-by-the-Sea but I told her forget it; we're staying put." He drapes his arm around Bennie's shoulders. "Hear you two are going up to the lake. Feel free to use the boat while you're there. Bennie knows where the key is. Take it out for a spin."

"Yes, sir. Thank you."

"Thanks, Daddy." Bennie smiles, looking Randy right in the eyes, like she knows he wants this to be over and have faith. It will soon. She turns to give her dad a peck on the cheek. "Excuse me a second. I need to go tell Javier to put everything in Randy's Jeep." Then to Randy, "There's room in the back, isn't there?"

"Sure. I'll go load it up."

"No, it's fine."

He can tell she's about to go check on things and he'll be left alone with Mr. Jenkins. He anticipated loading the Jeep for her, forgetting they'd have servants.

"You and Daddy can talk for a few minutes, and I'll be right back." She sees the fear in his eyes. *Must*, because she squeezes his shoulder before she walks away.

"Sit down, Randy. Have a drink with me," Mr. Jenkins offers, sitting down as Rosa walks over with a tray after speaking with Bennie.

"Another Arnold Palmer, Mr. Jenkins?" she asks.

"Sure," he answers as she places his tall glass on the tray. "Thanks, Rosa."

Rosa turns to Randy. "And what can I get for you, sir?"

"Uh. . ." Randy sinks into the patio chair. "What he's having."

"Yes, sir." She goes back into the house.

"I never know with young people these days," Mr. Jenkins says. "Do you happen to know who Arnold Palmer is?"

"Oh, yes, sir," he replies. "I know who that is."

"Thank God," Mr. Jenkins sighs. "Makes me not feel quite so old."

"Well, you certainly don't look old. Bennie hasn't told me how old you are, but you seem very fit." Saying that, he can't help but think of his own dad: constantly stressed, overweight, only occasionally able to take the grandkids to see a Giants game because it's gotten so goddamned expensive. Now that Ronnie, Sr., is dead, let his other two kids, Ronnie, Jr., and Alison, pony up their own dough for a good, old-fashioned family outing.

"Do you play golf?" Mr. Jenkins asks.

"No, sir. My brother was on the golf team in high school. He still plays sometimes." At least Randy thinks he does. Hasn't spoken to Ronnie, Jr., since the funeral. "My experience with golf is pretty much watching the Masters on TV."

"If you ever want to go see it in Augusta, I'll give you and Bennie my tickets."

"Thank you, sir." What Randy had left off was that golf puts him right to sleep every time. Before he acquired prescription tranquilizers, he could always count on the Golf Channel to knock him out. Except when they show *Caddyshack*. Classic.

"Did you play sports in school?"

"Catcher on the baseball team."

"Giants fan?"

"Yes, sir."

"I have a box at Oracle Stadium if you and Bennie ever want to use it." Then, "Bennie tells me you were in the service. Army, wasn't it? And after that, you were a policeman?"

"Yes, sir." Randy's throat tightens. He wishes Rosa would hurry back with those Arnold Palmers.

"Bennie says you plan on getting your private detective's license. What made you decide to go that route? Anything to do with your time on the police force?"

His throat aches. "To a certain extent. Guess I'm inquisitive by nature." This is starting to sound like a job interview, with Mr. Jenkins clearly sizing him up. "I don't expect to get rich at it, but I think I'll do okay." *Goddamnit, Randy! That is NOT what this guy wants to hear, you underachieving fuck!*

Worrying so much about what to say makes him fuck up and fucking up so much makes him feel like he might start hyperventilating any second. *But there's nothing to be upset about*, he tells himself. Mr. Jenkins simply wants to think his youngest daughter is going away with a decent young man for the weekend. It's just that these are hard questions right now and he has to carefully craft a response that satisfies the man's curiosity and leaves out things that might make him blanch beneath his tan and call a servant to "Release the hounds!"

Mr. Jenkins sits back, folds his arms, sighs. "It'd be very interesting, the life of a private detective, no doubt about that." He gazes out at the hills. Randy can tell by the set of Mr. Jenkins' mouth that he knows he might be asking a delicate question: "Did you see a lot of action over there, Randy? You served in Afghanistan, right?"

"I guess I've seen my fair share," he answers, flashing back to the lean, ultra-wired days of point guard: sounds of bombs, smell of burn pits, the shattering things that still live inside him. Then home, still wired for electricity, to the beat, the caffeine- and Adderall-fueled nights. Always down for the night shift.

"My dad served in the Air Force," Mr. Jenkins says. "I was really proud of him for that. Is there a military tradition in your family?"

"My dad was in the Army, but I don't know if I'd call it a tradition, really. They didn't expect me to join until I came home and told them I'd done it."

"Even better. I admire you for serving your country the way you have."

"Thank you, sir."

Rosa arrives with the drinks and sets one before Mr. Jenkins, then turns to Randy. When she sets his drink on the table, her eyes meet his as she smiles. This woman has a backstage view of this world, and whatever Bennie hasn't told her, she's known since he arrived: Even though he walked in through the front door, he's completely out of his element.

"Yep, my youngest daughter thinks quite a lot of you," Mr. Jenkins says as Rosa walks away.

"I think quite a lot of your daughter." *Understatement of the year.*

Mr. Jenkins sips his drink. "And you've met Jessica as well, right? That's how you and Bennie met? Working security at the gallery."

"Yes, sir. That was quite a show. Jessica's really talented."

"Wish I could've been there. Pamela had already made plans she didn't want to break with some close friends in Florence. Jessica assured us there'd be other shows. Looks like there will be." Mr. Jenkins leans back, reaches into the pocket of loose-fitting, pleated khakis, and takes out a small, silver flask. "Care for a shot, Randy?"

"Normally I would, but we've got a drive ahead of us so. . . I'll just take a rain check."

"Of course." Mr. Jenkins pours clear liquid into his Arnold Palmer. *Vodka maybe? Gin? Could be rum.* "Have you met the young man who lives in Jessica's guest house? What's his name. . . Andrew?"

"Ambrose? Oh yes, sir. I've met him."

Mr. Jenkins puts away the flask, swirls the ice to blend the booze. "Do you know him all that well?"

"I've talked with him a few times."

"What do you think about him?"

If Randy were cold and calculating, and still as pissed off about Ambrose breaking into his place as he was at first, he could torpedo that motherfucker. But if Ambrose hadn't pulled that shit, Randy wouldn't even be here in this palatial compound, talking to Bennie's dad, about to go away for a weekend of hot sex and speed-boating. And Ambrose could do a number on him if he ever had a similar convo with Mr. Jenkins. The threat of mutual destruction. "Well, he seems like an all-right guy," Randy answers. "What do you think?"

"Hard for me to get a read on him. I must admit I've barely met him, but when I have been around him, he didn't talk much." Mr. Jenkins adjusts his sunglasses, settling back to catch a few rays. "Guess time'll tell."

"Yes, sir. Guess it will."

✳✳✳

Randy and Bennie make it to Lake Tahoe by mid-afternoon and it's a hell of a cabin: less like a weekend getaway and more like a lakeside lodge with vaulted ceilings. This fireplace is twice as big as the one in the Jenkins' living room. No servants, though. He's glad they're all alone and he gets to unload the Jeep himself. She puts groceries away while he puts the luggage in the master bedroom. It has a king-size bed and opens out onto a wide patio and heated swimming pool with a slide.

After an early supper of grilled fish and vegetables paired with pinot grigio from her uncle's winery, they walk to the lake. She takes him to the boathouse. The boat is a Chris-Craft inboard and looks like the one in *A Place in the Sun*, where Montgomery Clift speeds around with a bunch of wild rich kids. The vintage vessel is mostly wood, with a flawless finish. She says their other boat, with a cabin for cooking and sleeping, is docked along with her dad's sailboat at the marina in Sausalito. Something she says in passing sounds like there's an even bigger boat docked elsewhere in the world. *A yacht, maybe? Of course.*

"My dad said to take this out for a spin or two. We could go after breakfast tomorrow. How does that sound?"

"Great. This is really nice."

"It was my grandfather's. He loved to come up here. We used to join him and Grandmother here for the holidays, and Jessica and I would come up every summer for weeks at a time."

"I can see why." He runs his hand along the curve of the bow as the waves under the boathouse gently lap at the hull. "This place is incredible."

"Glad you like it," she says. "Thank you for coming with me."

"Are you kidding? Thank you for bringing me here." He turns to her, keenly aware that in the *Place in the Sun* scenario, she's Liz Taylor and he's Montgomery Clift. Only, unlike in the movie, he doesn't have a pregnant girlfriend moping around who he'd love to be rid of, like his checkered past and uncertain future. Things can change, Randy tells himself. *This story won't have a sad ending, because I'm not hiding some awful secret that would destroy everything. Amazing things happen every day. Look at her. This. Now.*

"What're you thinking?" she asks, noticing he's gotten quiet.

"How lucky I am to be here with you," he says, slipping his arms around her waist.

"I'm the lucky one."

"You really feel that way?"

She nods.

Tears fill his eyes. He'd been going to kiss her, but he's so completely overwhelmed, instead he pulls her closer. He doesn't want to cry in front of her, and he won't, he tells himself. Why would he when he's so goddamned happy?

THREE

Dimitri gazes out the window of the diner at the passing walkers and joggers as Lev inhales a jumbo breakfast of three eggs, ham, hash browns, bacon, toast, sausage and a short stack of hotcakes.

"I met the girl, at last," Lev says, barely looking up. "Quite extraordinary."

Dimitri sips his black coffee with feigned disinterest. "Margarite?"

"Saw her at her other job. She doesn't know I work for Alexei so I'm a stranger to her. I like it that way. Unlike you, I'm not trying to make a name for myself. I am quite happy to remain—as they say—in the back channel."

Dimitri watches with distaste as Lev gnaws a sausage link.

"With her you get two women for the price of one, yes? The one in black leather and latex is the pricier version. But worth it." He slices a wedge from the short stack with the edge of his fork, holding it up, watching the cheap syrup drip onto the eggs for a moment before he stuffs it into his mouth. "The demure side of her is no less alluring," he says, smacking his lips. "Something about those waitress uniforms. Tell me, which do you prefer?"

"Prefer?"

"Either would bring any man to his knees, but she has most surely found her true vocation. She had Yuri and me both eating out of her hands." He breaks into a smile, a carnivorous show of teeth under the mustache. "Most joyful surrender. You and 'Lexei are the luckiest of men, yes?"

Dimitri clenches his fists under the table as Lev continues stuffing his face. Dimitri's expression remains much the same, even as his eyes wander slightly, searching for an answer he should know but doesn't. And yet the fat turd in front of him seems to know the secrets of the universe. "Yes," he says finally. "Most fortunate."

Lev swallows what's in his mouth, "I know you and he share her separately, but," he leans forward, elbows on the table. "Tell me; have you both ever had her at the same time?"

Dimitri barely shakes his head, reaching for a cigarette then remembers he can't smoke in here.

"Mm," Lev bites a piece of toast, leaving crumbs around his mouth, in his beard. "That is something I would like to see." He drinks some coffee. "Although I would also love a nice high- quality recording of a few sessions with her and this other woman I've heard about. To get me through those lonely nights when I'm working in Bakersfield. Have you seen them together?"

Dimitri fixes him with a stare, willing him to shut the fuck up. "No."

"Mm," Lev nods. "Simply a thought." He sips coffee and stuffs the last of the bacon into that mouth. "If you would ever wish to have such a recording, I'm your man. I have state-of-the-art new equipment just waiting to capture such scenes for posterity."

Dimitri rubs the back of his neck, picturing himself reaching across the table and slamming this bastard's face into what's left of those disgusting eggs and potatoes, laced with ketchup. So what if the girl is a freak and a whore and everyone knows it? What else would one expect in these circles? He resumes gazing out the window. When he'd first met her at the tearoom he didn't know she was so embedded with Alexei and company, as dirty as all the rest. He'd hoped he could keep her clean. For himself.

✳✳✳

This time Mignon texts Jessica that she wants to meet up at 11AM at a motel near Los Altos, which is different. They've met in the city the last two times, on weekdays. Jessica's heart quickens as she gets dressed to go. This is a bit of an inconvenience and a huge risk but, in all probability, it's the last time, since she's immersing herself in her art again, reconnecting with Ambrose, and slowly regaining focus after this tumultuous year.

She tells Ambrose she has a last-minute appointment to meet with an art agent. Says she wants to meet with this guy before he leaves to go to Brazil for a couple weeks. Ambrose says he's happy to stay with Beau. She doesn't invite him along. He doesn't seem to mind.

No drinks this time. Mignon seems in a bit of a rush, kissing Jessica with urgency and stripping both their clothes without the usual tantalizing foreplay. "Where is your boyfriend today?" Mignon asks.

"He's at home," Jessica says as Mignon reaches around her, unsnaps her bra, and tosses it aside. Mignon's not wearing one.

"Does he suspect anything—about us?"

"I don't know." Jessica lies back as Mignon kisses her neck, returning her to the other day, when Ambrose had done that and went even further than that kiss on the neck Mignon gave her at the art gallery. The red lipstick was one of the first clues to Ambrose that Mignon was hitting on her. Something occurs to her as Mignon works her way down, still kissing, threatening to derail Jessica's tenuous train of thought. "Are you afraid he might've followed me?"

"Why do you ask that, *chère?*" Mignon murmurs.

"Because. This place is so out of the way." Then another thought occurs to her. "Do you think someone's following you?"

Mignon pauses. "Of course not."

"Do you have a boyfriend?" Jessica asks, flashing on Ambrose at home and wanting him just as much as she does Mignon. *Insatiable.* Never would have applied that word to herself before, but lately. . .

"No, darling," Mignon whispers, kissing her breasts and lingering there before moving downward again.

Jessica closes her eyes, body tensing at the initial rush before she gives herself over completely, getting lost in the moments to follow, wondering if he had believed where she was going. If it were him meeting Mignon here, she'd be beside herself with jealousy. She'd want to be there between them, greedily partaking in all they'd have to offer.

Whether such fantasies are the height of self-absorption or just good, clean lust, she doesn't know if she wants them both because she's that selfish or because of a vast, hidden appetite Ambrose awakened that first night they made love out at the guest house. Mignon stops and starts, teasing her until it almost hurts. As all rational thought slips away, she remembers the time she took the train back to college and went to grab lunch at the Chicago train station. She'd been starving for something good and everything looked delicious so she couldn't decide what to get because, in the moment, she wanted it all.

✳✳✳

Ambrose glances at his phone every other minute while watching Beau play in the yard. Jessica said she was going to meet with some art agent and he hoped that was true, but, just in case it's anything other than that, he promised to pay Rajit for his gas and time to follow where she went. That's it; just see where she goes.

The minute she distractedly mentioned some unexpected appointment and stepped into the shower, he called for Rajit to hightail it down here, then stalled her as long as possible. After topping off the gas tank and scoring two packs of Twizzlers at the Valero station closest on El Camino Real, Rajit parked around the corner at the other end of the block. He was to stay close, yet far enough behind she wouldn't think she was being followed. She doesn't know Rajit's car.

The phone rings. Ambrose answers, and now Rajit's parked in the back lot at a motel called Villa del Sol, at the end of a row of cars.

"She went inside?" Ambrose asks. "That's all you saw?"

"She knocked on the door, the door opened, and she went in."

"You saw her knock on a door and go in? What kind of motel is this?"

"A small one off the freeway. One with doors on the outside."

Just fucking great. "You didn't see who opened the door, did you?"

"No. Want me to stay until they come out?"

"They?"

"She, and—whoever?"

"Nah, that's it. You can go now."

"Don't you want me to see who comes outside with her later?"

"I think I know who it is." And he doesn't want Rajit to know it's Mignon. *Worst fears confirmed. Now leave.* Then Ambrose hears another guy's voice. "Who's there with you?"

"My friend, Terrence."

"You were not supposed to bring a friend. This is private."

"It's cool. He was my partner when we worked together. You don't have to worry 'bout him."

Ambrose starts pacing along the edge of the sunny patio, jaw clenching. "Goddamn it, Rajit," he breathes, thinking back to all the times someone told him it was cool when it really wasn't.

"Terrence says there's a guy over there in a black BMW, watching the door as well."

Ambrose stops pacing. "What guy?"

"A guy. Sitting there."

"How do you know he's watching that door?"

"Hold on a second. Terrence has the binoculars."

"*Binoculars?*"

"You used them when we were looking at that guy's apartment, remember? Bennie's new boyfriend. You left them in the car."

"You didn't tell this Terrence about that, did you?"

"I have the binoculars now," Rajit ignores the question. "He's a white guy, mid-30s perhaps. . . Staring at the door of that room."

"He's staring at the same door? You're sure?"

"Looks like it. Want Terrence to pull the pizza scam? He can come from around the other side of the building, and I can watch this man's reaction when someone answers the door. Might provide insight as to what's going on, exactly." Then quieter: "It's what I think, isn't it?"

"Do not pull the pizza scam. Just— Does he look dangerous?"

"Terrence?"

"No." Ambrose grips the phone in frustration. "The guy in the car."

"He does not look friendly."

"You think he's a jealous boyfriend?"

"I thought you were the jealous boyfriend."

"I'm not—" Ambrose pauses, takes a breath. "I just wonder what he's up to, that's all."

"It's very hard to tell. You're sure you don't want Terrence to do the scam? We were planning on getting pizza for lunch anyway."

"No pizza scam," Ambrose says, sitting down in a nearby chair as Beau toddles toward him, dragging a foam baseball bat.

"If you insist. What now?"

"I'll call Jessica and tell her something's come up and she has to get home. When she walks out and gets in her car, just make sure he doesn't follow her. If he does, follow them, and call me. If he doesn't, you can go. Got it?"

"Got it. If he does not follow her, don't you want us to wait until the other person comes out, and see what he does then?"

Beau hands Ambrose the baseball bat, smiling up at him before he starts across the grass to the swing set. Ambrose follows. Yes, he does want to know what this mysterious guy would do if he sees Mignon, but then Rajit would see Mignon and know about her and Jessica. If Jessica's leaving fast for a fake emergency, Mignon probably wouldn't leave at the same time.

Rajit already found out per Ambrose's request that the number that called the office phone all those times was Maxim's, but Rajit hadn't asked any questions, besides wanting to know if it was business or personal. Maybe Rajit's starting to realize those two things are blurring more than they used to. And Ambrose still has to think of some plausible reason to ask Jessica to come home.

"No," Ambrose says, sounding surer than he feels.

"You're the boss," Rajit sighs.

But before he hangs up: "Hey, Rajit? Can you get that guy's tag number?"

"Certainly."

"Look it up this weekend. Find out anything you can. I'll pay you extra."

"Will do."

"You're sure Terrence won't say anything about any of this?"

"I give you my word."

"Okay. Thanks." He ends the call, slides the phone in his pocket and picks up Beau, warm from the sun. Would it throw a wrench into whatever she's doing if he calls to tell Jessica he's afraid Beau has a sudden fever and he's about to rush him to the doctor? After all, Beau does look a little flushed. His cheeks are deep pink and he's sweating.

Though abundant California sunshine'll do that, too. . .

Still. Worth a try.

✳✳✳

On the drive down to Palo Alto the following week, Bennie's mind drifts back to last weekend. She hadn't brought any other guys up to the lake cabin since she and Rob broke up and he moved out. That seems like ages ago. Rob loved to captain the boat, jet ski, and to show off. She has a feeling he liked to pretend it was his boat and she was a pleasing accessory along for the ride. In hindsight, it wasn't just her imagination he was looking at other girls, on other boats and docks, the young waitresses at the supper club, and at the bars and casinos they'd drop by afterwards. Randy, on the other hand, seemed to want to do only the things she wanted. Spend quiet time together cooking, sitting on the porch, sipping wine or maybe a beer and listening to music. He also liked building a fire in the fireplace, making popcorn in the old-fashioned popper or roasting marshmallows for s'mores.

Just the two of them.

Another thing that's different about him is that, unlike Rob, when it comes to getting naked, he's almost bashful, wanting to keep his T-shirt on unless they're in the dark, like he's self-conscious. It's sweet in a way, but she wants him naked. Sometimes, he looks vulnerable and it's like she's assuming some stereotypical male role, coaxing him out of his clothes. He brings out the deepest part of her female sensuality without even trying, more than any guy ever has, and she's comfortable with him, trusts him, and wants him to know he can be that way with her. She still wants to know everything about him. He's told her things most guys wouldn't share, but she senses there's more to be discovered.

By the time Bennie arrives in Palo Alto, Ambrose has already gone into the city and Jessica's way more distracted than usual. When she's focused on her art nowadays, she's a little unfocused on everything else but today especially. She has an appointment at the eye doctor at 10:30 and then she's meeting Pamela for lunch. Bennie still thinks of their mother as Pamela. Jessica calls her "Mom" and Bennie calls her "Mother," and sometimes under her breath *"Mommie Dearest,"* but thinks of her more as Pamela.

Whereas Jessica is the golden child, Bennie gets the third degree from Pamela with a certain amount of attitude. She gets defensive when Pamela starts in, and that's why, when Jessica invited her to join them for a little shopping and lunch, Bennie politely declined. She'd rather supervise this play date with Beau and his little friend Phil than be grilled on why she's not doing what someone else's phenomenally accomplished daughter is: raking in the dough, getting featured in *Vogue* or *Elle* or at least *Sunset*, and engaged to a CEO, real estate mogul, or hedge fund tycoon.

The only reason to string along might be to see if Jessica's halo has slipped a little in Pamela's estimation. A few well-placed, snarky remarks disguised as astute observations from a concerned mother and grandmother? A couple comments about seeing Mike in the *Chronicle*. Only last month, Mike had appeared in the Sunday edition, showing off his new condo and casually posing in the living room with its commanding view of the Bay. There was a French bulldog in the photo, wearing a red collar with silver studs. Perfect. Mike's reinvention is officially complete. Pamela notices these things, but, to Jessica's credit, she's stayed focused, steadily building a name for herself.

Now it's extending east with interest from a gallery in New York and another in Miami. The growing pressure may be working on her nerves, which is understandable, but there's something else going on. She's flat-out evasive when Bennie asks how things are with Ambrose. Even though she sees Ambrose at work, his life with Jessica has become shrouded in mystery, and he seems distracted, too.

Jessica bathes Beau in the master bathroom while Bennie looks through Jessica's roomy walk-in closet to see what's new. As she flips through the latest highlights, one thing makes her stop cold. It's toward the back of the closet like it's not a part of the daily or even weekly rotation. She pulls it out: a candy apple-red satin jumpsuit with ribbon ties down the back. The moment she sees it, she thinks of the story Randy told her, about the couple whose house he was watching in the city. And now here's the same outfit.

"Hey, Jess," she calls out, starting into the bathroom with the jumpsuit. "Where'd you get this?"

Jessica looks up from the sunken tub where Beau is playing with a toy whale, splashing it around. "At Saks a couple years ago."

"Can I try it on?" Bennie turns to start out. "If it fits, maybe I'll wear it to the Stafford-Stoneman wedding."

"What?" Jessica straightens, looks at her. "You can't wear that to a wedding."

"Why not?"

"I read somewhere that you shouldn't wear a jumpsuit or a pantsuit to any wedding. And it's red. You're not supposed to upstage the bride"

"I read somewhere that it's fine to wear a dressy jumpsuit to a wedding. And that thing about wearing red's not really true anymore."

"Mom'll be there, you know."

"So?" Bennie turns to go back into the bedroom. She puts it on while Jessica brings Beau into the bedroom. She places him on the bed, helps him dry off and get dressed. He's resistant. "What do you care if I upstage Jen? She's the one that introduced you to Mike, remember?"

"I remember," Jessica says.
"It's not like she's our favorite cousin," Bennie mutters, flashing back to her early teen years: a family trip to Hawaii, where the bride made Bennie think a boy really liked her when he hadn't. Bennie made a fool of herself, only to realize that she'd provided a day's worth of entertainment for Jen and her bitchy clique of prep-school friends who'd wormed their way along as her entourage. Now, Bennie buttons the closure at the waist and holds the top up to her breasts. "When you get a chance, would you tie me up, please?"

When Jessica finally gets Beau's shirt on, a sporty little rugby, she sets him on the floor.

"I hungry," he declares.

"Aunt Bennie'll feed you lunch when Phil gets here. Don't you want to wait and have lunch with Phil?"

He looks at the floor, shrugs.

"I'll get you some fruit for a snack; give me just a couple minutes, okay? Go watch TV. I left the channel on your cartoons." She sets him on the floor, and, as he heads for the hallway, she walks over to Bennie, observing her in the mirror. "You sure are looking happy these days," she says as she ties the ribbons. "Does it have anything to do with Randy?"

"Pretty much everything."

"Are you inviting him to the wedding as your plus one?"

"Yep. Is Ambrose coming with you?"

"He said he'll let me know." She finishes tying the last ribbon. "That does look good on you," she says. "But I still don't think you ought to wear it to the wedding."

"Maybe I'll wear a nice wrap and take it off for the reception. This'll be perfect for dancing." Bennie turns to see the back. Yes. It's a go. Plus, Randy will freak when he sees it. Then: "What do you mean Ambrose said he'd let you know?"

"He'll let me know, Bennie." Jessica turns to gather up Beau's towel and pajamas laying on the bed.

"You and him are really together, right? I mean, it's not like he's just becoming a tenant here or something."

Jessica tosses the pajamas into a hamper and takes the towel into the bathroom to hang it on a rack, with Bennie close behind.

"I keep thinking the next thing I'll hear is that you and Ambrose are getting married."

"It's too soon to talk about marriage," Jessica says quietly. "Things are still evolving."

"Since when?"

Jessica sighs. "I have to get ready. Can we finish this later?" She goes over to the vanity, takes some of her make-up out of the drawer.

"Have you two been fighting about something? You don't think he's seeing anyone, do you? Because I'm sure he's not."

Jessica smooths some lotion from a small, jewel-like container onto her face. "How can you say you're sure about something like that?"

"Because I just know. And it's not like you're seeing anyone else." She fully expects Jessica to confirm that, but Jessica just brushes her hair back. Bennie watches as she sweeps it into a loose up-do, which she pins into place with a tortoise-shell comb. "Is it?" Bennie asks.

"Of course not." She starts applying eyeliner.

"He loves you, you know."

Jessica faces her, only the upper lids outlined in kohl. It makes her look intimidating. "I said I'm not seeing anybody else, Bennie," she begins, "and now that you have a relationship that makes you happy, maybe you should focus on that and not worry about me and Ambrose."

"Fine," Bennie says. "If you want to fuck around and lose the best thing you ever had, be my guest. I'm borrowing this jumpsuit to wear to Jen's wedding and then I'll have it cleaned and bring it back good as new." She reaches around to untie the ribbons as she starts back into the bedroom. "I'll change and go get Beau a snack."

"Bennie!"

Bennie ignores her, steps out of the jumpsuit and back into her favorite retro cotton polka dot dress. "Better get ready," she says. "You don't want to be late." She leaves the room, still buttoning the dress, not looking back. But she knows Jessica's standing there staring, before turning to go back into the bathroom. Bennie can just feel it.

Struck a nerve.

FOUR

There's an envelope stuck in Randy's apartment door when he comes home from today's walk. It was a huge effort to drag himself off the sofa and put on his sneakers. Lately, he'd only put them on to go do laundry or go to the store, whenever he did those things. It seemed futile to exercise before but he's been making more of an effort to get off his ass, even if he's not sure what difference it'll make.

He kicks off the sneakers, flops on the sofa and opens the envelope addressed to **Burke, A-05**. It's the new lease. There's a substantial rent increase and a new garbage disposal fee. He has until the end of next week to sign and return it if he plans to stay. Otherwise, he'll need to notify management and vacate by the first of the month. He tosses the paper aside and looks around, reality having just bitch-slapped him hard.

This place sucks, but it's been home for a while, and he'd been looking forward to watching TV tonight. Maybe order a pizza, with some green peppers on it for a vegetable, have a beer and call Bennie, but, as he feels the world falling out from under him, none of that will happen. Even watching TV won't be the same, knowing this may be the last few days of TV he'll get if he has to hock it just to buy enough food to keep his body and soul together when he starts living in his Jeep. Even that might be too rich for his blood, because where to park it? Have to be near enough a bathroom, and far enough away from security cameras.

Even pitching a tent in a campground costs a lot. He doesn't know where he'll have to go to afford to live and work, and what happens in the interim? And if he has to sell the Jeep. . . It's hard to even find a spot to sleep on the street nowadays. You can't without getting rousted, and he once did his share of the rousting. Now when he's out there, he'll be the one stiffening at the sight of a cop.

When he realizes he's seriously contemplating the consequences of no place, no money, no job, nor anything that had given his "new normal" post-breakdown life any structure, he feels sick to his stomach. No need to look back at how it all happened because he doesn't have the luxury of time for reflection. He's run out of time and maybe if he were a better, smarter, industrious, more honorable person, this wouldn't be happening. On the other hand, there are plenty of people with those qualities out there on the street already, so that has nothing to do with it. If he were really crooked, he'd probably be rich. As it is, he's been bush-league, nickel-and-dime-crooked. Just crooked enough to get fired and not criminal enough to kill those cock-sucking, fat-assed sons-of-bitches who turned down his appeal.

And he's been looking for another job, but not hard and fast enough. It takes him forever to fill out online applications for even the lowest-paying positions. He suspects those pseudo-psychological questions on some of them raise a red flag, so he overthinks things, trying to outfox whatever entity may be trying to tap his brain to deem whether he's sufficiently controllable. He finds himself answering the opposite of his gut-impulse. He went on a "group" interview and the same thing happened. Also, he tends to sweat knowing he's being judged, or evaluated. And the way that lady at the last interview was looking at him made him paranoid, like she knew some kind of dirt on him already. She wouldn't quite look him in the eye, but just above him. So, he kept looking over his shoulder, which made him look shifty, like he has something to hide. And he does. He's desperate.

He's just had some new business cards made, real ones this time, with **R. Burke, Security** and his e-mail and phone number. They really look nice, too. He'd put them up around the neighborhood anywhere he could find, hoping to get more gigs like the hippie craft fair just to keep going a little longer. Anything until something bigger breaks, and then he can get his detective license.

His buddy, Jeremy, had said they'd need updated records for any further Stanford jobs and a new copy of his resume—no rush, no side gigs coming up soon; there's a bit of a lull now. More art gallery-type jobs would be so nice, but he only got that because of the situation with Ambrose, and then he met Bennie and— Bennie!

She already knows he doesn't have much of anything. He's been letting on like his prospects are brighter, as if he were a real boyfriend, but now time's run out on that, too. That's the most crushing thing of all. What does a princess like her want with a stone-cold bum like him? That's what really makes him wish he were dead again. He used to go to bed when this feeling happened but knowing even that won't be possible for much longer nauseates him.

He hasn't talked to his mother nor his brother or sister in quite a while. His mother called a couple times when he came home from the hospital after his war flashbacks but, even if the conversation started out normal, it always devolved into a black hole of guilt and recriminations as she started remembering her hopes for him and how those are forever dashed. His father had a massive heart attack not long after the police department started the investigation on him. Ronald Burke, Sr., was already dead and buried by the time the verdict came down. She blames him for his father's sudden, stress-induced death and so do his siblings.

And maybe they're right. That's something else he'll have to deal with for the rest of his life. Just one more reason that the thought of curling up in bed with a pistol had flitted through his mind so frequently in recent months. Though if he did decide to do it, he more than likely wouldn't blow his brains out on the bed. He always thought doing it in the bathtub would be better. That way, the crime scene clean-up crew could just scour the tiles and rinse everything down the drain. There wouldn't be a blood-soaked mattress to dispose of or a pool of blood dripping through the ceiling of the apartment below, though that would at least let someone know to check up here before the smell got really bad, because no telling how long he'd lie here. His neighbor/ex-fuck-buddy Brianna would probably find him. He'd leave the door unlocked.

And why should he care what kind of mess he leaves? They'll just clean up whatever, nothing to them. Just another crazy veteran/ex-cop living on the fringes who decided to end it all. Not too many left to wonder why, either.

A sob rises in his throat as he thinks of his mother again. *Would she want a note? Would Bennie?* He wouldn't even know what to put in one. Maybe people who knew him would just figure he had too much baggage to carry, others thinking *What a loser,* or smirking because they hated his guts anyway, don't even know the half of it.

And now a golfball-size pain forms in his throat, more sobs building up. He canceled his music app subscription to save a few bucks so no good way to even stream Sinatra's "My Way" without ads popping up if he goes out in a blaze of glory. Some people would say that's a cheesy selection for a suicide song, but those people can goddamn go fuck themselves.

He wipes his eyes, sighs, having sat tensed up for so long, it's like he's been holding his breath. Maybe he could go get the .38 out of his nightstand and bring it in here to clean, just in case. Maybe turn on the TV to drown out all this goddamn fucking sorrow. And there's a coupon for half-priced pizza in the kitchen drawer. He has enough money for that. . .

As he gets up off the sofa, he remembers he already hocked both pistols along with some other stuff last week, and he doesn't really want to use the shotgun for this. Might fuck him up without getting the job done. Then he'd be dependent on his mother. Or somebody. Or just die in complete agony. So, if he really and truly decides to end it all, he'll have to wait. Figure out some sure-fire, final method.

✳✳✳

Bennie's on her third batch of cookies from the Martha Stewart cookbook she found last week at a used bookstore. She's rolling little balls of dough in powdered sugar when there's a knock at the door. She walks over to answer it, wiping her hands on a dishcloth. "Who is it?"

"Terrence," comes a voice from the other side. "Remember me?"

She opens the door.

It's Rajit's partner from his last job: a young, black techie in jeans, retro Devo T and backpack. She'd met him at the coffee shop around the corner one day when he was there with Rajit. He wears thick-framed glasses, short dreads, and a rock-steady gaze that gives her the feeling, like with Rajit, that the nerdy vibe masks something else. "Hi," he says. "Sorry to bug you."

"Hi, Terrence. You're not bugging me. Come in."

He walks inside. "I'm supposed to meet Rajit at his apartment, but he's not back yet. Mind if I wait for a few minutes?"

"Make yourself at home. I've just been doing some baking." He leaves his backpack by the door and follows her to the kitchen.

"I can see that," he says, noticing the ginger snaps cooling on the counter along with strained raspberry jam, chopped walnuts, cookie cutters, and other accoutrement. "Making these for some party?"

"Just for fun. Can I get you a coffee? Tea? Beer?"

"Glass of water, thanks." She gets it while he looks at a tray of pale cookies with scalloped edges. Some solid, others with a heart cut-out in the middle. "Sugar cookies?" he asks.

"Linzer hearts," she says, handing him the glass of water. "You can eat the first one. Have a seat." He sits and she spreads a spoonful of jam on the solid cookie before placing one with a hollow heart on top of it so the red shows through. She places it on a small plate and sets it before him. *"Bon appetite!"*

"Thank you." He takes a bite. "This is truly amazing."

"I'll pack you and Rajit each a box."

"You don't have to do that," he says. "But—if you insist."

"I do," she says, joining him at the table. "So, tell me, what was it like working with Rajit?"

"Never a dull moment." He laughs like thinking of something funny that happened earlier, but he doesn't explain it like she hoped.

"Why's that?" she asks.

He drops his gaze. "You know you could totally package and sell these," he says, referring to the cookies.

"Maybe someday." She assembles another. "What exactly did you and he do to get fired?"

"You heard about that, huh?" His eyes are calm behind those glasses.

"Rajit said he couldn't really talk about it, but what happened?" She sets a ginger snap on his plate. "Promise I can keep a secret."

And he tells her the story, keeping it in layman's terms, which she is glad for because even though her grandfather was a tech genius, and so's her dad, she and Jessica inherited none of those genes. The company Rajit and Terrence worked for was resurrecting one of its projects for law enforcement, this time on steroids: police "smart glasses" with new Big Brother data-harvesting features, making it possible to target individuals just walking down the street or at a rally, riding by in a car or sitting in the park, by recognizing faces, scrutinizing characteristics, of which skin color was a factor, retrieving any prior arrests, tickets, scrapes, run-ins, reports, or warnings, and displaying that information before the officer's eyes, literally. There's already a similar program in China and now. . .

At the roll-out, there were a bunch of high-ups, along with a slew of police brass, sheriffs, and high-powered private security firm CEOs. Rajit, Terrence, and a few insider kamikaze workers knew what they were about to do and that it would spell the end of their career at this place. Nonetheless, they walked around the room, watching the bigwigs in prototype glasses. Flashed on the screens around the room were rap sheets: complaint reports, restraining orders, DWIs, and other infractions committed by many present, replacing the high-production promotional video with faces of the accused, sitting right there, over their quinoa and pomegranate avril salads, for all to see. Pandemonium ensued. Rajit, the mastermind behind the whole thing, Terrence, and other members on board with this "colossal prank" were kicked out on their collective ass, which they knew would happen. But reality set in when all their money quickly ran out.

"So where do you work now, Terrence?"

"I'm doing a little free-lancing: trouble-shooting, consulting, you know. Trying to piece together enough gigs to get by. Rajit's helping me brainstorm some ideas and update my resume."

"I hope you find something soon. Any leads?"

"A couple."

"Maybe you can find a way to start your own business."

"That's just what I've been thinking," he says. Then, adjusting his glasses: "If I can get something going, I'm thinking of maybe moving in with Rajit so we can share the rent. I'm really tired of living in that group house. It's like I never left college. Sometimes it smells."

"I'd hate living in a group house, too," she says, assembling another cookie.

"So, it's—okay with you? If Rajit and I share an apartment here?"

She looks up. "Sure, why wouldn't it be?"

"Well, you own the building, right? I just wouldn't want to ask Rajit to do anything that'd violate the lease."

"I don't personally own the building."

"But your dad does, correct?"

She sprinkles powdered sugar on the next Linzer heart. "Uh-huh," then, looking at him as she puts a dollop of jam on another: "How'd you know that?"

"Did some checking."

"I see."

"You're not mad, are you? I wasn't trying to snoop into your business." He laughs nervously, recognizing the irony, given what they'd just been talking about.

"I'm not mad," she says, spreading the jam.

"Rajit was pretty crazy about you, you know."

She looks at him. "He told you that?"

"Well, yeah. I mean, about when you and him were kinda dating, or at least— and then he left to go home for that wedding. And to see that girl his parents wanted him to meet?"

"Ah, yes." Rajit had shown her a picture of that beautiful girl on his phone, and—though he'd seemed less interested in meeting her than in pleasing his family—that's when Bennie knew another heartbreak could be lurking around the corner. When Rajit left that night, she'd gone to bed and cried. "Meera."

"Right. Wow, if he'd known then what he knows now. . ." He trails off, glances at her, eats a cookie.

"What were you going to say?" she asks, though she has some idea. That, maybe if he'd known who Bennie is, who her father is, Rajit wouldn't have been so concerned about his future here in the States? About letting his parents down? But then, his parents' successful arranged marriage made a case for adhering to tradition.

"Oh. . . Nothing."

She realizes she could be somewhat offended by what Terrence might've been suggesting, but she isn't. "Well, none of us know what the future holds. Do we?"

Terrence laughs softly. "No, we don't," he says. "Live & learn."

✳✳✳

Bennie calls Randy to tell him she got him some things at the market along with a few special treats so would like to come over and drop them off. He says okay but doesn't sound like himself.

She knocks, expecting him to welcome her with a kiss but he just says, "Come in." When she does, he's sitting on the sofa. He doesn't look well so she sets the burlap grocery bags on the counter and takes out the homemade cookies in their plastic container, then the organic fruit and a bottle of fresh-squeezed orange juice. She comments on how bare his kitchen is. She'll help him pick out some staples to keep on hand and more raw vegetables to cut up and keep in the refrigerator for healthy snacks. She's wired on matcha, prattling on so she doesn't notice at first he's barely talking.

"Want some strawberries?" she asks. "I'll rinse them for you. I thought I'd see if you want to go to lunch—my treat—then you could come over to my place and hang out there for a while."

"I have to tell you something," he says.

She walks over to sit next to him. He looks too serious and fear grips her heart that something's really wrong. "What is it?"

"They're going up on my rent and I have to find another place."

"Oh." *Looking around at this place, maybe moving isn't such a bad idea.* "I'll help you look if you want. There's this lady I know who—"

"I can't afford it," he says.

"How do you know? I was just going to say she lives in my building and has some rental property—"

"I can't afford anything around here, not even a worse place than this. I don't see how I've stayed here this long."

She'd hoped to help him find something where there would be less distance between them, not more. "But you can't move out of the city," she says.

"I haven't been getting any security work and I'm having a lot of trouble finding a job around here. And when I say, 'around here,' I mean within a 50-mile radius. I keep getting turned down. Maybe I'm on a blacklist somewhere."

Now that she's sitting down, she can see he really is in a bad place. And he looks like he's on no sleep. "Why would you be on some blacklist?" she asks.

"'Cause I'm a total fuck-up."

"You are not!"

He turns away, facing the blank TV screen.

Even though she can see that he's upset, there's something else, too. Something's missing. Besides just sleep, she senses a vacancy where her guy used to be: sweet, funny, affectionate Randy, the one she met at the gallery that lovely night and has been head-over-heels for ever since. She decides to go out on a limb. "Hey, I know. We could hire you to do regular security detail down at the building where Ambrose and I work. I don't know what the pay would be, but—"

"That's just it, Bennie. There's no job I can get that'll pay enough for me to live here or— I gotta leave."

"Leave?" She glimpses the pill bottles on the trunk he's using as a coffee table. "But we can work out the pay and we need someone watching the place. And since we're expanding, we hired someone to do IT work, and you can be head of security." She slides closer. "This would be tailor-made for you, right?"

"It's sweet of you to care, but I don't want to be a charity case."

"You're not a charity case! You can still study for your detective license, but in the meantime, you'll be helping us and—" She pauses. "Unless. . . It's not that you don't want to work with me, is it?"

"It's nothing at all to do with you."

"You don't have to move away, though, Randy." She does have an idea that's been in the back of her mind. *Hadn't wanted to pitch it too soon, but this calls for bold measures.* "Move in with me."

"What?"

"Move into my apartment. With me."

He doesn't say anything.

For a moment, she feels like when she was 10 and fell out of a friend's treehouse, the breath completely knocked out of her. She knows she should wait and let him speak next but the panic is starting to well in her chest. "I realize we haven't known each other that long, but, whenever you're not there, I wish you were. You're more than welcome to come and live with me. . ." She pauses. No reaction. Her heart cracks into pieces but she smiles anyway. "Why won't you say anything?"

He finally looks over at her and the shadows in his eyes are like nothing she's ever seen before. "And then what happens when you get sick of me? You don't have to feel responsible for me."

"I don't and I'd never get sick of you!"

"You can't know that."

"I know I love you."

"Bennie," he breathes. A tear slides down his cheek.

"I do. You don't have to say it back."

He smiles, giving her a glimmer of hope, but it's a sad smile. He rubs his face, wiping away more tears. "I love you, too."

"If I love you and you do love me, what's the problem?"

"The problem is you don't need me being dependent on you. I mean, whatever job I get and wherever I live, we might still see each other. If I ever. . . If you still want to. But I can't right now, that's all."

Now, big chunks of her heart are falling apart. "Why are you doing this?"

"I'm just trying to be. . . prudent."

"Well, don't!" she cries. "How can you say you love me and then—" She feels like she's about to hyperventilate. "I don't understand—"

There's a quick knock at the door and then a girl wearing yoga pants and a big sweater just opens it and walks in. "Hey, Randy, I—" She sees them and pauses. "Oh, I didn't know you had company."

Randy looks up, tears still streaking his face. "Brianna, we're in the middle of something. Do you mind?"

She steps back, makes a face like *oops!* "Sure, sorry. I'll see you later." She looks at Bennie, backs out, and shuts the door.

"That's my neighbor."

"Right." She tries to hold in the sobs that are building. "But, I wouldn't want you to feel trapped or anything." It hadn't occurred to her that he could feel trapped with her, but a girl just came walking into his apartment like it's a normal thing. Like it happens all the time. She hadn't really thought too much about that and the realization there could be other girls hits her in the face like a splash of cold water. "I didn't mean to pressure you."

"You're not. I've been trying to make things seem better than they are. Way better. But I just can't swing it anymore."

She reaches into her purse for a tissue. "I thought you knew you didn't have to pretend for me." She thinks of how she let herself go wild with him, the way she's never done with a man, and how worlds of possibility open up whenever she looks forward to seeing him, to the ringing of the bell when he arrives downstairs, cooking and baking for him, even buying these groceries for him, all the things they'll do, places they could go. Any amount of time they spend together doesn't seem enough already and now he's talking about moving away?

Yes, they could still see each other, but would they? What if there's a Brianna at the new place he moves to?

She reaches into her purse again, fishing for her phone.

"What're you doing?" he asks.

"Calling a ride. I've imposed on you enough. You can't help it if you don't feel the same way I do."

"But I do."

"No, you don't! You can't or you wouldn't even be talking about—*moving away*—when you don't really have to, if you'd—" She stops herself, a wave of tears coming on, but takes a breath, trying to hold it back. She can do this later, the crying. There'll be lots of it and nothing will ever be the same. She wipes her eyes. "Never mind," she says finally. "I want you to be happy. I don't want to be with somebody who doesn't want to be with me the same way."

"It's not that at all."

"Yes, it is."

"It is not!" he insists.

"Then what is it?"

"It's just. . . better this way for you. Trust me. It'll save you the trouble of kicking me out. You don't know about all my messed-up shit you might have to deal with."

"You don't know everything about me either but that's what it means to love somebody, in spite of all their messed-up shit!" She pauses to wipe her nose and get her breath. "Right?" She turns away. Such a beautiful day outside and so dark in here, silence stretching out like a long, lonely road. Can't even call a ride right now, too emotional. The way she feels, she'd just as soon start walking. Maybe call Ambrose from somewhere. But there's nobody who can help. Maybe she'll just take some time off and go to the cabin for a while. Too many memories there already though. Maybe just disappear. Maybe it's time for a faraway vacation to some remote place. A pain-filled vacation where all she can do is think about how it would be if Randy were there. . .

Already what-ifs and past tense. This is the last thing she expected when she decided to come over and surprise him. And she's the one who got an awful surprise.

"I can't do this anymore," he whispers. "I'm sorry." Such tenderness and yet so harsh at the same time.

"I'm sorry, too," she says before she walks out and shuts the door.

✳✳✳

Ambrose rings Bennie's apartment from downstairs. When she doesn't answer on the intercom, he calls from his mobile. No answer. Voicemail. *Another date with Randy?* He hopes not, because he ran up on an old acquaintance from his club days, a guy who used to sling for his boss Lang. He has a real job now working for an A/C company but still has a good line on some molly, and when they were talking outside the coffee shop just a little while ago, he went out to his truck and gave Ambrose a couple hits. The last thing Ambrose wants is to look suspicious around more people.

According to this guy, Lang's still in business with a smaller operation now because Lang knocked up his goth girlfriend and, in addition to dealing, he's working as a bouncer at a strip club just to have some form of legitimacy. "Still an asshole, though. Just because his expansion plans didn't work out doesn't mean he's not still looking for ways to screw anybody who'll let him" and Ambrose is glad that's no longer him. Those days are over. Still. Lang seems small-time compared to what's out there now. That, he'd rather not think about.

Anyway, it's Friday and this molly's burning a hole through his pocket.

He'd do it with Jessica, if she'd even want to, but she's at an overnight, indoor camp-out at the children's museum with Beau, his friends, their mommies, and some daddies, but nobody he really knows. And he's still rattled after that incident the other day, knowing she went to see Mignon just when he thought things might be getting back to normal. At least the guy who Rajit and Terrence thought were watching the motel didn't follow her. That could've been something else entirely; hard to know, having to hear about it without being able to get a read himself. Anyway, at least while Jessica's at the museum, he knows she's not with Mignon. So, there's that.

He shoots Bennie a text before giving up. He'd cool his heels at the Italian coffee shop in the next block, but he's already wired on a triple shot of espresso. Though he could head on back to Palo Alto and have the house to himself, he's a little nostalgic for the old days when Bennie and he used to hang after work, or even join Miss Dover and a couple of her friends for drinks. Anyway, maybe Bennie's not out with that stupid son-of-a-bitch tonight. They've been seeing too much of each other, as it is. Just for the hell of it, he rings the bell one more time.

"Yes?"

"Bennie! It's me. Are you busy?"

". . . No."

"Buzz me up. I've got a surprise for you."

A pause. "Okay. Come on up."

The buzzer sounds, the door unlocks and he goes in. He turns and takes the stairs to work off some of this manic, caffeinated energy. When he gets to her apartment, the door's ajar and he pushes it open just as she's getting settled back onto the sofa. She doesn't look well, like she's suffering from a cold or bad allergies. Her eyes are red and puffy. She looks miserable.

"Hi," she says. "You must've worked late."

"Yeah. . ." He walks around to the front of the sofa. Something's way off. Never really seen her like this before.

"Have a seat," she says, pulling her covers further toward her to clear a place for him. "Can I get you anything?" She reverts to her default hospitality even though he can see it's stretching her to the limit.

"No, thanks." He sits down on the sofa. One of her black-and-white movies is on TV, with well-dressed people in an upscale drawing room, making droll comments. The look in her eyes makes him wonder if maybe someone died. "What's the matter?"

She wipes her nose on a tissue and tosses it into a nearby wastebasket. He notices the wastebasket's almost full of them. "What makes you think something's the matter?"

"Only that you look like hell," he says, relieved to see her smile, slightly. Then she tears up again. He moves closer, his heart going out to her. "What happened?"

"Randy doesn't want to see me anymore."

"He said that?"

"He's losing his apartment. I think there's more to it, though. But it kind of threw me for a loop."

He's glad to hear it's over, but not to see her devastated, of course. Tempted as he is to go into all the reasons why Randy is so wrong for her, looking at her now, this just doesn't seem the time. "I'm sorry to hear that."

She looks up, sniffles. "What's going on with you? Are you meeting Jessica somewhere later?"

"She's on an overnight at the museum with Beau."

She nods, shrugs. "So, what's the surprise?"

✳✳✳

When Bennie closed the door, Randy sat on the sofa until dark shadows gathered in the corners. He wanted to go after her, but like that misguided gunfighter he'd seen on a TV western, he'd cut her loose because he's no good. Because she doesn't even know how bad things are, and, once she realizes, she'd just kick him to the curb anyway. The happiness—joy—he'd experienced for the last few weeks was a delusion. He'd put on a good act, had a good run, and now that he's on this downward spiral, all the demons who ever dogged his steps are running to jump into the whirlpool that is his life. What's left of it.

He doesn't remember how he got to the bedroom, but that's where he wakes up as night falls and something about this pitiful feeling reminds him of his dad's funeral. There've been other bad days, too, God knows, before and after, but that one was for the books. No uniform, no badge, just him in all his naked villainy, a pageant of failure from start to finish, on a day that should've been only about his father and honoring his memory: pure chaos.

It would've been bad enough that he arrived late, hungover, but then there was that skirmish with his brother at the graveside. His uncles tried to handle it, but his mother had to break it up, and when the service was over, mourners yet to disperse were treated to a brawl that ended with him at the cemetery with only the undertakers, a blackening eye, and a cracked rib. His mom, crying hysterically, was escorted away by his siblings, and their in-laws and outlaws who he barely knows just gave him dirty looks. The dirty cop with no regard for anyone but himself. And he's been alone ever since.

'Til Bennie. And now she's gone.

The darkness grows without and within until he's enfolded in it. He hasn't taken his meds the last couple days and, now with all this, the wind seems to be picking up outside. Whether or not he finds the guts to end it all somewhere in the night, "what dreams may come" will be punctuated by sandstorms, an occasional scream from down the hall, angry voices, and the eyes of an Afghan girl who once served him tea.

The rest is anyone's guess.

✳✳✳

Things are settling down at the museum now that the arts & crafts session ended a half-hour ago in the main lobby. The kids are in pajamas, getting ready for a bedtime story read by one of the City's leading children's authors. The docents dim the lights. Beau is sitting with some of his friends near the front of the group, supervised by Caitlyn, while Jessica visits the snack table, gets a bottled water, and eats from a bag of Sun Chips while slowly walking past the kids' artwork on the tables by the wall. Beau's flower collage rests with the others, glue drying. He included a butterfly in the center, which she thought was a nice touch.

She takes out her phone and dials Ambrose. No answer. It is late. *Maybe he's asleep.* No texts from Mignon or anyone else, which is actually a relief. Even though Jessica hadn't been looking forward to this camp-in, it has kept her so busy she hasn't had time to think of anything else. Things have been intense, and she needs this moment to catch her breath. One wouldn't think a person could do that with all these rambunctious kids and activities, but now that the noise has subsided, this place seems almost Zen.

She tosses the empty chip bag into a trash can, wandering down the nearest darkened corridor to the restroom, taking her time. On the way back, she pauses at a "moving" painting of undulating blue waves with animated sea creatures cruising past. When she returns to the main lobby, story time is well underway. The author does a great job holding the kids' attention, and most of the adults' too. Normally, she'd be closer to what's going on, holding Beau on her lap, enjoying his reaction to all the goings-on and exchanging glances with the other parents, bonding over this experience to make lifetime memories.

These are moments with children you'll never get back, so make the most of this time, everyone says. That's true. All true. But tonight, she feels more like a spectator and less like a participant. Watching herself move through like one of those animated sea creatures. . . Can't explain all these contradictory actions and emotions that have possessed her lately. Looking at the scene around her, she feels like she's in this world, but not of it.

A loving, involved parent and responsible human being, level-headed and mature.

She's all those things and none.

On the one hand, maybe it isn't the wisest choice, but on the other, what better time to do molly? Bennie isn't so sure it will help, starting from below sea-level while Ambrose is in a better place. Or so she thought. They watch *Dinner at Eight*, and Jean Harlow's platinum hair gets even brighter, her silk evening gown glowing incandescent, clinging to her body in such a sexy way. She's like a goddess lit from within even as she talks back to Wallace Beery in that streetwise patter. Gradually, the whole black-and-white movie looks like it's in color under silvery tones. After *Dinner at Eight*, Bennie's about to turn off the TV and put on some music, but *Scaramouche* comes on and the MGM colors are so riotously rich, textures so sensuous, they become transfixed by it, what with the period costumes, voluptuous wigs, Eleanor Parker's warm, buxom Lenore playing off against Janet Leigh's cool, platinum Aline. By the time the raucous, elaborate sword fight between Stewart Granger and Mel Ferrer ends, she and Ambrose are flying.

After a while, the apartment, which felt spacious, no longer seems big enough to contain the sense of expansiveness and obscure, sweet anticipation that envelops them. They head up to the rooftop garden, walk around to work off some excess energy. She'd left some plants up there that needed repotting and thinks this would be a perfect time to do it, while Ambrose is here to talk to her, only it's hard to focus on a single task, because tonight, anything is possible. Then her legs start getting shaky and she has to sit on one of the patio sofas, not hungry at all but realizing she hasn't eaten anything since this morning's pastry, which seems like a year ago.

Finally, Ambrose collapses onto the other patio sofa, and they gaze up at the strings of white lights as the sky goes indigo like it does, and the lights of Columbus Avenue brighten below. Getting antsy as another wave of euphoria advances and sensing a "party" atmosphere building below, they look over the edge of the building to the delicious, bustling jumble of neon and headlights. She notices she's been clamping her jaw and tries to mindfully loosen up and relax as Ambrose paces, smoking a couple cigarettes. They both marvel at the view and perfect weather, but, every so often, even feeling so good, she's aware of the undertow from earlier that's waiting for her on the other side of tonight.

After going back down to her apartment, she grows more attuned to Ambrose's vibe, picking up that things aren't quite right with him either. "But you've been talking to Miss Dover, haven't you?" she asks, tossing some blankets and pillows onto the floor. She plays some music while he paces around the living room, looking at her artwork and books and curios like it's for the first time.

"Not in the last few days. But I'm sure everything's fine."

"How can you be sure if you can't get in touch with her?"

"I'd know if it wasn't."

"How would you know?"

He clasps his hands behind his head as she switches off a couple of the brighter lamps, and switches on a lantern she got in Japan Town. The paper shade is printed with cherry blossoms and the bulb inside slowly rotates, projecting subtle pink flowers around the room.

"Are you psychic?" she asks, sitting down on one of the blankets to roll a joint on the tacky San Francisco tray she uses to serve tea.

He walks over, slips off his shoes and sits down across from her on the blanket. "Yeah," he says. "I'm psychic." The pink of the Japanese lantern casts everything in a dramatic, painterly tone and the shifting light on his skin looks velvety and rich, like a close-up on a movie screen. He's so different from when they first met, that day Miss Dover introduced them. He was so cute in this careless, rumpled way. . . The change just reminds her how young he was, and that wasn't even long ago. She had no idea what she was doing when she called Jessica and asked if he could stay in the guest house while he hid out from that blowhard he was dealing drugs for, or how just the act of helping a friend would alter the course of all their lives. And it was because of him she'd met Randy.

Now, Ambrose's staring at her, too. She has no concept of what she must look like.

He smiles. "Still with me?"

She snaps out of it, resumes rolling the joint. "Maybe Miss Dover's decided to ditch us and move all operations to Paris."

His smile fades. "She wouldn't do that."

"Maybe she met someone and ran off to Cannes for a week."

"Maybe." He looks momentarily distracted, then: "So? Randy. What happened?"

Shaken, she licks and seals the joint, hands it to him and flicks the lighter. "I don't want to talk about that now. It's just over, that's' all."

"You're better off." He draws deeply.

"Why? You never really liked him, did you? Even after he let you go that night instead of arresting you."

"Didn't say I never liked him. Just that he's all wrong for you."

She's not in the mood to debate, and certainly not to admit he may be right. "O-kay. Change of subject. How come you didn't want to save this molly to do with Jessica instead of your old pal Bennie?"

"That's just it. We never get to party anymore." He takes another hit. It smells of earth & citrus: grounded & comforting. Takes the edge off. "Besides," he says, passing it back to her, "Jessica's been pursuing other interests."

"Other interests?" She flashes on her conversation with Jessica the other day when she'd neither confirmed nor denied seeing somebody else. "Like what?"

"Like Mignon. I think it's at least partly my fault."

"What are you talking about?"

"I put the idea in her head that Mignon was flirting with her that night at the art show. It must've gotten Jess thinking that she wanted to see what it was like."

"What *what's* like?" She asks, taking a hit.

"You know. Sex with a woman. At least, I think it's just the sex. I don't really know."

Bennie is speechless, clutching the joint between thumb and index finger. She lapses into a coughing fit, making the buzz more intense and causing her to doubt what she thought she heard. She halfway gets over it, looks up, eyes watering. "Did you say—"

"Yep. Can I have another hit?"

She passes to him. "We are talking about the same Jessica, right? My sister?"

He nods, eyes meeting hers.

"That just can't be true."

"It be true," he exhales.

"Why didn't you tell me? Why didn't she tell me?" He's clearly had time getting used to the idea, even if he doesn't like it. Or does he? "Did you and Mignon and Jessica ever have like. . . a threesome, or something?"

"No."

"Fooling around, at all?"

He shakes his head. Between the molly and this earth-shattering news, he's succeeded in taking her mind off Randy. After another hit, he carefully places the lit end in his mouth, indicating for her to come closer for a shotgun. She leans forward, taking in the smoke he blows into her mouth, giving her another massive rush. She holds it then exhales, sinking further onto the blanket and pillows, the utter unreality of this whole day rendering her limp and exhausted. Jessica and Mignon? "I just can't believe it."

His eyes are glassier as he takes another hit.

"How does that make you feel?" she asks.

"Not good."

She rearranges the pillows and settles back again, floating. "Do you still love her?"

"Let me get back to you on that."

"You must still care. . ."

"I do." He passes the joint, but she waves it away. He smokes some more, gazing at her, like she must've been staring at him before in that pinkish light. One more hit and he places what's left in an old tiki bar ashtray, moves it to the side just off the blanket, then turns back to her, drawing his knees up to his chest. "I care about you, too, Bennie. I'm sorry he hurt you."

Whether any of this euphoric residue will last into tomorrow, she doesn't know yet. It'll probably all wear off, leaving her mired in those awful memories of yesterday. Or is it still today? "I care about you, too. You're sweet."

He sighs. "I really should go home soon. It's getting late."

"You can't go now. Aren't you still fucked-up?"

He laughs. "Yeah." He lies next to her on the pillow. "Want me to order some food?"

"You're hungry?"

"Might be in a half hour or so."

"Me too. . ." She rolls over, getting vibes of slumber parties past, along with a chill. She reaches for the nearest plush throw, pulls it over her, but then reaches out to touch his face while it still looks so velvety. "You're my best friend, you know."

He grasps her hand. "You're more than a friend to me." He leans up on his elbow. "Can I tell you something? Just between us?"

"Sure."

"I was crazy about you from the day I started working at Miss Dover's. I know stuff happened after that, and changed everything, but I'll always care about you." He leans closer. "Don't let that porn-addicted bastard get you down. He was lucky you gave him the time of day, let alone—" He stops. "You're just so much better than him."

She looks at him, one thing he said having fallen outside that sweet haze of warm, fuzzy words she can sort out later. "Porn-addicted? Where'd you get that?"

He pauses, like he forgot he even said it. "Just seems like the type, that's all. Anyway, if there's anything I can do to help you get over him, say the word and I'll do it."

"Like what?"

"Anything."

Maybe it's that it is late, or emotional overload, but she senses meanings could get distorted if they're both not careful, and he doesn't mean it like that. "You're Jessica's man." She smiles.

"I always wanted to kiss you back then and never got the chance . . ." He's close enough, all it would take is a slight move. "Can I this once?" he whispers. "It'll be our secret from now on."

Bennie, you bad girl. The worst. "That's the molly talkin'."

"It isn't just that, I swear." Then: "Got any Vicks?"

Ah, the Vicks VapoRub. . . "I haven't used any in a while," she says. "There may be some in the medicine cabinet."

"I'll be right back."

"But it's too cold for that," she says after he's already gone to get it. "I'm too cold," she says to herself.

When he comes back, he opens the jar, sets it down and rubs his hands together for warmth. He pulls the blanket off her and straddles her at the waist, causing her to flash on that poster for *Blow-up*, the Antonioni movie where handsome, blond, 1960s heart-throb David Hemmings plays a fashion photographer. In the poster, he's straddling a gorgeous model, taking her picture. And now Ambrose is sexy David Hemmings, applying vapor rub to her chest, her shoulders, and then he leans down on his hands and knees to blow on the places he rubbed. It gives her goosebumps, making her skin tingle, like those York Peppermint Pattie commercials.

Minty. . . "Cold," she whimpers.

"Yeah, but doesn't it feel good too?"

She nods.

He moves further down, pulls the hem of her faded jersey nightgown off her thighs and applies a thin layer. "Spread your legs," he says.

"Ambrose. . ."

"Just a little."

She does and he rubs Vicks on the inside of her thighs, leaning down to blow on her skin. "Relax," he whispers. "Take a deep breath."

She does, and the cold she felt earlier's not so harsh now. She raises her arms over her head, pretending to be the model from the movie poster, feeling pretty for the first time this evening.

"Feel good?" he asks.

She nods. "You should let me do this to you," she whispers. "I feel like I'm having all the fun now."

"You can do me later," he says, moving up to where he can look her in the face. "I feel like I'm having all the fun." He lowers his head and blows along her collar bone, then smooths her hair away from her face. "And it's not just the molly."

"I don't believe you."

"Believe whatever you want," he says, just before softly touching his lips to hers. He pauses, and does it again, longer this time.

Still lying there in an altered state of consciousness and imagination, she has to wonder if it's really happened, but when it happens again, she knows it's real. "This is wrong," she whispers.

He kisses her forehead and the side of her face. "You'll forget it tomorrow like it never happened. And pretty soon you'll forget all about him."

Maybe it isn't just the molly after all 'cause its last sparkling effects are only now starting to dim. Forget all about him. Even Humboldt County's finest isn't strong enough to make her forget all the things that happened with Randy. As bad as today was, tomorrow will be emptier because at least this morning there was hope. And now, here with Ambrose, idly passing her fingers over an open flame, in the grip of the most illicit drug of all: this past fantasy come to life.

He kisses her again, reaching down, gently sliding his hand between her legs, rubbing through her underwear and, getting no resistance from her, sliding his hand inside her panties, kissing her again, and touching her, deeper. There's a little of the vapor rub residue still on his fingers and his touch there nearly takes her breath away.

She flinches, holding onto him.

"I'm sorry," he whispers. "Want me to stop?"

"No," she admits. She leans up and kisses him on the neck, which he seems to like, fingering her deeper. It feels good but then a part of her has to wonder if all these minty sensations are glossing over the guilt she should be feeling. "Even if Jessica hurt you, you're not giving up. If that's true, what you told me. Is that true?"

"It is." Then: "He hurt you, but you'll move on."

"We're just trying to heal."

"We are."

"You'll never say anything. . ."

"Neither will you. 'Cause this never happened."

"It's not like we're—"

"We're not." He kisses her, leaning into her as she leans into the sensations building inside.

She worries he's having to work too hard for what he's trying to make happen. Gentle, but insistent, going deeper. He's starting to sweat, and she's no longer cold. *This is so wrong.* Sometimes she wishes that part of herself would shut up.

He whispers into her ear. "You're not holding back, are you?"

"This is our secret."

"It is." He presses closer, watching her, his lips close to hers. It's about to happen. "Is there anything else you want me to do?" he asks. So close now. His breathing mirrors hers. He wants this as much as she does—more. "Just know this," he whispers. "Before I met her and before you met him, I—"

She gasps. The wave crests, words scattering like lacy foam on the shore. She flashes on the last time with Randy and her heart breaks. She cries out.

"What's the matter?" he asks, panicked, as she scrambles to sit up.

"Nothing, it's just. . . This was a huge mistake!" She manages to get to her feet, run to the bedroom, then madly retreat into the bathroom and into herself, where she should have stayed all along.

✳✳✳

After Bennie ran out, Ambrose heard the bathroom door close. Unsure what to do, he looks around at the pillows, the candles, the lantern casting its rosy shapes. All of a sudden, he's drained with a growing sense of guilt that'll only get stronger. *Should've gone on home, saved the molly for later and let Bennie work through whatever she had to.* The last thing he ever wanted was to make things weird and now he's done that in spades. She might think he was taking advantage of her while retaliating against Jessica at the same time, and it wasn't like that. It wasn't. What was it, then? He got caught up in the moment, that's all. So caught up, balancing her on the tip of his finger, like a butterfly with shimmering, silver wings.

Hadn't meant to betray anybody or say things he shouldn't. *Fucked up enough calling Randy a porn-addict. Q: How do you know he's a porn-addict? A: Broke into his apartment and saw all his porn. And you should see the porn video he took of me and your sister!*

He looks at his watch. **3:35AM**.

Even though fatigue sets in, he crawls to the edge of the blanket to retrieve his shoes. *Should try to talk to her but that might upset her worse, so just leave quickly and never speak of this again. Already agreed it never happened, so—*

She walks back into the room, crying subsiding for the time being. She kneels on the blanket, watching him put his shoes on. "What're you doing?"

"I'll sleep on the sofa at the office and go home early."

"It *is* early in the morning. Sleep on the sofa here."

"I'd better just go."

"You don't have to go." She places her hand on his shoulder. "I didn't mean what I said, the way it sounded. I'm sorry." She swipes away a tear. "It'll take time to get over him, that's all. I still love him. And I really didn't mean to betray my sister—"

"Neither did I. Bennie, I swear."

"And I didn't mean spending the evening with you was a mistake. We're friends, aren't we?"

"I'm the one that's sorry. Coming in here like gangbusters when you're already dealing with so much stuff."

She settles down on the blanket. "Don't leave. I'll get you up in the morning."

"You're sure?"

She nods, leaning forward to hug him.

He lets her cry on his shoulder. He can feel hot tears through his shirt. For him, there's everything that's been tamped down and repressed, along with the harsh realization that things are changing again and the fear he won't be able to keep up. He holds her tighter, fighting back tears of his own.

✳✳✳

Walking arm-in-arm with Sergei to place flowers at Ivan's grave at Cimetiére de Monaco, both of them wearing black, they make a dramatic couple. The turquoise waters beyond the terraced grounds and blazing blue sky give an operatic feel to the whole task. Miss Dover's silk scarf ripples in the breeze as she and Sergei sit on a bench, admiring the white roses in the black marble urn.

"Have you thought of what you're going to do to stay safe when you return to the States?" he asks.

"Not really," she confesses. "Beyond just packing a pistol everywhere I go."

"What do you know of Alexei's new bodyguard? I hear he's dangerous or could be. Maxim is quite afraid of him."

Feeling a chill even in the sunshine, she pulls up the collar of her coat. "I wouldn't know." She misses Ivan in the worst way. "Maybe I'm crazy thinking I can hang onto that place and make all this work."

"You are not crazy. It can work." Sergei places his arm around her shoulders. "There are ways." He hands her his handkerchief at the sight of her eyes welling.

Always the gentleman. How she got involved with these shady, older Russian men sometimes escapes her, then she remembers Ivan's kindness and Sergei's, too. "I don't mind hustling to get my stuff off the ground," she says. "It's just that's enough without always looking over my shoulder, you know?"

"You should not have to live like that."

"Everything I ever wanted seemed so close at one time, but now it looks so far away. So far, I may not live to see it happen."

"Perhaps it can be closer than you think." He's smiling, but hard to tell what he means exactly, behind those dark sunglasses.

"How's that?"

"All the things you're hoping for, for your business, and yourself. Maybe there is a way you can have your candy now."

"My life doesn't work that way," she says, standing to walk to the foot of Ivan's grave.

Sergei joins her, takes her hand in his. "It can, but only if you completely let go of the past."

"Which one? I got a lot of past lives."

"All of them." He looks over the horizon. "*Tabula rasa*, my dear."

✳✳✳

Ambrose meant to get up and put Bennie to bed at some point, then crash on the sofa, but he fell asleep beside her and, next thing he knows, it's light out and someone's knocking at the door. Before he can remember where he is, Jessica walks in, carrying Beau on her hip.

She stops short. "Good morning," she says.

"Morning," he responds automatically, eyes beginning to focus as he catches her staring down at them, and realizes just how this looks.

"Am I interrupting something?" she asks.

"We fell asleep."

"I can see that," she says, setting Beau on the floor.

He makes his way over to Ambrose and hugs him. "Am!"

"Hey, Buddy! How was the camp-in?"

"Fun!"

Bennie rolls over and sits up. There are dark circles under her eyes, but she smiles to see Beau. "Hi there, you!" Beau turns, hugs her. She returns his hug. "Sounds like someone had a good time!"

Beau plops between Bennie and Ambrose. "Slumber party!"

". . .You could say that." Ambrose smooths Beau's hair, glancing up at Jessica.

She looks pissed.

"Kind of."

"What are you doing here?" Jessica asks. "I would've thought you'd be at home."

"He stopped by after work yesterday evening," Bennie tells her. "I wasn't feeling well, so he sent out for Chinese food and Rajit stopped by, and time just got away." Then: "Hey, would you turn on the coffee maker?"

Jessica goes into the kitchen. Bennie glances at Ambrose.

He quickly straightens himself, folding one of the blankets. "I worked late and thought I'd just spend the night at the office and meet you and Beau for breakfast, but—"

"Time just got away," Jessica finishes for him.

Bennie slips into her kimono. "I'll be right back."

When she walks out, Jessica looks at the bedding scattered on the floor. "Looks like the two of you did have a slumber party."

"Camping," Beau says, grinning. "Like us."

Jessica looks at Ambrose. "Well, maybe not quite like us."

"We were, sort of," Ambrose says, gathering the remaining blankets and pillows and tossing them into a chair in the corner, before heading into the kitchen. "Coffee?"

"Yes, please." Jessica picks the remote off the arm of the sofa, turns on the television, and selects a kids' channel. Beau climbs onto the sofa as Jessica turns back to Ambrose. "Well, at least you weren't home all alone. I'm surprised you guys didn't go out on the town."

"Nah," Ambrose says, watching the coffee drip into the carafe. "Just hung out, that's all. Got high." *Shut up, Ambrose. Less said, the better.*

"Have fun?"

"Considering." He reaches into the cabinet for coffee mugs, glances at the bedroom door, speaks quieter. "When I got here, she was lying on the sofa, crying. Something happened with her and Randy. She wouldn't really talk about it."

"What happened?"

"I don't know, but I think that's over," he says, realizing too late that might not be the best thing to tell her either. The coffee can't brew fast enough. "I don't know what there is 'round here for breakfast. Why don't I go down to the bakery and get us something?"

"Okay, if you don't mind."

Bennie comes out of the bedroom, looking somewhat refreshed. "What are your plans for today?" she asks Beau, joining him on the sofa.

"Swimming at Grandma and Grandpa's," Beau informs her.

"Not today, honey," Jessica says, then, looking at Ambrose: "Mommy needs a nap."

Ambrose hands her a cup of dark roast, then takes another over to Bennie before pouring his own. His impulse is to gulp it, but it's too damned hot and the lull in conversation leaves too much space. He feels a need for fresh air. "What do ya'll want from Broccato's?" he asks.

"Almond croissant," Jessica says, going to sit adjacent the sofa.

"One of those big palmiers," Bennie answers.

He walks over and looks down at Beau. "Want to come with me and pick out yours?"

"Yes!" Beau responds.

"You can grab one of those cloth shopping bags by the door to take with you," Bennie says.

He looks at the chair by the door. "I don't see any bags."

"Oh," she says. "Never mind."

"Do you need money?" Jessica asks.

"I've got money." He starts out, carrying Beau. "We'll be right back."

He closes the door behind them, wondering if it's a good idea to leave Bennie and Jessica alone. Maybe best to just hurry.

Rajit is just getting off the elevator with a bag of groceries and a bouquet of sunflowers. He looks surprised to see them. "Good morning!" Then to Ambrose: "What are you doing here?"

"We're going to get breakfast for Bennie and Jessica. I don't think you've met Beau. Beau, this is Rajit—Mr. Sharma. Rajit, Beau, Jessica's little boy."

"Hello there, Beau! Pleasure to meet you."

"Hello," Beau says softly before hiding his face against Ambrose's shoulder.

Ambrose looks uneasily at the flowers. "Who're those for?"

Rajit shrugs. "I got them for Bennie. Kind of a... peace offering. To let her know no hard feelings and I wish her all the very best."

"You're not dropping them off now, are you?"

"Is there a reason why I shouldn't?"

Ambrose glances back toward Bennie's door. "She's not feeling well."

Rajit looks concerned. "Is she ill?"

"No, but— She had kind of a rough night." Quieter: "Some stuff with her and that Randy guy happened and—"

Rajit looks elated. "Oh?"

This is all too much before a full cup of coffee. "I don't know the whole story. Would you do something for me?" A step closer, Beau still clinging to him. "If you do drop those off, and anybody asks, remember you, me, and Bennie had take-out last night. Dim-sum from Formosa Gardens."

Rajit stares at him. "We did?"

"We totally did. And we were up really late."

Rajit's eyes narrow. "You will explain this later?"

"Yeah." Ambrose starts into the elevator with Beau. "Thanks, Rajit."

✳✳✳

Having changed the channel to the classic movie network after Ambrose and Beau left, Bennie steps out of her slippers and tucks her feet under the hem of her kimono, sipping coffee, watching a Traveltalk reel of *Motoring in Mexico*, circa 1943.

Jessica sips coffee, too, waiting. "So, spill it," Jessica says.

"Spill what?"

"Ambrose says something happened with you and Randy."

"Nothing. It's just over, that's all."

"Did you have a fight?"

"It wasn't a fight, and I don't want to talk about it."

"Is he seeing someone else?"

"I really don't want to do this right now."

Jessica settles back in the chair. "But just the other day, you were so happy and it was all going so well. You know you can talk to me."

"You know you can talk to me, too. Do you have something you want to tell me?"

Jessica looks at her and the silence speaks for her: It's clear she doesn't want to do this now, either. They're both exhausted and the risks in having some kind of a hashing out or sisterly heart-to-heart far outweighs the desire to "get to the bottom" of what's going on. Jessica sets down her coffee, sighs, gets up and stretches. "Know what? I really would love to go take a shower. Are some of my yoga clothes still here?"

"In the bottom drawer of the dresser."

"Thanks. I'll be right out." Jessica goes into the bedroom and shuts the door. All alone, she's able to exhale. At first, she hadn't thought Ambrose told Bennie about Mignon and her, but now it feels like he has, for sure. Jessica paces momentarily, then looks in the drawer for the yoga clothes she'd left here in case she and Bennie ever go to a class when she's in the city. She finds the olive-green, bamboo sweat pants and off-white, organic-cotton top. She'd left a couple pairs of underwear here, too, and selects the most comfortable to put on after a shower.

As she takes off the clothes she's worn since yesterday, when she and Beau had left for the camp-in, her mind begins to clear, and she resents letting herself be put on the defensive so quickly. After all, she did walk in on them lying on the floor. As she removes her blue jeans and places them on the bed, she notices it hasn't been slept in. *What did go on here last night?* She peers into the wastebasket near the bed, but it's empty, then walks into the bathroom. Nothing in that wastebasket, either, by way of used condoms or anything else. But there probably wouldn't be if they started in here and went in there. More likely though that they'd start in there and come into the bedroom. But they didn't. That's what Ambrose said, and doesn't she trust Ambrose—and Bennie?

She turns on the shower, then looks at herself in the mirror as she takes off her bra and tosses it on the floor. Maybe Ambrose wonders if he can trust her. She was exactly where she said she'd be last night. Maybe she hasn't always been lately, but last night, she was. Maybe this time, they should give each other the benefit of the doubt. By the time she gets out of the shower, he'll be back with Beau and the pastries, and this won't get mentioned anymore this morning.

And maybe Ambrose didn't tell Bennie anything about Mignon after all, and she's just being paranoid. As she steps into the welcoming antique tub and under the massaging stream of hot water, that's what Jessica chooses to believe.

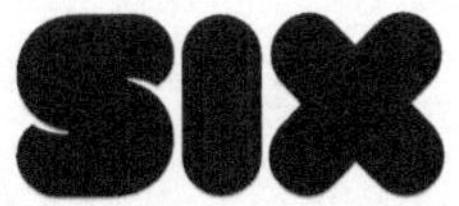

SIX

When Randy wakes up, daylight fills the room. No idea what time he managed to fall asleep nor what time it is now. He'd been awake the entire night so, even though his brain was humming with grim activity, it must've finally quieted long enough for him to drift off. He rolls over as the events of the last couple days return to torment him. He'd been contemplating suicide and decided that, since his pistols are still in hock, drowning might be an option. However, he didn't know if he could successfully accomplish that. Doesn't know if he could keep himself down long enough without bobbing up for a gasp. *And then— sharks. . . Nah.* He'd also considered walking across the freeway in heavy traffic, making a point to wait for a semi-truck and time it so there'd be no chance of survival. He'd put a note in his pocket, absolving the driver of all responsibility. But now. . .

Not so sure about that either.

He slowly sits up, realizing he's in the same clothes as two days ago. Hadn't even showered, having gotten back from a walk when he received that letter from the leasing office. Then yesterday morning Bennie came over. She'd looked so pretty, too. He doesn't really remember everything he said, just that it was awful and he'd made her cry. She was so nice, offering to help, and he turned her down because he felt so far beyond help. A lost cause.

He sighs, managing to heave himself up. He stumbles into the kitchen, thinking to get a cheap pot of coffee started. If he's not going to kill himself right away, he should at least shower. He drinks half a glass of tap water. The strawberries Bennie had rinsed and left for him in a bowl are still out on the counter along with a container of baked goods, and her two burlap shopping bags. He leans over the bowl, propping himself on his elbows, staring into the strawberries. She bought these for him because she thought he'd like them. He eats one, then a few more before he opens the plastic container and sees the beautiful cookies. He picks up a heart-shaped one and looks at it like it's a piece of art. She made these and brought them here. Even though he doesn't even feel he deserves it, he takes a bite, and it's the best thing he's tasted in his life.

He shuffles over and picks his phone off the end table. It's almost out of power but shows **11:20AM**. He flops on the sofa. Maybe it's just the smell of the coffee, or the strawberries and cookie kick-starting some brain receptors that had shorted out, but he feels a need to do something.

Doesn't want to go back to bed and doesn't feel like taking that last walk over to the freeway. What would the old Randy do? Hard to remember. He flashes on the last time he found himself on this sofa, unshowered, unshaven, wavering over his next move after a traumatic event. And what he did after that changed everything.

He runs his fingers through his hair. Needs washing. *Go shower first. Or coffee, then shower* . . . His heart beats faster, throat tightening as he becomes acutely aware of each passing minute, then each passing second. Somehow, he can feel the time that dammed up while he was out of it quickly flowing again. The world is moving outside while he sits here, and it'll go on with or without him. If he decides to stay here in it, what's the most urgent thing he should do in this moment?

For once, it's right there in front of him.

✳✳✳

After Ambrose, Jessica, and Beau left, Bennie thought of getting dressed but decided to lie back on the sofa to rest up. She really should go lie in bed after sleeping on the floor last night but there are vivid memories in there and, after the last 24 hours, she just wants to lose herself in an obscure comedy from the 1930s. Some family of grifters meets a rich, old lady on a cruise and goes to live with her. It has the kind of offbeat humor she likes but most people don't really get anymore. Except for—

She rolls toward the back of the sofa, pulling the blanket over her head. It won't always be like this, she reminds herself. Where everything reminds her of him.

The phone on the coffee table rings.

What fresh hell . . .? She sighs, pushing back the blanket. Why bother getting it? If they leave a message, she'll call back later. All talked out. She picks it up just to look, then quickly sits up, nerves jangled. *Why would he be calling?*

It rings again. She impulsively smooths her hair. No reason to get excited, she reminds herself. *Probably just left my sunglasses at his place.* But glancing toward the kitchen, she sees the sunglasses on the counter. Also on the counter is a slim, clear vase with the sunflowers Ambrose said Rajit must've left outside the door. The phone rings again.

"Hello?"

"Hey." He clears his throat. "Do you have a minute? I mean, are you busy?"

"Not at the moment."

"Oh, good." A pause, then: "I don't know 'bout you, but I really don't like the way we left things yesterday."

Her heart falls. Maybe this is the final goodbye. Things he'd meant to tell her before she walked out. She bites her lip, waiting for him to go on.

"I'm sorry for everything I said to you, that. . . I just really need to talk in person. Can I come over, like, in an hour?" Pause. "Please?"

". . . Okay."

It sounds like he's catching his breath. "Great. Thank you. I'll see you soon."

"All right."

"Bye." The call ends. She sits still for a moment, unsure how to feel. Looking around, she realizes her place is in disarray. The blankets and pillows still on the chair, pastry boxes from breakfast still on the table. She has to straighten up. But first things first.

She leaps to get ready.

✳✳✳

The rest of the day, Jessica tells herself there was nothing odd about finding Ambrose and Bennie together on the floor. It was just. . . jarring. She lies across the king-sized bed, trying to put all that out of her mind, gazing at her phone. There's another reminder e-mail from Echo at Infinity Gallery about the deadline for applications to the Emerging Artists retreat in Provence. Echo said that if she wanted to get away to concentrate on creating works for a fall show, this would be an amazing opportunity. Jessica said she'd think about it, but then there's Beau and Ambrose. Echo said Beau could come with her; there are recommended au pairs she could hire, or she could bring Caitlyn. As for Ambrose, he could certainly visit. And maybe a new setting would inspire her.

She switches from e-mail to another app, scrolling through her feed. Mike hasn't posted in a while, but his new friend posts quite often. It's a guy who frequently shows up in Mike's photos: good-looking, always wearing somewhat sporty clothes. She doesn't follow the friend but found him through one of the tags she just checks every so often. Today, it's a view of the Greek shoreline. Looks like it was taken from the deck of a yacht. Apparently, if they are an item, they're living their **#bestlife**. *Good for them.* She hasn't posted in over a week and that's pretty long for her. She switches to the photo app to see if there's anything worthwhile she might share, but nothing spectacular. Just some photos of her, Bennie, Ambrose, and Beau when they were cooking out a couple weeks ago. She snapped a selfie of her and Bennie in front of the rose bushes closest to the patio. The rosebuds had blossomed and everything looked bright and vibrant. Just the act of posting ought to show she's not threatened or paranoid in the least. *No reason to be whatsoever. Everything is fine.* She types a caption, **In the garden with sis**, a couple of hashtags about flowers, gardens, **#beautifulday, #saturdayvibes**. She sighs, rolling onto her back. Napping and phone time's over.

She rises to get painting again.

✳✳✳

When the downstairs bell rings nearly an hour later, Bennie buzzes Randy up. She paces beneath the chandelier by the door, waiting for him to knock. *Make him knock.* And when he does, she waits a beat, heart pounding, so glad to see him but trying to maintain a neutral expression until she finds out what this is all about. Like her, he looks as though he's had no sleep, but freshly scrubbed, hair damp from the shower, wearing jeans and a polo shirt.

"Hey," he says.

"Hey yourself. Come in." She closes the door behind him.

"I missed you," he says.

"You did?"

"I've been thinking about everything you said. I must've sounded like the most ungrateful bastard God ever put on this earth." He's smiling, seems like he's on the verge of laughter, tears, or both.

"I missed you, too," she confesses, eyes watering. *So much for the poker face.* "Guess you were just saying what you felt."

"It's not really what I felt. I mean, it was but it came out all wrong. It might come out wrong again, but. . . You already know I'm a fuck-up. Just going out with you was more than I could've ever hoped for but then, when you asked me to move in. . ." He stops, leaves her hanging.

"I never meant to pressure you. And you're not a fuck-up."

"Will you marry me?"

She's pretty sure she heard him right, but: "What?"

He nears, placing a hand on each side of her face, pulling her close. "I said, 'Will you marry me?'"

She stares at him. "Do you mean that?"

"I do," he says. "If I move in with you, it can't be temporary, or just living together. It has to be for the long haul." His eyes are bloodshot, naked and raw. "I don't have anything to offer you 'cept my broke-ass self," he goes on. "I know I've got some hell of a nerve asking, but even though you can do a million times better than me, you will never find anybody that loves you more than I do."

Her spirit rises from the ashes of yesterday so quickly, she can barely breathe.

"Swear to God. It's just— I got nothing, Bennie; that's all. And I'm not asking so I can get my hands on any of your money. I'll sign an iron-clad pre-nup, anything you want. I just want you."

She reaches up to caress his face and he grasps her wrist and kisses her palm.

"I've been too afraid to say it, but I've felt this way ever since the night we met." He pulls her closer. "I want to move in with you if you'll still let me and if you'll promise to marry me."

She can only put her arms around him and feel his around her. She can't help but think of that line from *A Streetcar Named Desire*: "Sometimes, there's God, so quickly." Maybe he feels the same, because his arms tighten around her and no hug has ever felt better.

"Is this a yes?" he whispers into her hair.

"Yes," she answers.

✳✳✳

Ambrose finally receives a brief text from Miss Dover, informing him that she's decided to sell the building, but all will be fine and not to worry. She'll fill him in on the details later. He was unsettled by the news, but relieved to hear from her. He called her right away but got no answer. Maybe she didn't want to hear him complain. He settles back in her desk chair, looking up at her portrait.

But why complain? She is the boss. Besides, she might have her eye on a much better place. No need to wax sentimental about a location that looks like some generic office building from the outside. But inside, in this part of it anyway. . . He walks out into the hallway and strolls toward the ballroom. Maybe it's just that this was home more than his shitty apartment when he first came here. Miss Dover'd shown him kindness when no one else did, introduced him to Bennie and Momo and others who weren't out to use or abuse him before kicking him into the gutter. That won't happen again, though, he tells himself. There are those who don't understand what goes on here, but it makes more sense in its own way than all the senseless pain people inflict on each other in the so-called real world.

Miss Dover's teakwood "queen's" chair is still in the center of the riser, and off to the side of that there's an antique wheel she'd bought in Vienna. It's a white, wooden wheel about six feet high with a blue star painted on it, faded but still in good condition, with two handles, two foot-rests, leather straps and buckles to secure a person in place, most likely a knife-thrower's assistant in a spangled leotard, like an act from an old carnival sideshow.

He whirls it around. It makes a clicking sound, spins nicely. Smooth. As the clicking slows, he sits in Miss Dover's chair, the one she'd been sitting in that evening she'd tried to wise him up—about what he'd do if left to his devices, if everything he'd come to depend on disappeared. She was trying to teach him something and he'd been a willing pupil, but now. . .

Why this feeling?

***

Randy's late grandmother's engagement ring is in a blue velvet box, along with the matching gold wedding band, in her old bedroom upstairs at his mother's house. He'd loved Nana Delacroix's stories and she encouraged his rebellious side. Laughed at his creative profanity and, before she got so sick, mixed herself sidecar cocktails and they'd sit on the patio to play matchstick poker. She said Hemingway and Fitzgerald drank sidecars back in 1920, Paris. She'd been to Paris once and said he should go there some day. And when he found the right girl, he could have this engagement ring, the one his grandpa bought at Adler's in downtown New Orleans, and the wedding ring that went with it.

On Mondays and Wednesdays, his mother volunteers at the senior center from 1 to 3, then helps with refreshments for AA meetings in the church basement from 3:30 to 4:30. If he leaves within the next hour, he can make it down to Gilroy while she's out. He'll park down the block, go to the back yard to check inside the stone turtle in the flower bed to see if that's where she keeps the back door key. He can get the rings and get the hell out before anybody's wiser. It's not like he's going to steal anything. That blue velvet box belongs to him.

He sits to put on his shoes. A knock at the door. He stops, expecting Brianna to come walking in. She'll be able to tell from the pile of boxes he collected from the liquor store that he's moving. He won't tell her exactly where to. He can't remember if the door's locked.

He softly walks over and peers out the peephole. It's Bennie. He opens the door. Turns out it wasn't locked. "Hey," she says, smiling, holding out a white paper bag. "I brought you some lunch."

"Thanks, angel." He kisses her. Is this the first time he's called her that? It won't be the last. "Want to ride with me down to Gilroy?"

She shrugs. "Why not?"

When they get there, Linda Burke's car is at Our Lady of Prompt Succor Church so he drives to the house, walks to the back yard for the key, and goes in the back door with Bennie trailing.

She stops to look at some framed photographs on the wall: a hodge-podge going back to when he and his siblings were kids, a few from when his dad was in the Army, and then all those pictures of his nieces and nephews. Loads of grandkids.

"I'm just going upstairs to my room," he says.

"I want to see!" She follows him up to his old bedroom and he's surprised to see it's pretty much like he left it. He goes over to the closet.

"This was really your room," Bennie says in a hushed voice, looking at framed photos of him in his dress uniform and then in desert fatigues at the training base with four soldiers. Two of them made it back; two didn't. She stares at one in his combat uniform, another incarnation of himself like the cop picture she likes so much. He used to have a copy of it framed on the wall of his apartment bedroom. But then he'd taken all his pictures down.

In the closet, he gets out an old weekender tote and quickly looks through the clothes to see if there's anything worth taking that would fit. He turns to see her snapping a picture with her phone of the framed newspaper article where he'd taken off his catcher's mask, arguing with the batter: a lanky boy from Sunnyvale, sneering as Randy yells at him, poking his finger into the guy's chest. The umpire approaches to break it up and other players in the background laugh while some seem to boo. His team lost.

"I didn't know you were so into sports," she comments.

"Not sports. Just baseball."

She sits on the bed, leaning back, swinging her feet just off the floor. Sexy shoes. Mary Janes with solid but not-too-thick heels. And that short, plaid kilt. Very Catholic schoolgirl, today of all days. Sitting there looking at him, thighs spread just enough to be casual. She knows what she's doing. She doesn't know he's on a top-secret mission.

"I'm going to get something from the other room," he says. "Wait here?"

"I'll wait," she says, looking him up and down. "What time's your mom getting home?"

"Sometime after 4:30, but I want to be out well before that."

"Then you'd better hurry."

"Hurry and do what?"

"Whatever it is you want to do," she says, lying on the bed, legs hanging off the side. "I'll be waiting right here."

He glances at the clock. No telling when he'll be over this way again. In his old room. With this honest-to-God princess. He goes over to draw the blinds, then unbuckles his belt and unzips his jeans as he joins her on the bed, figuring ten minutes ought to do it. Fifteen tops, under the gun like this. The possibility of getting caught is kind of hot, but he knows they've got enough time. Plus, those few minutes are intense and totally worth it. There's no way he'd doze off after that but, when Randy looks at the clock again, it's somehow twenty-five minutes later. He stands, panicked. "Jesus Christ!"

Bennie sits up. "What's the matter?"

"We need to get out of here. I've just gotta get something." He strips off the condom and, not wanting his mom to find it in the waste basket or under the bed, tosses it in the weekender bag. He hands her the panties he'd taken off her earlier with such haste. Black and silky with a lace panel in the back. She puts them on as he zips up.

"Can I take a few more pictures of your room?"

"I really don't know why you'd want to," he says, slipping his shoes back on. "But sure, be my guest."

She reaches for her phone as he goes into Nana's bedroom, top drawer of the maple chest where she kept her jewelry. He picks up the gloves and wallets to look underneath but—no blue velvet box. He shuffles through the contents of each drawer without disturbing things too much but—nothing! What if his mom took it and put it in some safe-deposit box God-only-knows-where?

He looks everywhere he can think of in the room: the lower drawers, the dresser, the closet, the nightstand. *Nada.* "Goddamnit," he breathes, walking back into the hallway.

Bennie comes to the door of his room. "Everything okay?"

"Just trying to remember where I left something."

"What is it? Maybe I can help."

"I just need a couple more minutes and it'll come to me." He starts toward his mother's room, then turns back toward his own. "Bennie?"

She's looking in the dresser mirror, applying lipstick. "Yes?"

He hands her the car keys and zips up the tote bag. "You want to take this and go wait in the Jeep? I've just got to find that one thing and then we'll get the hell out of here."

"Sure." She takes the bag by the handles and grabs her purse, slinging it over her shoulder. "'Anything else?"

"Just yell if you see my mom coming."

"'Kay." She kisses him and starts down the stairs with the bag, pausing to look at baby pictures at the stair landing. "Hey," she calls. "Are you the one in little blue overalls?"

"Yeah, that's me," he calls back.

"I knew it. They're adorable!"

"Thank you!" He walks into his mother's bedroom and opens the jewelry box on the dresser. It has little drawers and sections. The velvet box nor the rings are in the main part so he opens the first little drawer. Nothing but junk. When he opens the second one, the blue velvet box is there. The moment he sees it, Bennie yells out, "Hey, Randy—I think your mom's home!"

✳✳✳

Mrs. Burke is in her mid-50s, shorter than Bennie imagined, with long, dark hair that has a few gray streaks. She walks into the kitchen from the garage, wearing a denim jacket over a sweater and jeans, glasses with multi-color frames, new track shoes. She does not look happy.

"Hi there." Bennie smiles. "You must be Mrs. Burke."

"Hello," Mrs. Burke responds. Then: "Who the hell are you?"

"I'm Bennie," she says, gift of hostess-y gab temporarily disabled.

"Where's Randy? I saw his Jeep out there."

"He's up in his room."

Mrs. Burke heads for the living room, tossing her purse on the sofa. "Randy?" she calls.

No answer.

She stands at the foot of the staircase and yells: "Randall, get your goddamn ass down here!"

Bennie remains in the doorway to the kitchen. She was about to walk into the living room to comment on some of the family photographs, but this woman's in no mood for chit-chat.

Mrs. Burke turns to her. "So, what're you? His girlfriend?"

Bennie almost tells her *No, his fiancée*, but she gets the feeling Randy doesn't want his family to know yet. "Yes, ma'am."

"Uh-huh," Mrs. Burke says, taking in the short skirt, the Mary-Jane shoes. "Where'd he meet you?"

"At a gallery in the city. He was the security guard at my sister's art show."

"He's actually been working?"

"Yes, ma'am," she says, relieved to see Randy rushing down the stairs, sweeping past his mother.

"We're leaving," he says to her. "I just had to come get some things from my closet."

Mrs. Burke follows him into the kitchen. "Excuse me? I haven't laid eyes on you for months and that's all you can say?"

He stops, turns to her. "What do you want me to say?"

"How about, 'Hello, Mother, how've you been? I'm sorry I haven't called you in fucking ages!'"

"I haven't called because I can feel like shit all by myself. I don't need any help."

"You're right about that; you don't need any help." She takes a step closer. "You're paying a fortune for a crap apartment, unemployed, disgraced, and you're doing everything in your power to alienate yourself from your family. So yeah, you're doing just fine, Randy. Keep up the good work and you can feel like shit for the rest of your life!"

"That's just what I'd expect you to say. That's why I can't stand to talk to you anymore." He looks at Bennie. "Let's go."

Bennie feels like she should say something, but she's got nothing constructive or healing to say, so just turns toward the door with a quiet, "It was nice meeting you, Mrs. Burke."

Mrs. Burke nears. "Why don't you go out to his car and play the radio, sweetheart? I need to talk to my son."

"You and me got nothing to talk about," Randy informs.

"Well, I have some things to say." Her voice gets husky, eyes moist. "Next time you come to my house, you call me first and don't come sneaking in here when I'm not home."

"I didn't sneak in here. There are still some things upstairs that belong to me, and I have every right to come get my stuff."

"You do not have every right. This is my house and I want to be here when you come over."

He stares at her a moment, then turns toward the door, past the refrigerator decorated with artwork by the grandkids.

"You hear me?"

"I hear you." He opens the door for Bennie.

Mrs. Burke follows them into the garage. "And I don't like you bringing people in the house, either. This time, you claim it's your girlfriend, next time it could be somebody you picked up off the street."

Bennie manages a weak smile and continues walking into the daylight of the driveway with Randy close behind.

He turns to his mother. "Bennie is my girlfriend. And since when have I brought a parade of strangers into your goddamn house?"

"Since when do I know what you're up to? You never talk to anybody, and you hole up at that rat-trap place you live in for weeks—months—at a time."

Bennie opens the door, throws the tote into the back seat, gets in and closes the door. She places the key in the ignition so he won't have to fumble around when he gets in the driver's seat. The window's down, so she can hear them.

"Are you still drinking?" Mrs. Burke asks. "Even when you were on the police force you drank too much, so I can only imagine now."

"Not so much," he tells her. "I'm on pills these days."

"Pills?" she repeats, watching him go around to the other side of the Jeep. "What kinda pills?"

"The kind that numb you out, so you don't keep obsessing over bullshit." He opens the door and gets in, cranks up, and, after a moment of her standing there, says to her as he's shifting into reverse, "Goodbye, Mother."

SEVEN

Ambrose already knows what he'll wear today to her cousin's wedding. He splurged on a custom suit by a tailor Bennie recommended in Chinatown. It's cream-colored linen, and he'd ordered a shirt made from pale blue Egyptian cotton and gotten a purple Italian silk tie to go with it. The shoes are Italian, too. No matter how badly he feels inside, slipping on that suit and stepping into those shoes will be some consolation. Plus, now he knows where to get a suit made like the ones that preacher wears. He can bring them a picture and they'll take it from there.

Mignon won't be at the wedding, unless via text message. Jessica claims she hasn't heard from her in a while, but he doesn't believe her and hates that he doesn't believe her. He also hates the implication that he's not enough for her.

He looks at Jessica sleeping beside him in the early morning light. She stirs under the covers, and he moves closer, trying not to wake her. Soon, he'll gauge what she's feeling by how she responds to him gently touching her shoulder, by how she says, "Good morning," and then the shifting clouds in her deep blue eyes if she senses he's getting too possessive. Best to appreciate every moment, show her he can be mature and open-minded and not give in to the impulse to be the guy who's not.

She's been working long hours and turning out incredible artwork. Maybe one person, male or female, just isn't enough for her anymore. Maybe he'll have to share her with someone from now on. He's reluctant but hasn't told her he's willing to, if that's what it takes to be with her, like this. He draws closer, sliding an arm around her waist. She shifts again. Almost time to get up. She rolls over, still sleepy. "Good morning," she says. "We have someplace to go today, you know."

"That's why we shouldn't waste any time."

"Is the coffee ready?" she asks while he reaches into the nightstand for a condom.

He slips it on, rolls on top of her.

She's warm and receptive and it feels so good being inside of her. Pulling him close, she remembers something. "I haven't had a chance to brush my teeth, you know."

"That's all right, I brushed mine earlier."

"Okay. . . But I still have morning breath."

"I don't care about that; your breath smells fine."

She starts to protest but he stops her with a kiss, just to prove it. She doesn't say anything else about it, but he notices she doesn't look at him that much and it's more hurried than he wanted, even after waking up early. Then he'd gotten turned on thinking about things that maybe he shouldn't. *No telling what she's really thinking about, either.*

Afterwards, she gets up to go to the kitchen, still in her nightgown, no panties.

He settles back into the pillows as she comes back with two cups of coffee. She sets one on the nightstand next to him. "I'm going to take a shower," she says.

"Okay."

She pauses. "That was a nice way to wake up."

"Really?"

"Yes, really."

"Glad you think so."

"I do." She leans down to kiss his forehead, then lips.

He looks deeply into her eyes, which seems to disarm her; he wants it to. He doesn't always feel this intense in the morning but knows they're going to a fancy social function and she'll look amazing, and others will be looking at her, too. Her parents will be there. It'll be ages before they're home and can be alone together again.

She goes to the closet and looks over her dress. It's peachy-pink, light and swirly. "You like this?"

"I do."

"Sounds like Bennie and Randy made up, so I guess he'll end up being her plus one after all. Did she tell you? That they made up?"

She *would* have to bring that up. "She told me."

"Anyway, Caitlin's coming over soon. Would you mind getting Beau dressed in some play clothes while I'm in the shower?"

"Not at all."

She takes her coffee, disappearing into the bathroom. He's about to get out of bed when he hears the faint text notification on her phone. He sees it laying screen-down on her nightstand. He takes a sip of coffee, walks by the bathroom door. When he's sure he hears the shower, he goes to sit on the bed, knowing he shouldn't be looking. But here he is.

Sure enough; it's Mignon. No contact name, just her number. He sighs, dithering over whether to read the message. Then it won't show as new and Jessica will know he read it. Unless he deletes it. He opens it. All it says is **good morning**.

He texts back **good morning** and regrets it. There's no time to engage in a texting game with Jessica's other lover. The notification sound again: **r u still going 2 the wedding**.

Yes, he texts back. **getting ready now**.

Im sure u look lovely darling have him take many photos of you.

I will.

Then from her: **would love 2 c new nudes. It's been a while**.

He pauses, thumbs trembling over the screen. Finally: **will soon-u send 1 now**.

And she does. It's of her in bed with a seductive gaze.

He's seen her in her various outfits at work, like when she's wearing corsets, garters and stockings, latex and stilettos, but he wasn't quite prepared to see her totally naked. Her breasts are bigger than he thought. She's not wearing much if any make-up, just sultry and natural. He feels himself getting turned on, even though this isn't the time for that. Mignon thinks Jessica's the one looking at this, getting turned on instead. *So, they do this—they swap nude pictures.* Ambrose can't help but wonder exactly what they do together, and want to watch, in secret, so they'd be totally uninhibited. . . A hard-on already. He flashes back again to the other night with Bennie, when she said, "This is so wrong." **beautiful**, he responds.

I have a confession 2 make, she says.

He glances toward the bathroom door. **Tell me**.

The other day u were right I think I was followed

His shoulders tense. **Who followed u**

a man not my boyfriend. I did not lie promise I will speak w/ him, she answers, then: **I think he's possibly someone from the other place I worked who likes the way I look**

Ambrose sits on the edge of the bed. *Wonder if that's true. What would Jessica say? First, she'd probably be concerned*. . . **Oh no! R U scared that he followed you?**

Not scared. could've even been imagining things. If it was him, I musta lost him on way back so m safe.

As long as yr safe. He wants to know more, but, keenly aware Jessica'll be getting out of the shower, Caitlin's on the way, and he still has to get Beau and himself dressed, he tries to think how to wrap this up. **I just wouldn't want to think yr in any danger. You would tell me, right?**

Of course! Mignon texts back. Then: **I will let u get ready now, have a wonderful time today. au revoir**.

He texts back **au revoir**, then deletes everything through the first **good morning** and, shaken, places the phone back on the nightstand. He goes back over to listen at the bathroom door. Water's still on. He wants to get into the shower with her and forget ever seeing those texts. *Is Mignon talking about Rajit, or that other guy sitting there in a BMW, watching the same place? Should've asked for more details but might fuck it up. But it could be fucked already if Jessica finds out I was snooping. She won't though; how could she?*

He lets her finish bathing in peace, slips on some boxers and a T-shirt to get Beau ready for a trip to the park, a play date with his friend Dudley and, no doubt, a trip to the ice cream shop. He almost wishes Jessica were going to the wedding with her parents so he could be the one hanging out with the kiddos today. But then Jessica might decide to take Mignon as her plus-one, and everyone would think they're just good friends and after the wedding they'd go off for one of their trysts. And he wouldn't get to wear that gorgeous suit that looked like one in that '60s French movie set in Italy they watched the other night.

And that would be a shame.

✶✶✶

Randy was worried he'd be running late to pick up Bennie, but he's right on time. She buzzes him in and the door to her apartment is ajar when he gets there. Won't be long before it's their apartment. Just bring over one more light load of stuff he packed last night, turn in the key, and he's out of that old place. He's staying here tonight and giving her the ring. He walks in just as she's coming out of the bedroom and, when he sees her, stops cold, because she can't know.

"Well," she says, radiant, smiling. "What do you think?"

He watches her turn around in the silky, candy-apple jump suit like Jessica was wearing the night of the great fuck-fest sex-video. The one that presaged the failed pseudo-blackmail attempt. It looks perfect on Bennie, too, only. . . She's waiting for a reaction. "Wow," he says finally. "You look great!"

Her smile fades slightly. "Do you really like it?"

"I love it. It's—you're beautiful. I mean, wow. . ."

"You do recognize it, right?"

He gets weak in the knees. "Um. . ."

She draws closer, straightening his tie. "The phone sex," she says. "Isn't this like the jumpsuit you said the woman was wearing?"

"I guess so. I had my mind on other things. . ."

"But you described it to me, in detail." Getting a little exasperated: "Remember?"

"Uh. . . Oh, yeah. That's exactly like it, I do remember now. Where did you find that?"

"Can you believe Jessica has one just like it and I borrowed hers?"

"No, I can't."

"I came across it in her closet and just had to try it on." She puts her arms around his neck. "I was thinking when we come back, you could untie the ribbons and let it slide off me and then we could do the stuff you saw that couple doing through the window. You said you'd fuck me all those ways and then some. Remember?"

He embraces her, the shock starting to wear off. "I remember." He kisses her on the cheek not to mess up her lipstick. She does look wild and kind of dangerous today. He was expecting her to be wearing one of her vintage-y outfits and here she is all sleek, modern, and about the sex she's anticipating later. She reaches inside his tweed jacket to hold him closer, and he can look straight down with a great view of cleavage. He likes the feel of her hands underneath his jacket and it's sexy she wants to hold him closer this way. "Goddamnit," he says quietly. "What are you trying to do to me?"

"I've just missed you, that's all."

"I missed you, too." He kisses her, lipstick and all.

She doesn't seem to mind. When it's over, she rubs a smudge off his lower lip. "Better not start anything we can't finish. I'll go get my wrap and purse and we'll go. Want some coffee for the road?"

"No, I'm fine," he says.

She goes into the bedroom, then returns, looking at him through the doorway. "By the way, you look fantastic. You'll be the most handsome man there."

After the sundrenched drive up to Napa, they start down the shady road to the winery, where there's an elaborate, ivory-colored bow tied to a tree every few yards. It keeps going on and on and then finally, at the end of the road, is a what looks like a splendid chateau with meticulously tended grounds and lush, rolling hills beyond. "This is the winery?" he asks.

"This is their house; the winery's down that road we passed, remember? Follow that car up to the front. There's valet parking."

His throat tightens as he sees the line of luxury cars and SUVs pulling up to the front. "Do we have to use the valet parking?"

"Sure." She pulls down the visor and looks in the dull mirror, touching up her lipstick. "That way we can make our entrance."

He sees a Mercedes convertible behind them in line, then looks down at the cigarette butts in the ashtray and wishes he'd vacuumed those out along with the bits of trash on the floorboard. At least he'd cleared out the fast-food containers and stray French fries. If Bennie knew it'd be this swanky, they could've brought her car but she doesn't seem to give a damn they're arriving in his jalopy.

He pulls up to the front steps, stops and opens the door to get out while a valet on the passenger's side opens the door for Bennie. Another valet appears to hold his door open. "Thanks."

"Quite welcome, sir." *Another "sir."*

Bennie has the wrap around her shoulders, over the jumpsuit, toning it down a little, but she still looks like a wild child, waiting to take his arm to walk down the steps together. There are stone steps going up to the main entrance, but these go down, like into a moat. Only this is some wide, stone passageway around the side of the house. The flow of well-dressed, beautiful people heads that way, moving in couples or little groups, some gathered in chatty knots around small, wrought-iron tables. Bennie's outfit is turning heads but she doesn't notice, holding onto his arm: a nod *hello* here, quick air-kiss there. A young woman with long, blonde hair and an ice-cream pink dress approaches. "Hi, Bennie!"

"Michelle!"

"I haven't seen you for so long. Where've you been keeping yourself?"

"In the city, mostly." She glances at Randy. "Michelle, I'd like you to meet Randy Burke. Randy, this is Michelle Delaney. She and I went to college together in Virginia."

"Hello," he says on automatic. "Pleasure to meet you."

"Same here," she says, eying him like trying to place him, but can't. "So, Bennie, are you still working at that. . . legal aid center, wasn't it?"

"For the time being. What about you? What're you up to?"

"I just made junior partner at Metcalf, Menger & Powell."

"Congratulations! Your folks must be thrilled."

"We're having a little get-together at the Cliff House next Saturday afternoon. If you're free, you're welcome to join us. Janie's coming in from Seattle, and Beth's driving down from Sacramento. It'll be like a reunion!" She looks at Randy. "And you, too, of course. Any friend of Bennie's. . ."

Bennie takes Randy's hand. "Actually, Randy's my fiancé."

He looks at her, shocked she'd come out and say it like that.

"Oh, really?" Ice Cream Blonde glances at Bennie's left hand.

She's looking for a ring, goddamnit!

"Congratulations to you both. Have you set a date?"

"Not yet, but we're working on it," Bennie informs. "As soon as we do, you'll be getting a save-the-date announcement."

"Wonderful." She looks at him in a new way. "You're a very lucky guy. Bennie's quite a catch."

"Don't I know it." He smiles.

"And what do you do, Randy?"

"He has his own security firm," Bennie answers. "It started out kind of small but now it's growing leaps and bounds. Keeps him really busy but we manage to carve out quality time." She turns to him. "Don't we?"

"We manage."

"What's the name of your firm, Randy?" Blondie asks.

"Burke Security," Bennie answers.

A male voice calls out, "Michelle!"

She glances around to a guy in a seersucker suit beckoning up ahead. "Well, congratulations. Cliff House next Saturday at 3—love to see you both there!"

"It was great seeing you!" Bennie says as the girl goes to join her date, husband, whatever.

Randy hadn't noticed if she was wearing a ring. "You really want to go to that Cliff House thing?"

"Nah." She shrugs. "I'd rather hang out with you next Saturday."

He looks for someplace semi-private: a nook, a niche, a grotto away from the crowd. He can hear music striking up from somewhere around the corner, but people are still arriving. There's time. "Let's go over here a minute." He pulls her further down the passageway and into some open space as the well-heeled herd continues toward chairs beyond a massive white tent. The sides of the tent are closed while caterers prep for the reception. He guides Bennie in that direction: around the hedge, near the service entrance to the tent.

"Where are we going?" she asks. Then, "I hope you're not mad I told her we're engaged. I'm just excited. I want people to know."

"Me, too," he says, reaching into his pocket for a velvet drawstring bag that—until this morning—held his Army pins. He opens it to take out the ring. "I wanted to do this tonight but, if you're going to start telling people now, I can't wait." He takes her left hand in his. He wasn't going to say this part in case she had second thoughts but, if she's excited and wants people to know, that's a very good sign. "Bennington, one more time, will you please do me the honor of marrying me?"

She grins, tears in her eyes. "Yes, Randall. I'm honored to be asked and proud to marry you."

He sighs, right on the edge, but no bawling. It'll make him look crazy and ruin her make-up. He slips the ring on her finger and kisses her. A couple of servers walk past, carrying baskets of flowers. They smile seeing them kissing, then disappear into the tent.

Afterwards, she holds out her hand, gazing at the ring. "My God, Randy. It's beautiful! When did you get this?"

"It was my grandmother's. I hope you don't mind I didn't take you shopping for a ring, but— Do you like it? Really?"

"I love it." She kisses him again. "I love you. Thank you."

She looks like she might start bawling and, if she does, he will. One more kiss, then, "You're welcome. I love you, too. Shall we go?"

Just like at church, he prefers to sit on the end of a row, so he doesn't feel hemmed in. They find a couple of seats near the back. She can't stop looking at the ring and it's hard for him to stop looking at her. Would she want a big wedding like this or something intimate? His preference would be to elope. Run off to Vegas. But whatever she wants. At least now it's official.

It's hard to focus on what's going on up front during the ceremony because he doesn't know these people and his mind's going a million different directions. He looks around the crowd. They all have the same country-club, rich-as-hell look as Bennie's dad. So secure, polished. Even all dressed up, none of them look like they're trying.

It's itchy inside this tweed jacket. He doesn't see anyone else wearing tweed. Cashmere, maybe. A lot of ladies wearing hats. He fixates on a pretty hat a few rows ahead, a woman with blonde hair pulled off her neck and tied into a loose bun. When the guy next to her looks around as the minister talks about love and what it means being gathered together in the sight of God, he can see it's Ambrose. That's Jessica in the peach hat and, to the left of her, some lady wearing a sherbet-green hat with a big bow. To the left of her sits a man with a nice head of silver hair, distinguished even from the back: Bennie's dad. The one in green is Bennie's mom. The future in-laws. His throat tightens as he runs his fingers along the inside of his collar but that's no help. He shifts in his chair. Bennie reaches for his hand to squeeze with a reassuring glance and sly smile.

When it's over, the picture-perfect newly married couple walks back up the aisle to that triumphant-sounding post-wedding music played by a tuxedoed ensemble from under an oak. The ensemble still plays as all the beautiful, sociable people mingle again, moving slowly toward the tent, in a prelude to the eats. He realizes he hasn't had anything all day except a convenience store Danish early this morning.

"Hey," Bennie says. "There's Ambrose and Jessica." She pulls him in their direction.

He lets her take charge.

"Hi, guys!" she says.

Jessica looks at Bennie. "I see you decided to wear it after all."

Having gotten an eyeful of the red jumpsuit, Ambrose shoots Randy an accusing look. Maybe just a knee-jerk reaction, seeing it on Bennie this time.

Live with it, motherfucker.

"I did. You like?"

"It's—fine," Jessica says, then adds, "I guess."

Ambrose fixates on Bennie's ring. "What you got there?" He reaches for her hand.

"It's my engagement ring. Isn't it beautiful?"

Ambrose pales, looking at Randy, then back at her. "When the hell'd that happen?"

"Little over a week ago but I got the ring today."

Randy finds his voice. "Yeah, it happened kind of sudden."

"This is really sudden, isn't it?" Jessica asks. "Do Mom and Dad know?"

"Not yet."

Jessica glances at their parents a few yards away, talking with another couple. "When're you going to tell them?"

"As soon as they come over here."

Randy looks at her, speaks quietly: "Well, you could tell them later. Maybe after they've had a few drinks. . ."

"Why shouldn't I tell them now?"

"Your mom hasn't even met me yet. Think she'll flip out?"

"Everything I do flips her out. Here they come."

Randy turns to see Mr. and Mrs. Jenkins heading their way.

"Jess, where's the men's room?" Ambrose asks.

"They usually have the guest house open for parties. It's over there." She points toward what looks like a mini-Victorian mansion by the tree line. There are sprays of greenery and white roses tied around the banister leading up the steps.

"I'll meet you inside," he says, walking away.

"I'll go with you," Randy says.

"No, stay," Bennie pleads, holding his hand. "You can go in a minute, I promise."

He stays, watching Ambrose continue toward the guest house. *Lucky bastard. Mrs. Jenkins probably likes him, too, although Mr. Jenkins seems suspicious of him. Wonder if he thinks Ambrose is some kind of con-artist.* That had been Randy's initial impression, but then Ambrose's initial impression of him was none too good, either. Ambrose looked more shocked about the engagement than Jessica. Maybe because of how this whole thing started.

"Hi, Randy," Mr. Jenkins says, approaching. "Bennie. You both look great." Mrs. Jenkins is right behind him, adjusting her hat.

"So do you, Daddy." She kisses him on the cheek just as Mrs. Jenkins looks up and sees Bennie's outfit.

"My God," she says. "What is that you have on?"

"Hi, Mom. *Great to see you, too.*" She gives her mom an air kiss.

Mrs. Jenkins is an attractive older lady but, unlike most of these people, there's that so-hard-to-find-good-help-these-days look.

"It's good to see you, but, honey, what were you thinking?" She turns to Jessica. "Did you know she was going to wear this?"

"What's wrong with it?" Mr. Jenkins asks.

"It's inappropriate, Parker," Mrs. Jenkins tells him.

Bennie doesn't look upset that her mother's giving her shit. In fact, she hardly seems to be listening. "Mother, I don't think you've met Randy," she says. "This is Randall Burke. Randy, this is my mother, Pamela."

He smiles. "Nice to meet you, Mrs. Jenkins."

"I had no idea Bennie was bringing a date." With the way she's looking at him, he has the sensation that his fly might be open, but he knows it isn't, so he's not looking down.

"He came by to pick up Bennie when you were away at Carmel," Mr. Jenkins says. "I told you, remember? That I'd met Bennie's boyfriend?"

"Actually, Randy's my fiancé," Bennie announces. Just like that.

Mr. Jenkins looks surprised but not necessarily upset.

Mrs. Jenkins looks appalled.

"Well, well! Congratulations," Mr. Jenkins says. "Must've been love at first sight." He shakes Randy's hand and gives Bennie a warm hug and kiss on the cheek.

"Fiancé?" Mrs. Jenkins echoes. She looks at Jessica again. "Did you know about this?"

"Found out five minutes ago."

"How long have the two of you been dating?" Mrs. Jenkins asks.

"Long enough," Bennie answers, holding out her hand, palm down. "Isn't this a gorgeous ring?"

"I'm going to find our table," Jessica says. "See you all inside."

Mrs. Jenkins approaches. "Where are you from, Randy?"

"Gilroy, ma'am."

"And what do you do?"

"He has his own security firm," Bennie answers. Again. The way she keeps saying it, makes it seem true. And it's not a total lie; it's how he met her, in a round-about way.

"Wonderful," Mrs. Jenkins says, like she doesn't believe it. "Where did you go to school?"

"I went to Peninsula College before I joined the Army."

"He fought in Afghanistan," Bennie informs.

"Is that so? Well. Thank you for your service," Mrs. Jenkins says in that cold, automatic way some people do that's just so fucked. "It's been a pleasure meeting you. Guess we'll see you at lunch."

"Yes, ma'am."

Mr. Jenkins smiles at them, winks as he grasps Mrs. Jenkins' elbow and walks her toward the tent, where the chatter is getting louder.

When they're gone, Bennie turns to him. "Shall we find our table?"

"I don't think your mom likes me worth a damn. What do you think?"

"She doesn't like anybody I like." She lightly kisses him. "Don't worry about her."

He glances toward the guest house. "I'd better go find the restroom. Be right back."

"I'll save your seat."

"You do that," he says, grazing her ass with his hand as he starts away.

She smiles, sweeping her eyes over him in that way that makes him feel naked without having to strip.

He turns to see an older guy, maybe Mr. Jenkins' age, walking toward the tent, staring at him as if wondering who let him in. He hadn't thought anyone was looking. He makes it up the steps to the guest house, and notices the porch wraps all the way around. He sees Ambrose smoking a cigarette on the patio and walks over to him. "Hey."

"How's it going?"

"All right. Mind if I bum a smoke?"

Ambrose offers him the pack. He takes one and fumbles for a lighter, but Ambrose lights it for him.

Zippo. Nice. "Thanks."

"You're welcome. Congratulations, by the way."

"Thanks again." He takes a drag. "I owe you one."

"Don't worry 'bout it," Ambrose says, thinking he's talking about the cigarette.

"No, I mean, I really owe you,. If it hadn't been for you, I would've never met her."

Ambrose looks lost in thought.

"Everything all right?"

"Fine. Why?"

"I don't know; you just seem. . ."

Ambrose opens and closes the lighter a couple times, distracted. He'd looked stunned when Bennie said they were engaged. Maybe it was more than just seeing her in the red jumpsuit that had gotten to him.

Let it drop, Randy decides. Along with the break-in, deleted video, and myriad of fucked-up things that somehow led to the sublime moment he slipped Nana Delacroix's ring on Bennie's finger.

"'Seem' what?" Ambrose asks.

"Huh?"

"You said I 'seem' something. What were you gonna say?"

"Nothing. It's really none of my business." Randy strolls a few steps away to look at the small babbling fountain at the end of the tile. There's a marble nymph in the center, flinging a banner into the air, in a state of perpetual exuberance under the effervescent spray.

Ambrose nears. "What is it?"

Randy shrugs. *Don't say it. It doesn't matter. So don't say it.* "Was there ever anything between you and Bennie?"

Ambrose had been about to put the cigarette between his lips but pauses. "Why would you think that?"

Shouldn't have said it. "I don't know. Forget it."

Ambrose looks down at the cigarette as he flicks some ash. "We met at work and became good friends. Maybe, at first, I had kind of a schoolboy crush on her."

Randy can see that he's choosing his words carefully.

"But she was with somebody else then."

"Who was she with?"

"This Coast Guard guy. He was tall and buffed out. A real dick. There was something cruel about him if you want to know the truth."

"*Coasties.*" Randy takes a drag, exhales. "Arrogant bastards."

"He cheated on her. She broke up with him, and then. . ."

Randy can feel there's lots more.

"Then she met you, I guess. So here we are. You'll be good to her, won't you?"

"Sure, I will. I'd fuckin' die before I hurt Bennie." Randy takes a last drag before he tosses the butt on the pavement and steps on it. "So, where's the bathroom in this place?"

There's a line of women waiting three deep downstairs, so he goes upstairs looking for a bathroom because he really has to go and there are too many people milling around to slip behind a tree without getting caught. He walks into an impeccably decorated bedroom with houndstooth wallpaper: a velvety, flocked pattern with big squares in bright red over a navy background. Something about the flocking makes it look like the design moves. *Probably causes seizures if you look at it just right. Weird.* Like a pattern a kid would pick out. Only this kid got his way.

He goes into the adjoining bathroom all done up in dark blue. There's a black sink, black tile and a black toilet with a mahogany-looking seat. He takes a piss and washes his hands. Just as he barely opens the door a couple inches, he hears the bedroom door close and women's voices mid-conversation.

". . .How could you be so thoughtless?" one of them asks.

"What are you talking about?" the other one asks.

Jesus, it sounds like Bennie! She's come looking for me.

"About you. Showing up here in that bizarre get-up with a perfect stranger you say you're going to marry. What on earth has come over you?"

"I've found the right person to spend my life with, that's all."

"You can't possibly know that."

"I know you think I've made some mistakes and they're mine to make, but marrying Randy is not a mistake."

"Keep your voice down," Mrs. Jenkins hisses. "What do you know about his background, his family? He could be lying to you about who he is."

He stands still, shocked Mrs. Jenkins would think he's capable of that, though she can't know her wonderful daughter is saving him from an echoing well of loneliness, madness, and, yes, homelessness. But if she did know, that means he's damaged goods and no daughter of hers should marry factory seconds when there are so many fresh out-of-the-box billionaires and Bennie could have any of them.

"He is not lying about who he is," he hears, then the sound of walking in high heels. He imagines Bennie looking in the mirror while her mother reapplies Pepto-Bismol pink lipstick in between maligning him. *Go out in the middle of all that or stay? What if one of them comes in here?* If he were a gentleman, he would've already made his presence known but he can't go out there now. He silently moves back from the door.

"I want your father to have him investigated. At least that'll be a step in the right direction before you sign a marriage license or any other documents."

"Investigate him like he's a common criminal?"

"No, Bennie. To see if he's a common criminal."

"Well, he's not," Bennie insists. Maybe she's thinking the same thing he is, that then they'll find out about the police department investigation, the stuff he did, the stuff they *said* he did, the firing, the meltdown, the stint in the psyche ward, the awful state of his finances and no telling what else. . . He feels weak, shorter of breath. Maybe he just needs some lunch or maybe it's the thought of her mother using her dad's money to put him under a goddamn microscope to show Bennie what she's settling for and therefore how much better she could do.

"If there is something off about him, we'll get to the bottom of it. Then we'll know what we're dealing with."

"I know everything I need to know about him. I've been to the house he grew up, I've met his mother, and I know what kind of person he is. He's gone above and beyond, serving his country, which is more than you can say about any of the brats I dated when I was younger, and I'm going to marry him, whether you ever accept it or not."

He puts his hand over his mouth, trying not to make a sound: a gasp, a shocked laugh, or some burst of profanity from deep inside from hearing the love of his life defend him like a goddamned tigress.

"And you will not sic any investigators on him."

"I don't suppose you'll let Bill draw up a pre-nup?"

"No, I won't." A couple of footsteps.

"My God, honey! What kind of a hold does this man have over you?"

"Couldn't you give him half a chance before you assume he's some scammer?"

"It's just that, after Jessica's and Mike's divorce, I don't know who or what anybody is anymore. We thought Mike was such a wonderful husband and father and now he's living so openly gay! And today she's here with that. . . tenant of hers who for all I know could be her live-in lover. . . Is that what he is? You know, don't you?"

"You'll have to ask Jessica about that. Or him. His name is Ambrose, by the way. I'm going back to our table; Randy must be there by now."

"Honey, I wish you'd understand we're trying to look out for you. We raised you for something better than this."

"Better than what?"

"Working as a general factotum at a rinky-dink charity, and marrying some common-as-dirt, enlisted man from Gilroy."

He hears a door close, hard. Not a slam, but it's final. He lowers his hand from his mouth. *Did they both leave?* He hears footsteps coming this way, panics down to his socks, and glimpses his terrified face in the mirror as he turns and somehow, in one fluid motion, manages to step behind the plaid shower curtain into the bathtub.

She comes in and he can hear her shifting her clothes around. Then she must be sitting down on that toilet with the wooden seat, and then the sound of urinating. He covers his mouth with both hands. Then the flush. Footsteps. She's looking in the mirror, maybe. Then a sigh: the weary sigh of the rich, disappointed, and put-upon. Like it's all such a fucking burden. If he were any kind of a man, he'd step out of this bathtub and read her the riot act about what a precious and loving woman her daughter is, and why she should fall back on being such a goddamn bitch to her.

But he just waits for her to wash her hands and get the hell out. When she's gone, he steps out of the tub, splashes water on his face, and wipes it with an embroidered guest towel on a brass rack. He can still smell Mrs. Jenkins' perfume in the air. It's flowery. Sweet. A touch nauseating. He looks at himself a moment, and sighs the sigh of the broke, enlisted, and "common-as-dirt." But then he notices he also can't stop smiling.

When he gets back to the big tent, he makes his way over to the table where Bennie sits with Ambrose and Jessica and another beautiful, young couple. Mr. and Mrs. Jenkins sit at the next table with two other couples. The wait staff from the catering service moves easily between the tables, serving champagne in glass flutes—not the plastic kind they had at his sister's wedding. He can hear the *clink* here and there and feels like he's killed a couple of drinks already but hasn't had a drop. No alcohol in a few days, actually. But still. . .

Bennie smiles and pushes out the chair for him. "Hey," she says. "I was wondering where you were." He sits next to her, feels her hand on his knee. "Everything okay?" she asks.

"Fine," he says, gazing at the array of silverware arranged neatly at each place setting. Napkins folded like swans. . .

She leans close. "You start at the outside and work your way in."

"Is that right?" He picks up the smallest fork and looks at it. It's not plastic either. Real stainless. Jessica's chatting with the other woman about their school days among the horsey set in Virginia. Ambrose has already downed one glass of champagne and looks like he could use another, pretending to look half-ass interested with frequent glances at him and Bennie. The other guy chimes in every so often about some themed frat party or road trip.

"What's so funny?" Bennie asks.

"Nothing's funny."

"Well, what're you smiling so much about?"

"I'm having a great time, that's all."

The musical ensemble on the riser strikes up, playing a jazzy, easy-going tune. Little kids go out on the wooden dance floor to play around like they do before they learn to be self-conscious. A white-haired couple steps out there and the man takes the woman in his arms. She looks delighted and they don't seem to give a damn either. A harried dad emerges to herd the kids back to their table but they just pull him out to the middle and a little girl with a neat pink bow at her waist insists he dance with her. He finally agrees and she puts her feet on top of his to move her around the dance floor.

He grabs Bennie's hand. "Let's dance."

She looks surprised. "Really?"

He stands. The dizziness has mostly passed and, if he can hold onto her, he'll be all right. "Take off that wrap."

She leaves it on the chair. He barely glances back but, when he does, sees Ambrose watching. *Eat your heart out, motherfucker.* He feels Mrs. Jenkins watching them, too, all pinch-faced when she gets the full effect of Bennie's red jumpsuit.

On top of that, seeing Randy hold her daughter in his arms, right here in front of God and everybody, must be enough to make her skin crawl.

EIGHT

It couldn't be colder or more impersonal, the way Ambrose finds out about the death of Miss Dover. A phone call from Paris says her body has been found in a hotel room. Cause of death has been ruled a massive heart attack due to overuse of stimulants.

Stimulants? Ambrose knew Miss Dover used drugs in the past, all kinds, but only in her stories of the bad, old days in Dallas and when she lived in New Orleans a while. That was another reason she was always so grateful to her benefactor who left her their building and paid for her sex change. He'd helped her clean up her act and schooled her on the finer things.

Ambrose asks for a number or someone he can speak to for more information, but it's difficult understanding the Frenglish at the other end of who's talking *at* rather than *to* him. They want to ascertain how the next of kin wished to repatriate the remains, if the body is to be cremated, because the funeral parlor in Paris needs approval or, in the event of no next of kin, a responsible party must pay all associated costs, and on and on.

The more he tries to ask specifics, the more information they throw at him in French and English. Ambrose rushes the cordless phone down the hall, looking for Mignon. He finds her in the dressing room, lacing up her black satin corset, and hands her the phone. "Miss Dover's dead," he babbles, shaken to the core. "I can barely understand what they're saying; ask them if I need to come over or what I need to do!"

Mignon takes the phone, speaking calmly in French as he paces, not understanding a word. She goes over to her dressing table, picks up a pen, and writes something on the back of a magazine. Then he hears, "*Merci. Au revoir.*" And she clicks off the phone.

"What'd you do that for?" he asks, panicked.

"What do you mean?"

"You hung up! Don't we need to get more information? Did you get their number?"

"*Oui.*" She hands him the magazine "Here is the number. When you call, you're to ask for Gille."

"What'd they say to you?"

"That they will send the ashes back, along with a death certificate if the next of kin approves a cremation. Otherwise, the process will be much more complicated. Do you know what her wishes were?"

"I could call her lawyer; she may have a will. . ." He walks over to a chair in the corner. His legs feel leaden. The news is starting to hit. "They said she had a heart attack."

Mignon continues lacing her corset. *She's shown no emotion at all, though she'd barely known Miss Dover.* In his shock, he'd forgotten for a few moments about Mignon being Jessica's lover. *Is that even the right word?* He doesn't know what he is to Jessica anymore and doesn't know exactly what Mignon is either. He thought he knew, but all that's blotted out by the reverberations of this awful news pulsating through his body and mind.

Mignon finishes lacing up, and fluffs up her dark, wavy hair in the mirror. She glances at his reflection. "You're pale. Are you okay?" She turns to him in her full gear: thigh-high stiletto boots, fingerless leather gloves, black eye shadow and lips painted the color of the pinot noir he and Jessica had with salmon steaks last night. She looks like a sexy angel of death. "You were very close to Miss Dover, no?" she asks.

"Yes."

She walks over to him and he looks up at her, towering above him at this angle. "I am sorry for your loss," she says. But she doesn't look sorry. He wonders if she means Miss Dover or what she's done to his and Jessica's relationship. She wouldn't be sorry for that either.

"Thanks. . ."

"If you need for me to speak with the French authorities again or translate anything at all, please let me know. I am most happy to help any way I can."

"Okay."

She smiles, leans down, and kisses him on the forehead. "I suppose you are the boss now, yes?"

"No. I don't know."

She caresses the side of his face. "I have a session in the Charenton Suite. A couple visiting from Pittsburgh. Courageux, *chers*."

He watches her walk out.

✶✶✶

It is one of those deliriously beautiful days in the park, when the friends—no family—of Miss Dover (first known as Reginald Ford, then Layla Bordeaux) gather to pay their respects. There are around fifty people gathered, the affair officiated by her good friend Reverend Kelly, a black, trans preacher from the Castro. Her vestments are bright purple with gold filigree around the bottom of the sleeves. Her hair is tinged purple, lips painted electric lilac. "...This woman was fearless," she says. "Having recognized that fear and greed are the two most destructive forces on the planet, she fought both with equal zeal."

"Amen," someone says.

"And she didn't just use her determination for her own purposes. In fact, some of you might not be alive if not for her intervention to get your act together."

"Right, ma'am."

Pacing before the podium, Rev. Kelly tries to bring aid and comfort to the downhearted in this half-sunny, half-shady little enclave on a Saturday afternoon. "She sought to inspire and empower others, particularly those of the next generation. Sister Dover wanted more than anything to make her mark in the world and she has left an indelible impression on this city, this community, and all those gathered here today to honor her memory. . ."

Bennie eases around the crowd, looking for Ambrose and Jessica. Randy sits in the back row, arms folded, head tilted to one side, listening. He didn't know Miss Dover, so he's just taking it all in. Ambrose has barely spoken since getting the news and had sat at the airport sleepless until the ashes arrived. Miss Dover's ashes are in an ornate urn on a table before the podium. Created by an artist from Berkeley Bennie contacted, it's shaped like a ceramic chalice, white with a purple *fleur de lis* jewel near the bottom, edged in gold. The stem of the chalice swirls upward, with a lid that rises to a point. Up to the lid is encased in sea-glass encrusted metalwork. Miss Dover's lawyer, Theodore "Teddy" Simmons, is to read her will at his office in Oakland on Tuesday, and he'd contacted Bennie and Ambrose to make sure they'd be there if possible.

Already here in the park are the sounds of birds chirping and the laughter of children playing in the distance, punctuated by a dog's occasional bark. And now, hanging over all that, the melancholy notes of someone crying. Many assembled had tears in their eyes, but this crying is unbridled heartbreak.

Benny pauses where she is, looking over the crowd to see where the hardest sobbing is coming from. Others are as well. It's Ambrose, sitting six rows back. Bennie takes a step forward, but it would be hard to get to him right now and Jessica's there with him, her hand on his shoulder, eyes darting around every so often as if she's self-conscious and really wishes he would stop.

When the eulogy is over, Rev. Kelly invites those who knew Miss Dover to come share some memories with the others. Bennie is surprised to see Ambrose rise and go forward. As he stands to the side of the podium, he spies Bennie, and their eyes connect for a long moment. She smiles. She had known Miss Dover first but Miss Dover and Ambrose always had a special bond.

"I grew to love this woman very much in the time I knew her," he says. "I worked for her, but I don't just think of her as my boss. She was very kind to me, along with some others who've helped me get through hard times. . ." He looks pointedly at Bennie, then Jessica. Jessica smiles, head slightly down. "When I came to town, I was alone, surrounded by strangers. . ." He wipes away a tear. "And even though I didn't know her then, she wasn't a stranger. We were both Texans and we both. . . I guess some people would say we had rough childhoods." He pauses, like he's trying to hold it together.

Bennie feels connected to him because she's about to cry, too, as it dawns on her that Dover, Inc., as it was, is gone forever.

"While I was listening to Reverend Kelly talking about everything Miss Dover's done, I was thinking how when I met her, I was a homeless runaway and. . ." He wipes his eyes again. "And she gave me a legitimate job and tried to teach me right from wrong, which seems simple, but for me it hasn't always been. I've never meant to hurt anybody, but Miss Dover taught me that, by compromising so much, I was hurting myself. Nobody's ever really cared whether I learned that before, but she did. And I'm grateful to her." He pauses, takes a half-step from the podium. "I'll miss her. That's all."

He returns to his seat. Bennie wipes her eyes and as she starts slowly making her way to check on the caterers setting up lunch at the picnic tables. She sees a familiar figure off to the side, standing in the shade of a tree, a part of and yet apart from the proceedings. A short, stocky, middle-aged man wearing a hat, sunglasses, and very nice suit. There's a flower in his lapel and a neatly folded handkerchief in his top pocket. He takes the handkerchief out and removes the sunglasses to dab at his eyes. It's Maxim Rusovich. Eccentric and pervy as he is, Mr. Rusovich really was crazy about Miss Dover, and seemingly about their whole little enterprise. She's never seen him outside the dungeon, so it's odd running into him in the outside world. *Wonder what he's thinking. Maybe the same thing I am:*

This is the end of an era.

✳✳✳

As planned, the will reading takes place at the Simmons' Law Offices in Oakland, above a gluten-free bakery. Mr. Simmons, to whom Miss Dover always referred as Teddy, had been her attorney for many years and makes for an imposing figure as he strides into the conference room where Ambrose and Bennie and a representative from one of the youth charities Miss Dover supported are waiting.

Teddy, a large black man in his mid-40s, wearing tortoiseshell frame glasses and a gray suit with a muted stripe, takes a seat at the head of the table. Hidden in his navy-blue tie is a tasteful design featuring music notes. Teddy plays trombone in a jazz band some evenings and Ambrose and Bennie accompanied Miss Dover to a few of his gigs after work. Noticing the details of Teddy's attire takes Ambrose's addled mind off the bad case of nerves he's had all day.

He doesn't feel grown-up enough to handle all this, which is a horrible admission to make, and Miss Dover would kick his ass for even letting such an idea enter his consciousness.

Teddy smiles his trademark smile: warm, laid-back, and wholesome on stage and, according to Miss Dover, devastating when deployed in the courtroom. "Good afternoon," he says. "Thank you all for coming today. As you know, you've been asked here because you're named as heirs in the last will and testament of sister Regina Dover. I know you're all busy people, so, without any further ado, I'll go ahead and read the document, and then I'll be happy to answer any questions you may have." And he reads the will.

And it really is the end of an era.

✳✳✳

Ambrose is on the patio, smoking a cigarette, about to get back to studying for an accounting exam when Jessica places a letter on the table in front of him. She stands there while he looks at it, as if she's waiting for him to take action. He reads the return label. It's from Dallas. He feels a tightening in his gut. **Law Offices of Daniel Mullins, LLC.**

"Aren't you going to open it?"

"Is it something I want to open?"

She pulls up a chair to sit across from him. "I would think you'd be curious. The mail carrier brought it to the door. I had to sign for it."

"I'm just not in the mood for any weird surprises."

"Do you want me to open it?"

"Knock yourself out," he says, using one of his older brother's favorite phrases.

She picks it up and opens it carefully, trying not to tear the envelope too much. The longer she takes, the longer he can spend in blissful ignorance about whatever it contains. "It's from your brother's lawyer," she says. "Your brother wanted him to tell you that your dad's terminally ill and would like to see you before he. . . dies."

Ambrose feels his face tense at "terminally ill," and "before he dies." *How achingly sentimental. Just like something the old man would come up with and that Butch would buy into.* He stands, walks over to the edge of the patio, folding his arms against the night chill. She leaves the letter on the table and walks over to him, places her hand on his shoulder and slides it down to rub his back. "I'm sorry it's bad news about your dad."

"I'm not. Good riddance."

She steps back. "How can you say that?"

"My dad was a real son-of-a-bitch."

"But still, he's your dad. Why are you already referring to him in the past tense?"

"Sounds like he's on his death bed."

"He asked to see you. Maybe he wants to make amends."

Ambrose suppresses a bitter urge to laugh. "I don't think so."

She folds her arms, too, as the air gets cooler. "Look, I realize I don't know the whole story with your family. . ." She really doesn't. The things he told her when he was pretending to be a graduate student were mostly bullshit. "Since you never want to talk about them, I gather it's not all that good, but I really think you'll regret it if you don't go see him. It might make things a little better. Not so much for him, but for you. It might give you some closure."

"I'm not going."

"Why don't you sleep on it and decide in the morning?"

"There's nothing to decide."

"What about your mother? Is she still living?"

"I guess."

"Your brother must want you to come back. Maybe you could at least see him?"

He doesn't have an immediate come-back for that. Butch went to the trouble to track him down and he's the only one in the family who would. He tried to be a good big brother, just steered Ambrose wrong about a few things. Like teaching him that the only way out of Riviera is breaking the law. And that he should hook up with Lang on the west coast. The thought of good-natured, baby-faced Butch sitting in prison puts a dent in his resolve, as the temperature continues to drop, and stars appear in the sky. "Maybe," he says.

"Maybe you'll go?"

"To see Butch."

"And your dad? I'll bet Butch would go there with you—if you wanted."

She doesn't even realize Butch is incarcerated. If he took Jessica to meet Butch in prison, he'd likely be his same, *aw-shucks* charming self. Unless prison turned him hard. But how hard can he be if he's gone to all this effort to reach out? And on the old man's behalf?

"He might if he's able," Ambrose says.

"Is he in bad health, too?"

"I don't know."

Jessica slips her arms around his waist, pressing close to get warm. He slowly puts his arms around her, eyes stinging a little. Not because of his dad but because this is the first time in a while that she's come to him like she really wants him to hold her, so he squeezes back.

He really doesn't want to make this trip. But thinking only about Butch. . . "You don't have to come along if you don't want to," he says.

"What if I do want to?"

He reaches up to smooth a strand of her hair.

She doesn't know what she's in for, but he doesn't really know what to expect either. "Want me to call my dad and see if we can use the private jet?" she asks.

Now there's something no one says back in Riviera, Texas. Ever. "Let's just fly commercial."

✳✳✳

He'd gone to bed with her that night with the vague intention of making love to her but he fell dead asleep and had bad dreams of running from something. Images of Miss Dover calling out for help and not being able to. Talking to Butch in a prison visitor's room and he's his affable self with a raven sitting on his shoulder. *Was it a raven or a crow?* Either way, a bird kept tugging on Butch's hair with its black beak. His dad doesn't appear in the dream and neither does his mother, but he knows it's them he's running from. Mostly it's them. The past. He thought he'd left it behind but it's still here and all the more because he hadn't really faced it.

Then the alarm and a shower. Mike arrives to pick up Beau and then somehow Ambrose finds himself in the San Francisco airport, going through security. Jessica goes through first. As he takes off his belt and shoes, putting them in the plastic bin to be slid along the conveyor and into the carry-on scanner, he sees Jessica step into that round glass booth that supposedly detects metals and weaponry. She stands with her arms raised; legs spread apart so the machine can get a clear picture of the outline of her body. She smiles at the TSA worker as she steps out to collect her things.

Ambrose places his change and watch into his right shoe and gives it a gentle push along the conveyor as he steps into the clear plastic tube. He places his hands on the designated handprints and his feet on the footprints. For him, the whole trip will be like this body scan. She'll finally get to see the things he's kept tucked away. All the hidden objects. Even though everyone must stand here and be scanned like a chip, most have nothing to hide. Why does he feel he does? Why an uneasy sense that buzzers, lights, and sirens will go off any minute?

He hasn't told Jessica but this is the first time he's ever flown on an airplane. He's ridden buses, trains, walked his fair share of miles, and caught rides with bootleg truckers, male and female, some of whom wanted something out of the deal to pick up a scruffy juvenile delinquent on his way west. Once he's snapped in, the plane is finally loaded and the engines start, he shuts his eyes and holds her hand. She must think he's in the throes of some strong emotion, but it's the sensation of defying gravity that makes him grip so hard.

They wait on you hand and foot in first class. He presses the warm towel against his face until the heat is out of it. It's nice behind that towel. Then he has two drinks and a glass of water before he gets up unsteadily to go to the restroom. Jessica watches him start down the aisle, then goes back to reading her magazine. He makes it into the restroom, shuts and locks the door. He heaves into the toilet but nothing much comes up; he's barely eaten anything today.

He takes a piss, flushes, washes his hands, splashes water onto his face, and dabs it dry with a paper towel. Can't tell if it's those drinks or the retrograde sensation of heading east that's making him feel so disoriented. Maybe both. Drinking on an empty stomach and hurtling at breakneck speed toward the last place he wants to go.

Back in his seat, he puts on sunglasses to block out the bright light and fall asleep for a few minutes before the plane descends into Dallas/Fort Worth International. As he and Jessica walk to baggage claim, he's vaguely aware of people staring, some with their phones out. When he glances at Jessica, he realizes why. She looks like a movie star with long, blonde hair and a stylish, loose pantsuit, all fresh and flawless. She's used to attention and pretends not to notice.

Guiding her past the knot of amateur paparazzi, he catches a glimpse of his reflection in a glass-encased cowboy boot display and realizes he's still wearing shades, so no wonder people are looking: her with that face and him holding her hand like he's Joe Hollywood. Still, he doesn't want to take the glasses off. Jessica had reserved a Cadillac SUV, so they place their collection of suitcases on a cart and roll it out.

"Big enough?" he asks.

"Guess I should've gotten something more environmentally friendly, but I asked for something roomy, good for desert driving."

"Desert driving?"

She shrugs. He puts their luggage in the back compartment, closes it up, then opens the passenger door for her. He gives her a hand up as she steps in. "I'll take you to the hotel, then I'll go see my dad."

"But it's early. We can check in, and then I was thinking I'd at least ride with you. If you want, I'll wait outside while you visit."

He pauses, unsure what to say, so he just walks to the driver's side. *Why am I here and how did I let myself get into this situation?* He feels her watching while he puts on the seat belt.

"Well?" she says. "What do you think?"

"I think you're welcome to come with, if that's what you want."

She smiles. "That's what I want."

He puts the Cadillac in gear, smiles back. "Then by all means. Come with me."

***

The town is so small, there's no chance of getting lost. Nothing much has changed, but, when he drives the Escalade into the parking lot, the nursing home looks different than when he used to visit his granddad. It had looked bigger then, but now, having been away, he realizes how small it really is. The trees around it have grown and the sign out front is missing an **H**. A swath of forest beyond the fence has been cleared for the construction of a mini storage center.

He parks and sits there a moment, staring through the windshield. Jessica turns to him.

"According to what your brother said, if there's anything you want to tell him, you should do it now."

"Uh-huh." He starts to get out, but stops when she says, "You were listening, right?"

"To who?"

She sighs. "To me. And what was in his letter. About your dad. This may be the last time you get to see him."

There are actually potholes to navigate as they walk to the entrance. A few heads turn as he and Jessica approach the reception desk. He asks the nurse where Carl Ballard's room is.

"Down this hallway, take a right, and it's the first door on the left," she informs him. Then: "Do you mind if I ask, are you a relative?"

"I'm his son."

"Really? I knew he had one son in jail. . ."

"I'm his youngest son. I've been away for a while."

"Oh." She glances at Jessica. "Well, I'm sure—He'll be happy to see you."

Why the hesitation, he wonders. Maybe she's heard Carl bad-mouth his youngest son, or he's not really glad to see anybody. Ambrose and Jessica start down the hallway. Some of the residents are sitting in wheelchairs in the doorway to their rooms. There's a whiff of dried urine as they walk past a man wearing worn slippers and baggy, stained pants held up by suspenders, shuffling along the wall's handrail, oxygen tank in tow.

Jessica leans closer to Ambrose, speaking quietly. "Your brother's in jail? Why didn't you tell me?"

"Federal prison, actually."

"What did he do to be sent to federal prison?"

"He got caught running drugs. Stooging for a Columbian kingpin." *Click*. And another X-ray image of his life is revealed to her. He's conscious of his heart beating faster as they round the corner. The door to his dad's room is ajar and he can hear the television. He stops.

She stares at the door, too, then reaches to take his hand. That catches him off-guard. One thing at a time. He pushes open the door and sees a worn-out, old man asleep in a hospital bed. Even though it seems like a lifetime since he left in such turmoil, it hasn't been long enough for Ambrose to think Carl would age this much. His father's hair's totally gray, his face craggier, painfully thin like shrunken. Ambrose glances at Jessica, squeezes her hand then releases it to draw near the bed. Maybe Carl's weakness shouldn't make him feel stronger but it does.

"Daddy?" he says.

The old man slowly opens his eyes, takes a deep breath, glances around like wondering if he's dreaming. "Who said that?" he asks in a scratchy voice.

"I did. It's Ambrose. Remember me?"

The old man sniffles, eyes starting to focus. "Well, I'll be damned. What the hell are you doing here?"

"Butch wrote and told me you were bad off. How're you feeling?"

The old man tries to sit up. "Like shit," he says, catching sight of Jessica. "Who's that fine piece of ass you got there with you?"

Ambrose glances at Jessica. She looks stricken, seeing he's just a dirty, old man with one foot in the grave and what's left of his mind in the gutter. "This is Jessica," Ambrose informs him.

"She your girlfriend?" the old man asks with a naughty smile.

"She's way more than my girlfriend."

"Hello, Mr. Ballard," Jessica says, pretending to ignore his earlier remark. "It's—a pleasure to meet you."

"Oh, really?" the old man asks.

Ambrose feels his jaw tightening but doesn't want Carl to see it. His dad's not sorry for anything he's done and will never, not that Ambrose even wants an apology. He doesn't want anything but somehow let Jessica and Butch talk him into coming back based on some sentimental idea that "If you can see him before he dies, you'll have no guilt when he's gone," and he'll die a little happier. But that's all bullshit. Age and alcohol haven't mellowed Carl but hardened him.

"Yes, sir, it is. Your son is a wonderful man," she tells Carl. "You should be very proud of him. He's kind and loving and my little boy looks up to him as a father figure."

"Little boy?" Carl looks at Ambrose. "She got you raisin' some other guy's kid?"

The color heightens in Jessica's face.

"She hasn't *got* me doing anything," Ambrose informs. "I love her little boy like he's my own."

Carl nods knowingly. "Uh-huh. Some other bastard got her all stretched out and now you the one having to play 'daddy.'" He looks at Jessica. "Course, I never expected him to be a real daddy anyway. We always thought he'd end up being queer as a three-dollar bill."

Jessica seems torn between wanting to remain Ambrose's moral support and get the hell out of this room. Ambrose turns to her, nods slightly toward the door. Not that she needs his permission, but. . . She looks at Carl. "Well, Mr. Ballard. It was. . ." She can't really bring herself to say, It's been nice meeting you. "I'll just step out and let you and Ambrose have a few minutes alone to talk."

Carl lies back on his pillow, having expended a good deal of energy already. Ambrose watches Jessica walk out. As she leaves, the slanting shafts of afternoon sunlight contain dust motes that swirl and dance, particles which have likely been around since he was here sitting at his grandpa's bedside all those years ago when the family gathered for his passing. Even Butch had been there, before that final caper had sent him inside for this longest stretch.

"You ran her off," Ambrose begins. "Just you and me now."

Carl can barely lift his head as he shifts his eyes to look at Ambrose. "Who is that gal? What's she to you?"

Ambrose quickly weighs the possibility that he'll ever have to see this old bastard again. Butch said he wasn't long for this world, and, looking at him, that seems fairly accurate. "Like I said, she's more than just my girlfriend. We're married."

"Married?" Carl repeats.

Ambrose shoves his hands in his pockets, realizing he's not wearing a wedding band. But so what? "That's right."

"When'd you get married?"

"'Bout a year ago."

"She said something 'bout a li'l boy. But that ain't your son."

"No, she has a son with her first husband. But she and I'll be having kids before long."

"Where ya'll live?"

"Out in California. I headed there the night I left home."

Carl gazes at him, slack-jawed. "That's the last time I seen you."

"That's right."

"What even happened that night?"

"You tried to burn my face on the stove."

"I did not," Carl claims. "You're full of shit."

"You did it, all right," Ambrose asserts. "And I made sure it was the last time, because I knew if I stuck around and anything like that happened again, I'd kill you."

"Might've done me a favor if you had," Carl says. "Maybe then I wouldn't be laid up in this place." He starts coughing.

Ambrose watches as he tries to regain himself, reaching for a small box of tissues on his bed tray. "Wasn't worth going to jail over," Ambrose says. "How're they treating you here? Pretty good?"

Carl coughs into the tissue, looks at it, wads it up, and tosses it into a wastebasket at the side of the bed. "What do you do out there in California besides bang that blonde pussy?"

"Don't forget that's my wife you're talking about."

"I ain't forgot."

"I run a dungeon," Ambrose says.

"A what?"

"A place where people go to get spanked and all kinds of other things."

"Who does? Queers?"

"Anybody. We have clients of every orientation, all walks of life."

Carl laughs. "Do ya now? And who does the spanking? You?"

"I don't do it myself. Not anymore, anyway. I got people for that."

Carl looks skeptical. "Sounds like some California liberal, Satanic bullshit."

"It's the truth."

Carl rolls his eyes. "What the fuck will they think of next?" Then: "You make a lot of money?"

"Mmhm. Most people who pay for that got money to burn."

"That wife of yours into that kinky shit?"

"Not really. It's just a business."

"It's a racket, all right."

"Well, if it ever goes out of fashion, it's a good thing Jessica's daddy's a billionaire. Otherwise, we might not be able to pay private school for Junior."

Now Carl squints as if trying to tell whether he's lying. *Could be jealousy, deep resentment, or both.* "Billionaire? What kind?"

"Does it matter?"

"I reckon not."

Seconds tick by. Ambrose feels the wheels turning in Carl's head.

"So, you got all that money and leave your old daddy to rot in a nursing home?"

"Thought you said they treat you pretty good. Don't you have any friends here?"

"You're a stingy, selfish little bastard."

"Why you say that? Want me to give you some money?"

"I don't want a goddamn thing from you," he says finally.

"Good," Ambrose says, drawing closer. "I don't want nothing from you either."

"Then why'd you come all this way? So I'd hug and tell you what a fine son y'are? Don't hold your breath."

"I really only came because Butch wanted me to, and I still love Butch as my brother."

Carl turns away. "*Boo-hoo-fuckety-hoo.*"

"At least he gives a shit, which is more than I can say for you or Mama. A hell of a lot more."

They sit in silence a moment, Carl staring at the wall, Ambrose staring at Carl, taking in every detail of that face. It's wrinkled like cheap, old leather or fake, new leather: slack and dull. Carl's lashes and eyebrows had always been light-colored and, along with his cool gray, slightly drooping eyes and blondish hair, always made him look a little detached, able to inflict lasting pain with fists or words, then maybe laugh about it later over at the bar or around a trash fire with his buddies in the backyard. "Are you even my real father?" Ambrose asks.

"What makes you ask that?"

"Thought it might explain why you hate me so much."

"I don't hate you."

"But you don't love me either, do you? Never have."

No answer.

"That's okay. I always figured as much." Another few moments of silence. Ambrose tries to think whether he has anything he wants to say. Nothing comes to mind. "All right, then," he sighs. "Guess I'll go." He gets to the door and, just as he's about to open it, Carl speaks.

"Hey."

Ambrose stops, turns.

"I don't hate you," Carl says. "I just don't got no feelings for you, that's all."

He didn't want Jessica to come with him to see his mom the next day. That's one X-ray snapshot of his life he refuses to show her. He hadn't wanted her to see the one of his dad but she'd insisted and he's not sure if she's glad or sorry she went now. Either way, she saw it and won't ever again picture him riding around in a red convertible checking on his dad's oil wells like she'd said that night at the country club fundraiser months ago. She knows about his white-trash roots, so no need to belabor the point by driving her all the way past the car wash, trailer park, and old recreation field to the house his parents moved to after his dad finally closed the gas station.

His mother had worked off and on at Family Dollar, and for a short time at the liquor store run by two Indian brothers, but that job proved too much for her. She lifted the merchandise, plus they caught her on camera slipping cash out of the till. They didn't call the police, but fired her, and she brought home a bottle of vodka with her last paycheck—minus what she'd been caught stealing. She and Carl downed most of it that evening, sitting out by the trash fire in the backyard, smoking cigarettes and a couple joints, lamenting that outsiders seemed to be taking over these days. "Before long they'll own everything and there'll be nothing left for real, honest-to-God Americans."

His parents had both run around on each other and even though they're still married, he has to wonder if his mother has a boyfriend now that Carl's out of the house. She did even when he lived there, but now she wouldn't have to hide it, and Carl no longer gives a damn, which would take most of the fun out of it for her. Wonder what she does for fun these days? She'd been kind of pretty before all the substances. Even though she'd dabbled around with other things from time to time, alcohol was her drug of choice, just like it became Carl's.

Driving out alone to see her, having talked Jessica into resting at the hotel, he tries not to anticipate what he might find. Coming back to this town, especially after Miss Dover's death, is like ripping off a Band-Aid, and coming to visit the folks is like ripping the scab off the sore. Yes, he lied to Carl just to blow his mind a little since he'd done nothing but put him and Butch down all their lives, but Carl saying he had no feelings for him whatsoever made him wish, once again, that he hadn't made this trip. Even though there's no way Carl can hurt him anymore, it's depressing knowing your closest kin doesn't give a shit about you, even if you feel the same. It's liberating, too, but—strange. So much for any kind of "healing" Jessica thought possible.

He rolls up in the yard. Not much has changed. The car his mom, Jackie, used to drive is on blocks and there are other vehicles in varying states of disrepair, and appliances scattered around the sides of the house, which badly needs a paint job. The patchy grass looks like it hasn't been mown in a while. *Maybe she's not here.*

He gets out of the Escalade, walks toward the sagging porch and up the cinderblock steps. He takes a breath as he approaches the screen door and knocks on it. Waits. No answer. It creaks as he opens it. He can hear movement inside, then someone says, "Who is it?"

Can't tell if it's her. It has to be her. "Ambrose."

No response but he hears a deadbolt unlocking and the door opens a crack. "Who? Ambrose?"

"Mama? It's me."

The door opens and he can see her. She hasn't changed much but she does look older, the lines in her face prominent. She has a skeptical expression, then a momentary look of surprise. "Well, I'll be damned. It is you!"

"Yes, ma'am."

She's wearing shorts and a T-shirt with flip-flops. Her hair's kind of a mess, but it always was. She used to tease it with a comb and try to set it with coats of hairspray and it looks like maybe she did that a couple days ago. She stares at him. "When I talked to your daddy on the phone, he said you'd come by to see him, but I thought he was hallucinatin'. And here you are. . ." She repeats, "I'll be damned."

He can't tell if she wants to hug and he isn't sure if he should try, but she does reach out to him, so he puts his arms around her shoulders for a moment. She smells of smoke, always.

She pulls away, looks him over. "I didn't know if I'd ever see you again."

"I didn't know if I'd see you again either," he says.

"You look like you mighta made something of yourself."

"Do I?"

"Come on in."

He walks inside, looking around the living room and kitchen. There's a game show on the widescreen and the window-unit A/C is running full-blast. "How've you been?" he asks.

"All right, I reckon. Your daddy told me you was living in California, married to a rich girl. I thought he's off his rocker."

"No, it's true. Butch sent me a letter that Daddy was in bad shape, so I decided to come see him." He glances toward the kitchen counter, thinking he might have seen a roach run across it. There are boxes of cereal and some canned goods sitting next to a cardboard box, and, on the stove, a frying pan encrusted with food, a couple of flies buzzing around it. The pan sits on the same stove eye Carl tried to press his face against that night. "Been grocery shopping?" he asks.

She looks over at the counter. "They brought that stuff from the food bank. Andy, that delivers my stuff from Sorrell's, volunteers down there and brings me a box every Thursday."

"Oh. Good." Sorrell's is the other liquor store in town. Mr. Sorrell was getting frail back around the time he left and probably didn't run it anymore. Most likely Ray, the son, runs it now: the one who used to buy pot from Ambrose and disappear into the storeroom with Jackie on a slow night. Andy must be one of Ray's flunkies.

He takes a couple steps into the living room. The carpet, the furniture, the curtains. Everything's pretty much the same. He'd expected memories and emotions to come flooding back but now it's all he can do to feel anything.

"How long you here for?" She scratches her head, sniffling.

"We plan on leaving tomorrow afternoon."

"Will I get to meet the new wife?"

"One of these days. She's back at the hotel." He glances over at the China cabinet from his grandmother's sitting in the corner. It used to have dishes displayed but there's only a half-gallon bottle of vodka, a fifth of bourbon, and a flashlight sitting there with the batteries hanging out, like she's going to replace them or maybe couldn't get it to work.

She grabs a tissue on the counter and blows her nose. Her eyes are watering, too, but he doesn't think it's from emotion.

"Jessica thinks she might have a cold. Wouldn't want her to give you some illness. Sounds like you're kind of sick yourself."

"It's this allergy," she says, swiping her nose over and over with the tissue. "Them goddamn pecan trees out there. Oughta have 'em all cut down."

If there's one thing that could make the place look worse than it does, it would be cutting down the only redeeming feature of this cursed property. But then he remembers they've been threatening to have them cut since he was in junior high and, just like the talk about cleaning up the yard or having stuff hauled off, it'll probably never happen. Carl could never bring himself to part with the junk, thinking he might have a use for it someday, and Jackie never seemed to mind what anyone thought. There are no neighbors close by so no one to really complain, and passersby just deem it an eyesore or a landmark for giving directions as in, "If you pass a little, white-frame house with lots of junk and old cars in the yard, you'll know you've gone too far."

"You want something to drink?" Jackie asks. "I got a couple of sodas. Or you want a shot?"

"No, thanks."

She sniffles again. "Well, hell. Have a seat." She walks over to the recliner in front of the TV. Ambrose sits down on the green and red plaid sofa. His other grandmother's crocheted throw is still draped across the back of it, more ragged now but still with that yellow, gold, orange color combination. He doesn't even know how to make conversation. There are things he's curious about but talking with her is like making small talk with a stranger, and he senses she feels the same. So here he sits, in the home of his youth, being treated like a guest by his mother, who seems strangely detached. She was Carl's biggest enabler and stood by while Carl abused him and Butch. He occasionally slapped her around as well, and she would threaten to divorce him, but the next night it was business as usual, like nothing ever really happened.

She turns down the volume. "What you doing out in California? Carl tried to tell me but didn't make sense. I think he got all mixed up."

"What did he tell you?"

"That you run a place where people get spanked and shit like that."

"No, it's true. He told you right."

"Sounds like you got mixed up with some weirdos out there. How'd you meet this rich girl?"

"I work with her sister, and she introduced us."

"And her sister works at this weird place, too?"

"Yes, ma'am."

She laughs, half like it's funny, half in disbelief. "That beats all I ever heard."

His mouth's gotten dry, and he'd like a glass of water but doesn't want to ask. She's so nonchalant about his being here. They both are. He'd dreaded any emotional scenes that might break out after all this time, and the circumstances under which he left. "Do you miss Daddy being here?" he asks.

She shrugs, looking at the TV. "Sometimes. I kinda like having the place to myself, to tell you the truth."

He leans closer to the edge of the sofa, so he doesn't feel he's getting sucked in. Feels like some springs are broken and it's sitting very low. He hadn't wanted to talk before, but he's starting to, now that he's traveled all this way, and endured the heaviness that came with thoughts of seeing them again. "Do you go visit Butch very often?" he asks.

"Not really. I ain't got a car now so I have to get rides. It's hard enough getting a lift to town. Who wants to drive all the way out to the prison? Then whoever takes you'll want gas money."

Listening to her and all the folks he's encountered anywhere in town makes him revert to his small-town, shit-kicking vernacular. "It ain't worth swapping a couple bottles of liquor to go visit your first-born son up at the federal pen?"

"How many times have you been to see him since you left?" she asks, which leaves him at a loss. *Touché.* With that, she turns back to the TV. He's struck by what she said, then realizes he doesn't even have her full attention as she yells at the screen, "Lower! Lower, you stupid bitch!"

He looks at the TV where a gameshow contestant has to guess the price of a car versus the one on the board. He stands, gets the remote off the end table, and turns off the TV.

She looks up at him. "What'd you do that for?"

"Because I'm trying to talk to you."

"I could hear you fine."

He pulls up a chair and sits, keeping hold of the remote. "Mama, do you remember why I left home?"

She shifts around in the recliner, a heating pad pressed against her lower back. Something in her expression conveys, "What'd you want to bring that up for?" but she takes a stab at an answer. "Well. . . you and Carl got in some kind of fight. And he hit you and you hit him and ya'll cussed each other out and then you ran out the house and we didn't see you no more."

"That's all you remember about that night?"

"I remember ya'll were always getting into it about something," she allows. "He never really meant to hurt you." She stretches her legs and arms as if she's bored with this conversation. "They's plenty of blame to go 'round. The men on your daddy's side all have hot tempers."

"You just think Daddy has a hot temper?"

"Kinda. Don't you?"

"Don't I what? Have a hot temper, or think he does?"

"Both."

He feels the temperature rising in his face, seeing her taking up for his old man, after all this time. "When I left, did ya'll ever even try to look for me? Or ask anybody if they'd seen me? Or wonder where I might've gone?"

She folds her hands in her lap, looking puzzled. "We just figured you'd come back if you ever wanted to. You know, after you got over it. We didn't want to bring the police in on it 'cause. for all Carl knew, you might try to get him in trouble telling God-knows-what about how it happened. Besides, Butch said he'd talked to you and that he was trying to hook you up with a job out west doing something."

He hands back the remote. "I see." He stands. *Looks like this is all the "closure" I'll be getting.* From their point of view, one day he was here and the next he was gone, and they really haven't given him too much thought since. "Guess I'd better be going."

"What's your rush?" she asks. He doesn't know if she means it or if she's being sarcastic. He suspects it's the latter.

"What're you using mine and Butch's old bedroom for?"

"Junk room. Storage."

"Can I go take a look?"

"Knock yourself out," she says, pulling back the lever to raise the footrest on the recliner. Then she reaches for the beer.

He walks into the short hallway to the end where the door is closed. He peers inside. The bed and dresser are there. Several boxes sit on the bed. Some contain magazines or junk mail, and there's an empty box that a space heater came in. A couple of white garbage bags full of clothes are piled next to the bed. *Can't tell if those are clothes she's donating or got from a donation and has yet to sort out.* Butch's junior high football picture is on the dresser along with one in a smaller frame of Butch and himself as kids. He bends to look closer, not having seen any photos of himself and Butch together in quite a while. He turns to look at the closet where he and Butch often hid from Carl. The door is missing so it wouldn't be a good hiding place anymore. Now he realizes they weren't really hiding, just trying to shield themselves from the yelling, and to stay out of the way of Carl's fists, belt, and anything he might throw.

He flashes on one particularly chaotic night with Carl drunk, screaming about money Jackie spent on the boys during a trip to Wal-Mart when he'd been saving for a car stereo. Ambrose was seven, Butch, twelve. Carl yanked Ambrose off the floor in front of the TV, nearly breaking his arm before Jackie flung a beer can at Carl's head, distracting him. Butch had rushed Ambrose into this messy closet. Butch wrapped his arms around him, holding his head against his shoulder. That was before Ambrose figured out crying wouldn't do any good, and Butch, trying not to cry himself, kept saying, "It's my fault; it's all my fault."

"What's your fault?" Ambrose had sniffled, wiping his face on his own shirt until finally leaning against Butch, exhausted.

"I'm the big brother. I'm supposed to keep you safe."

"You do keep me safe."

"Not like I should." Butch's hands were sweaty holding him close. The closet was dark, but Ambrose could feel Butch wiping his own eyes on a dirty T-shirt that had been laying among the pile of shoes they were sitting on. "Tomorrow, after school, I want you to get off the bus at Granny and Papa's. I'll tell Mama and Daddy you're spending the night there and then you can just stay with them a while."

"What if they don't want me to stay with them?"

"They will. They always want you to. The only reason Daddy don't let you sometimes is 'cause he's always on the outs with them."

"What about you?"

"What about me?"

"Are you gonna come stay at Granny and Papa's?"

"Nah, I can handle it here." He squeezed Ambrose close to him as they heard their parents' drunken quarrel moving to the bedroom at the other end of the hallway, and then the sound of an object—maybe a shoe, or a bottle of aftershave—hitting a wall. "Just do whatever they ask you to. You know, help 'em out around the house and all."

"Okay." They'd slept in the closet that night. The next day, Ambrose took a change of clothes in a bag to school and kept it in his desk until time to catch the bus. He'd gotten off the bus at the trailer park down the road. Sure enough, his maternal grandparents were glad to have him stay a while. They had a double-wide and some shade trees newer lots didn't have. He was on his best behavior the whole time, and Carl and Jackie were no doubt relieved to be rid of him a while.

After a couple of months, he'd split his time between the trailer park and house, always heading to the trailer park when things got too hot here. Butch had said he was fine, but Ambrose felt he shouldn't be here all the time with them. Then Butch started hanging out with some older boys and later, even though the coaches really wanted him for the varsity high school football team, he gravitated toward delinquency, then dropped out altogether. As Ambrose came of age, he'd done the same. As long as Butch was in the know about ways to make a little chump change, Ambrose was in the know, because there wasn't much Butch kept from him. Then Granny had died and Papa soon went to the nursing home. And Ambrose returned to living at the house all the time.

Now, he flips off the light and goes back down the hallway, glancing into the other bedroom as he walks through. Total time warp.

He walks back into the living room. "I have to be getting back." Since she doesn't care, it doesn't matter where or to what he has to get back, just that she can get back to her drinking and shows. "Is there anything you need before I go?" he asks.

"I don't reckon," she says.

"Okay." He takes one last look around. "Goodbye, Mama."

He turns to go and she grasps the lever on her chair, lowering the footrest. "I can walk you out," she says, moving slowly, like the effort of getting out of the recliner is exhausting.

"No need for that," he says, pushing open the screen door. "You just keep watching your show."

"All right then. Thanks for coming by." As he closes the door, he hears one more thing, maybe her effort just to try and not let this end like the stone-cold mother/child reunion it turned out to be. "Don't be such a stranger!"

***

Jessica had gone to the hotel gym, called Mike to check in on Beau, had lunch at the restaurant, then went back to the room for a nap. When Ambrose returned, he looked shell-shocked like he had yesterday when he'd walked out of his dad's nursing home. His dad was a real piece of work; he was right about that. She didn't know what was said after she left the room because Ambrose didn't want to talk about it, but it influenced him. *Maybe I'll broach the subject later.*

She talks him into joining her for a swim in the roof-top pool. She swims a few laps then sits in a lounge chair in the sun, drying off and sipping a glass of lime water while he continues swimming laps. He seems to enjoy it, relaxing, somewhat. She dabs more sunscreen on her face, slides on her sunglasses, and puts her feet up. Reclining, watching him swim back and forth, she thinks on when they first met. *Who is he, really?* But then, she realizes, he must wonder the same about her.

She thought he'd want to go out to dinner after a shower, but he just wants to lie in bed, watch TV, and order Buffalo wings from room service. She calls to place the order, adding a garden burger for herself, and a pitcher of iced tea. When room service arrives, he's in the shower so she signs for it and peeks under the stainless-steel domes of food while he dries off.

He walks in from the bathroom with a towel wrapped around his waist, his face and shoulders reddened from the sun, because after the swim he'd fallen asleep in a lounger for a half hour. He still looks tired and distracted, which is frustrating because she feels invigorated.

She watches as he slips into a T and boxers, pops open a beer from the mini-fridge, and takes his wings back to the bed. Watching him eat in bed, leaning against the headboard, occasionally licking orange sauce off his fingers, she's reminded he's over ten years younger than her. Not that it matters, really. A man of any age could want to sit in bed like that and eat chicken wings; it's just that something about this takes her back to her college days: spring breaks and skiing trips.

"Want one?" he asks, holding out a small, bright orange drumstick.

"No thanks."

He eats it himself. The TV is on, but he's not looking at it, just gazing straight ahead.

"You haven't told me about your visit," she ventures. "Want to talk about it?"

"Not really." He takes a sip of beer and starts in on the wings again. She takes her own plate over to the table by the window. When they're finished eating, she leaves their tray outside the door in the hallway. When she returns, he's under the covers.

She stands next to his side of the bed. "You've barely said a word since you got back from your visit."

He rolls over, facing the other way.

"I wish you'd feel like you can talk to me." She sits next to him, a hand on his shoulder. He's obviously not all right and she wants to hold him but doesn't quite know how he'll react.

"What was Mignon up to today?" he asks.

Ah-ha. "I wouldn't know. What does she have to do with anything here?"

"You tell me."

"Okay. Nothing."

He throws off the covers, which she wasn't expecting, rolls over and sits on the other side of the bed. "I'm going out by the pool for a smoke."

"Want me to come with you?" she asks as he puts on jeans.

"What is it you just had to come here with me to see?" he asks.

"I wanted to see where you're from."

"*Great*," he says, grabbing a shirt from the closet and slipping into it. "I hope it's been fun for you, like gawking at a bad car wreck for cheap thrills. Before you get rid of me."

"Get rid of you? Why would you even say that?"

He opens the dresser drawer, rummaging around, looking for his pack of cigarettes. "That was a nice show you put on for my dad, but the novelty's worn off, right?" He finds the cigarette pack and sticks it in his shirt pocket. "Isn't that why you'd rather be with your gal pal at some hotel back in the city, drinking cocktails and licking each other's cunt—"

She slaps him across the face.

He has a shocked expression and a reddening mark on his cheek but doesn't look angry.

Now that she's had a moment to think about it, she doesn't know if she slapped him for what he said or just the embarrassment of hearing it out loud.

"She must give you something I can't. But there's a reason you keep me around, too, right? At least for now?"

Jessica pulls her robe closer. She'd just wanted a quiet evening with him. "A lot of reasons," she says, almost in a whisper. "I meant what I said to your dad." She fully expects him to grab a room key off and walk out. *Then he'll go to the bar downstairs and women will flirt with him, some men, too, and he'll come back without a word, the way Mike used to.*

This trip was supposed to be about him finding a measure of peace, but it might have made things worse, so she shouldn't have talked him into it. And even after talking him into it, shouldn't have insisted on coming along.

"I'm sorry I slapped you," she says quietly.

He stands, watching her for a moment, like waiting for her to say more, but she doesn't.

She wipes her eyes, trying to hold back crying until he leaves.

Finally, he tentatively sits beside her.

She doesn't look at him.

"I'm sorry I. . . insulted you. I've been jealous, you know."

She can't articulate her mind, sensations coursing through her, and emotions surfacing in a terrifying way. If he wants an explanation, he'll have to wait until she has one. "I know." She wants to tell him she's been jealous, too, but doesn't even want to acknowledge that finding him and Bennie that morning alarmed her, even though she had no right to feel that way after the things she'd done. Plus, it would make her seem insecure, which she's fully aware is not attractive.

He leans closer. "But you're with me tonight, aren't you?"

"That's right," she says, picking up that she hasn't been present with him lately. He probably thinks she's texting Mignon whenever he sees her on her phone. He's confessing to jealousy when, if she thought he was texting another woman, "jealous" wouldn't be a big enough word for what she'd feel.

And she'd wanted to tell him she's not looking at his hometown and family like a gawker, but a stranger in a place she knew existed outside the bubble of her own but had never been to. She had no interest in stepping outside her little California dreamscape until hers had been upended. Exposed as a simulacrum. A false narrative. Then their false narratives merged. And she still needs Ambrose badly.

He places his hand on her knee and she puts her hand on top of his. Looking into his eyes, she senses emotional exhaustion, and sees hers reflected.

"Just make love to me," she whispers.

He leans forward and kisses her. She stands, letting the bathrobe slide off her shoulders and fall to the floor. Being naked while he's fully clothed reminds her of the night she slipped out of the red jumpsuit and gave herself over to pure pleasure like she'd never done before. He stands, takes her face in his hands and kisses before he pulls back. "I taste like Buffalo wings. Want me to go brush my teeth?"

"Not right now," she smiles, unfastening his jeans, kissing him, more aware of the Buffalo scent of his mouth.

He starts to pull her closer, then pauses. "Just a second," he says.

She goes to get under the covers, as he walks to the large window and closes the curtains.

"We're on the eighth floor," she reminds. "No one could see in here if we turn off the light, could they?"

"Never know."

✳✳✳

It's obvious she's never been to visit anyone in prison. The search of the vehicle, the pat-down, the scan. He asks her to leave her purse locked in the SUV unless she just wants to bring some quarters in it for the vending machine—no paper money allowed. He leaves his cigarettes in the car; God knows he'll want those when he comes out.

Since they made plans to come at the last minute, he'd barely gotten Jessica on the visitor's list, but she's with him when Butch walks into the visiting area. Ambrose feels his heart quicken when he sees him. Maybe it seems longer than it's actually been but still. . . nearly a year and a half.

Butch has put on weight. He looks like he's still been working out, but his rock-hard physique's gotten softer. His dark hair is short but still wavy, starting to gray at the temples: baby face and sociable disposition still intact. He grins and Ambrose feels like bursting into tears from joy and guilt. Jackie's words about when was the last time he'd been to visit Butch come back to haunt him, and he doesn't know if something in Butch's eyes might, too, for being so slipshod, selfish, and uncaring but there's nothing negative there at all, just a strong, welcoming embrace as they use one of the two hugs they're allowed.

Butch is a big guy so it's a hell of a bear-hug and lasts until one of the guards turns their way and Butch, smiling, in tears, pulls back to get a good look at him. "Baby brother," he says, maybe just to say it since he never gets to anymore. "You looking good," he says. "You are a sight for sore eyes."

"You are, too, Butch. I never meant for it to be this long."

"Aw, hell, I know you out there trying to survive and all. Times is tough, they tell me." His attention shifts to Jessica. "This must be the pretty lady I heard about."

Ambrose glances at her, unaccustomed to her shyness. Still, she has that beautiful smile and those bottomless blue eyes that are so mesmerizing. He places his hand on the small of her back to pull her closer. "Jessica, this is my big brother Butch. Butch, this is—"

"I already know. She's my new sister-in-law."

Jessica's eyes enlarge and she looks at Ambrose, puzzled. He'd forgotten about telling Carl and Jackie he and Jessica were married. He'd said nothing to Jessica, thinking he'd maybe tell her later and even laugh about it (or maybe not) but now he looks at her pleadingly, while Butch stands there grinning in his XL khaki outfit.

"Can I give you a quick 'welcome to the family' hug?" he asks Jessica gently.

"Sure. It's so great to finally meet you, Butch. Ambrose has told me so much about you." *Not really, but that's sweet of her to say.*

Butch leans forward to embrace her: not too close, not too tight, mindful of the watchful eyes of the guards around the semi-crowded visiting room. Since it's the middle of a weekday, it's not as crowded as it might be. As Butch hugs Jessica, Ambrose notices he's gotten new ink on his right arm: a human heart like you see in a medical diagram, but cracked, wrapped in barbwire and bleeding.

Butch releases Jessica, looks at Ambrose. "You got yourself an angel," he says.

"Didn't I, though?" Ambrose agrees. She's giving him a veiled look that says they'll discuss this later, but she seems to be playing ball on the "married" thing, which enables him to breathe a little easier.

"Hell, ya'll have a seat," Butch says, indicating for them to sit on the opposite side of the table. "I'm glad I found you," he tells Ambrose. "Hope you're not upset I had Danny's private dick track you down but. . . Well, I just didn't know what else to do."

"How long you think it'll be now, Butch?" Ambrose asks.

"Lookin' like another three; maybe sooner if I'm real good," he says. "I hope." He clenches and unclenches his hands, then lays them flat on the table, glancing at the guard closest to his line of sight as he keeps an eye on the clock. "Almost got my associate degree. Then I'm going for my bachelor's. Ain't that something?" he asks, still with that infectious enthusiasm Ambrose realizes he's been missing out on by not being around. No one's around. Not the way Butch deserves. Butch glances at the guard again. "Pardon my language, ma'am," he says to Jessica. "I almost forgot; we're not supposed to use profanity here in the visiting area." Ambrose wonders if he forgot because it's been so long since he's had any visitors. "So how long ya'll been married?" Butch asks. "Got any kids?"

"Jessica has a little boy named Beau from her first marriage. He's a real sweetheart and I'm crazy about him. . ." He glances at Jessica, quickly checking her reaction. She looks like she's still with him. "We don't have any of our own yet."

"We will, though," Jessica says, causing him to look at her again. "One day."

"Good, 'cause I'd just love to be an uncle," Butch says. "You can bring babies in to visit, you know." Then, "Aw, listen to me. You wouldn't wanna bring no baby in here. People do, but. . . Maybe I'll get out in time to see him while he's still—you know. A little kid." He smiles, but to mask the fact he's getting emotional.

Ambrose leans forward, following an impulse to grasp his hand, hold him, but the guards are watching. "Butch? You all right?"

"Hell yeah," he says.

Jessica turns to Ambrose. "Why don't I take those quarters and get us something to drink? . . .What kind of soda would you like, Butch?"

"Uh. . . Coke or Pepsi. Whatever. Thank you, ma'am."

"Ambrose?"

"Same."

"'Kay. I'll be back." She starts toward the vending machines in the corner, taking her time.

"Butch, I swear," he says, "I'm so sorry I haven't been back to see you." This feels like an echo of last night, with him and Jessica apologizing to each other before a session of wild-as-hell sex to rival the night of the red jumpsuit. Meanwhile, poor Butch is sitting here day after day, year after year, enduring no telling what. He asked Butch once if he'd ever had to fend off guys looking for sex and he said he could handle himself—he was really buffed out then—and then again later when the subject came up, he'd said, "It is what it is."

"You're living your life. That's what I always wanted for you. I didn't mean to drag you away from it by sending you that letter. I just wanted to find you." Despite the tears in Butch's eyes, a smile tugs at his lips. "Daddy told me you're running one of those S&M places. Is he crazy or is that true?"

"It's true."

"What the hell's that like?"

"It's not quite as fun as it sounds. The woman who owned it left it to me in her will. I was working there most days and slinging for Lang nights, then a bunch of stuff happened. I don't even know where to start to tell you everything."

"That goddamn—" Butch remembers the guards and drops his voice to a whisper. "Did that bald-headed motherfucker screw you over? If I ever see that bastard again—"

"I owed him some money for a while, but I paid it all back," Ambrose says softly, glancing toward the guards. And he did pay it back. Facing his fear of Lang that day had given him the courage to return to Palo Alto and ask Jessica's forgiveness. Now that seems like forever ago. "I think I might've even scared him."

Butch grins. "Well, that's good to hear. I oughta know you can take care of yourself by now. Tell me 'bout it one of these days?"

"Sure." Ambrose turns to see Jessica making a selection at the vending machines. "You think Daddy's days are really numbered?"

Butch places his hands flat on the table, eyes downcast. "He had a bout of pneumonia last winter and things were looking grim." Finally, he looks up. "So, I'm not a total egg-sucking liar."

"Liar? About what?"

"Well, Daddy is in bad shape, by all accounts. I don't know how much longer he'll be around. Could be a week, a month. Hell, he's so fucking mean, he might last another year or more. He could outlast me."

"Don't say that, Butch."

"And Mama's drinking herself to death, 'cording to some folks I hear from ev'ry once in a while. Guess you could tell. You went to see her, didn't you?"

"Yesterday."

"Well, anyway. . . The reason I told you all that 'bout Daddy in the letter's 'cause. . ."

"Yeah?"

"I missed you, Baby Brother. Guess you could say I exaggerated some. Hoping you'd write back and I'd see you again. Ain't that some shit?" He says the last almost laughing but not quite. Then silence.

Ambrose sits still, staring at Butch, absorbing the fact that he went to all the trouble to get him here because he's lonely and desperately needs to know there's someone left who gives a damn. And the fact that he had to doubt it for a minute is sad beyond words. "God, Butch," he says. "I've missed you, too." He has to swallow hard to dispel the lump in his throat. "I'm sorry it's taken me so long to come back, but I'll find a way to make it up to you."

"You don't have to make anything up to me. I'm glad you're here now. Just wanted to find out where you were and if you're all right. And tell you I love you, and. . ." He sees Jessica, tentatively hanging back before approaching the table. "You can come on back," he says to her.

She sits at the table. "I didn't mean to interrupt. If you guys need to talk, I can go pick out something else from the vending machine."

"Stay," Ambrose tells her. "I was just telling Butch how we won't be strangers anymore. We'll come to see him a lot. I will anyway."

"Me, too," she says, opening Butch's soda and setting it in front of him. "I'm so glad I'm finally getting to meet you." She smiles, charmed by him. Many women are. It's just that he goes for the dangerous ones. Like playing with matches.

"Does Callie still come see you?" Ambrose asks.

Butch smiles but looks downright wistful. "I ain't seen or heard from her in a damn long time. Hell, she could be living in Barcelona with some baron or count, or in some Mexican jail. Or she could be dead, for all I know. They's no telling."

"Sorry to hear that," he says.

"Well. Shit happens. Ya'll going home today?"

"We're flying out at 5. Are you feeling all right?"

Butch looks up, eyes moist, red around the edges. "I'm fine."

"I notice you keep clenching your hands. Are you having some trouble?"

"They get numb sometimes. Might be bad circulation. I'm all right though."

"Let's see your grip," Ambrose says.

Butch smiles like it's much ado about nothing, looks him in the eye, gripping his hands. It's still a firm grip, but not what it used to be. "How's that?" Butch asks, releasing him. "Not bad?"

"Oh, I want to see," Jessica says, reaching out to him. "Squeeze."

He glances around to see where the guard is, then takes her slim, delicate hands in his large, angular ones. He grips her hands, glances around for the guard once more, leans forward and kisses her left hand. Ambrose notices she's not wearing a wedding ring—and neither is he, for that matter. Butch notices; his eyes shift briefly to Ambrose. Ambrose can read his mind. He's thinking, *You little fucker. What the hell are you up to now?*

"You have a very nice grip," she tells him.

"Why, thank you," he says, releasing her. "Ya'll just make the most charming couple I ever saw." He sips from his soda. Ambrose notices Jessica watching Butch intently. *Yeah, you big fucker. You still got it.* "I'm kinda surprised though," Butch says.

"'Bout what?" Ambrose asks.

"That you ain't put a ring on that finger. Seems like you'd want to let everybody know she's taken." Then, "Well, the both of you are. But, I guess ya'll are living that swinging lifestyle out there on the west coast. Maybe I'm just old-fashioned."

Jessica places her hands in her lap, giving a sideways glance to Ambrose, slightly embarrassed. She smiles, blushing. "Um. . . I wouldn't exactly say 'swinging.'"

"All right, Butch," Ambrose says finally. "I'll level with you about something."

"Whatever could that be, I wonder?" Butch asks, sarcastically furrowing his brow.

"Jessica and I aren't married; I just told Daddy that because I thought it would piss him off. And he told you and Mama so I just played it as it lays since I started it." He glances at Jessica. She's staring at him, blushing deeper, put on the spot. "And Jessica knew nothing about it 'til now and was just going along with me—I guess to keep from embarrassing me or whatever."

"Ambrose!" she cries, whiplashed at being roped into complicity then outed, all within a few minutes. "What made you tell your dad that in the first place?"

"He was being so rude to you. I just thought it'd get his goat."

Butch finally laughs. "Well, boy, it did. When Mama called me, she said he was fit to be tied."

"Why would telling him you're married to me 'get his goat'?"

"Because he doesn't want me to have anything, least of all a good-looking wife."

"That's the God's honest truth," Butch agrees. "Our daddy is one contrary, bitter, old sumbitch." He takes another sip of his drink. "But we're not," he says, looking at Ambrose. "Thank God we're nothing like our old man."

TEN

Ambrose walks into Miss Dover's former office, his for a finite number of days before it fully belongs to the new owner. Since the sale was done before her death, it's all going through, and there's nothing he can do to stop it. As for the stuff that's here at Dover, Inc., the things that go with that, such as equipment, décor, bed sheets and curtains, outfits, whips, and chains are his. Now to find a place to put it all: a whole new locale, which is way easier said than done.

He places his lunch in the mini-fridge, turns, and is shocked to see a thin, middle-age man in a double-breasted suit standing in the doorway.

"Good morning," the man says. "You must be Mr. Ballard." He speaks with an accent that's hard to pin down: part Dracula, part world-weary diplomat. He has a grim smile, silver hair and gray, flinty eyes. The suit fits perfectly. *Must be custom-made.*

"And you are?"

"Alexei Rusovich, purchaser of this lovely property," he declares, looking around like the first order of business will be to have everything placed in the dumpster out back.

Rusovich? Ambrose stands behind the desk, recalling Miss Dover's ominous warning about a man named Alexei. She said he runs a tearoom in the Richmond. *But that last name. . .* "How'd you get in here? I mean, so soon. I was told the new owner wouldn't take possession until—"

"I didn't mean to startle you."

Ambrose watches him move around the office.

"I simply had to see the interior myself. My brother Maxim is most familiar with this place."

"So, Maxim is your brother?"

"He handles many of my business and legal matters. . ." Alexei's eyes come to rest on the framed photograph of Miss Dover, along with her "fairy godfather," and an older man with white hair, wearing Wayfarers. Miss Dover said that was the last time they'd all gone to the Riviera, the real Riviera: blue and sparkly in golden sunlight. Alexei walks over and picks up the photo. "Ah, the late, great Miss Dover. I'm glad she saw the wisdom in accepting my offer." He sets the picture back down, turns to Ambrose. "And to you she only left this. . . entertainment enterprise. Pity, she didn't see fit to bequeath you both that and the property, but alas. I suppose the money now goes to her. . . estate."

Ambrose eyes the drawer where Miss Dover's pistol—one of them, anyway—is stored. Pearl handled, nickel-plated. Loaded. She said she had it in case any would-be thieves ever tried to rob the place or mug her while leaving. Now he realizes it was more likely her fear of this Russian she'd told him about. The one standing in her office right this moment. "We'll find someplace else."

"On the other hand," Alexei begins, "if you want to sell me said enterprise, I could make it worth your while, pay you a generous salary if you would perhaps like to remain and run the day-to-day affairs."

"I don't think so."

He doesn't look surprised. "If you change your mind, give Maxim or myself a call and we will draw up the necessary papers. Could be very lucrative for you." That Dracula gaze coupled with the voice is somehow hypnotic. Ambrose tenses as Alexei reaches into his interior coat pocket, takes a business card out of a silver holder. "Here is a card for a free drink at my tearoom. You can find me there most days. I look forward to seeing you again soon." He smiles that grim smile. "I will let myself out. Good day."

"Good day."

Ambrose follows several feet behind to the reception area until he sees him leave through the entrance. Ambrose looks down at the card, still reeling from the fact that that's the guy. He told Miss Dover he'd never let this Alexei in the door, and somehow he'd gotten in. But even worse, before she died, Miss Dover sold out to that snake.

The phone in the office rings. He rushes to answer it. "Dover, Inc."

"Eh. . . Mr. Ballard?" Still the accent, but without the vampiric seductiveness.

"Maxim?"

"I saw my brother leave," he says. "I have to speak with you."

"If you're going to try and talk me into working for him, forget it."

"Quite the contrary. I'm just around the corner. I cannot discuss this over the phone. One moment, please. I will come to the back."

Ambrose goes to the back entrance and guides Maxim into the ballroom. Maxim's hair is a bit out of place, and he looks like he got dressed in a hurry. "I must warn you: Do not make any deals with my brother. Get out of this place as soon as you can."

"Why didn't you tell me the client was your brother?"

"It might have seemed odd, like I wanted this sale to happen, but I assure you, I did my best to dissuade him." Maxim approaches. "Alexei hates to be crossed. And he resents—*resented*—the Duchess deeply."

Ambrose thinks back to that day in the ballroom, the day Miss Dover tried to slap some sense into him and warn him about this guy, but she'd been sketchy on the details. It had something to do with her fairy godfather, Ivan, and that other man in the photo, the one in sunglasses. That part of her life had always been shrouded in mystery but with Count Alexei showing up in the flesh, it's coming into sharp focus fast. "What the fuck, Maxim?"

"A long story, Mr. Ballard, but the gist: After her lover Ivan, passed away, she inherited money and property that Alexei thought rightly belonged to him, and when he did not get it, he went a little crazy."

"Why'd he think it should go to him?"

"For being a longtime, loyal *associate*. But then he did some very disloyal things and fell out of favor with the boss. Our boss at the time," Maxim clarifies, taking a couple steps toward the riser, where Miss Dover's favorite chair still sits empty. "Alexei has come to embrace some rather. . . *grotesque* beliefs, causing him to behave oftentimes in a manner that is precipitous at best and violent at worst."

"How violent?" Ambrose asks, then realizes what a dumb question. Violence is violence. If they'd cut off an ear, what's to stop them from gutting someone like a fish, or blowing a person's brains out? He feels weak at the thought he was just talking to a man who deals in such things on a grander scale than Lang.

"Quite," Maxim answers. "It is true that Sergei—he was our boss and Ivan's best friend—made Alexei many promises. Alexei felt cheated, believing he had come through for Sergei time and again, with little to show for his efforts." He sits heavily on the riser. "Forgive me," he says, fanning himself with a handkerchief. "My blood pressure medication sometimes makes me lightheaded." He dabs at his forehead. "There is a vast difference between the lifestyle of Sergei and that of Alexei running the tearoom, rustling honeybees, and raising fake caviar while Sergei, and Ivan owned racehorses and cruised the Mediterranean on yachts. Keeping Alexei in his place was Sergei's revenge on him for over-reaching. He tried to insert himself into Sergei's and Ivan's business. He wanted a bigger role for a bigger cut of the money. Not just the occasional ride on their yachts; he wanted his own yacht. Not that there's anything wrong with ambition, mind you, but. . . revenge is a different story. For Alexei to take it out on the Duchess. . ."

"Are you saying she was murdered?"

"I cannot say with utmost certainty. But my brother is like a shark, I tell you, and this bodyguard, Dimitri, his golem."

"Call me Ambrose," he says blankly, not having felt this out of his element and dislocated since posing as a Stanford grad student when Bennie put those reading glasses on him and told him to act smart.

"Ambrose," Maxim repeats. "Alexei still has a few contacts in Europe and knew that the Duchess was travelling there. He's alluded to extreme measures before. . . He wants this place for his headquarters."

"Headquarters for what?"

Maxim looks at the cavernous ceiling in the ballroom until his gaze turns toward the upper windows where the morning sun filters in, filling the space with white light. "It is practical, with soundproof suites, ample office space upstairs, a private entrance and garage. He already has a stable of prostitutes in the valley, and more set to arrive next month."

"He wants to turn this place into a brothel. Is that what you're saying?"

"This is the perfect front, don't you see? If you sell out to him, he could place Margarite in charge while he runs his other enterprises from a suite upstairs." He looks around the ballroom. "Unless of course, he decides to use this as his office."

"This?" *The guy wouldn't really use the ballroom as his office, would he?* Then, the more pressing question: "Who's Margarite?" he asks, though he has a sinking feeling he knows.

"You call her Mignon," Maxim tells him. "Alexei knows that she and your girlfriend are casual lovers. Dimitri has been seeing Margarite also and is quite smitten."

Unease turns to all-out panic at the thought this touches Jessica in any way. And he'd talked about Miss Dover in front of Mignon, about where she was, the hotel she was staying, chatting with Bennie and Rajit when Mignon was around. . . *And this guy, Dimitri. The one Rajit and his friend saw in the motel parking lot that day?*

"Margarite is a sometimes-waitress at the tearoom, though less so now. I have learned that Alexei met her in French-speaking Canada on a vacation last year They became lovers, and she followed him back. It is my belief that—" He cuts himself off, glances around. Ambrose nears and sits on the riser, knees suddenly weak. He thought his problems were receding into the background like chattering gremlins, but now real monsters are stepping into the fore. Maxim continues, shifting closer: "That she and Dimitri are plotting something. I don't know what. I could be wrong. I simply do not know where her allegiances lie. Alexei uses her as something of a spy. . ." He pauses as a thought comes to him. He glimpses Ambrose's panic, looks away.

Ambrose has the feeling Maxim fears he can't handle the truth. "What?" he asks.

"Let's just say that Alexei likes to play games with people for his own amusement. I would not be surprised if he were looking for a way to make your Jessica his *belle du jour.*"

That French word sounds familiar, but Ambrose isn't entirely sure what it means. There's a movie by that name on the list of films Miss Dover wanted him to watch but he hasn't. *"Belle du jour?"*

"His star prostitute, like Catherine Deneuve in that film."

"Jessica would never do such a thing," Ambrose says, then remembers there's no telling what Jessica might do anymore and, if he's to stay with her, he has to be okay with that. But not this.

"Perhaps. But someday. even if she only thought she was having an adventurous afternoon with Margarite and a handsome stranger, I can assure you there would be video footage."

"For what?"

"Kompromat! Blackmail. Your girlfriend and her family are very rich, no?"

Now that Maxim has drawn him a picture, Ambrose has an impulse to call Jessica, just to check in, see what she's doing and who she's with. Whatever Margarite/Mignon, some guy named Dimitri, and this Alexei son-of-of-a-bitch could be up to makes Randy's bungled attempt at sex-video blackmail look innocent by comparison. Not to mention what Alexei and company could've engineered, and what he could be responsible for just by being stupid enough to hire Mignon. Miss Dover had signed off on getting extra help while Momo was away, but then Mignon showed up here, so sexy and French, looking to learn the ropes, and he and Bennie fell for it. Him, especially. He'd been so naïve or trusting—same result either way—to run his mouth about Miss Dover's movements. "Tell me straight up, Maxim: Do you really think your brother had Miss Dover killed?"

"As I said, I cannot speak with utmost certainty." Maxim looks him in the eye. "But all signs point to yes."

✳✳✳

It was Ambrose's idea to go to the beach, and Mike's weekend to have Beau over, so Jessica got him dressed and packed his things. While she was getting ready in the bedroom, Ambrose answered the doorbell. Mike came in for just a few minutes, but Jessica can't help but wonder what they're discussing before she comes to kiss Beau goodbye.

As usual, Ambrose doesn't volunteer information. He's been on edge since his boss suddenly passed away in Paris, and now there seems to be something going on with the property being sold. No texts from Mignon lately, so he need not worry about that, but it seems like something is wrong.

She thought it'd be more practical to drive the car, but he wanted to ride the motorcycle. Said he didn't want to take more than a couple towels and sunscreen.

They stop for lunch at a taco stand between Palo Alto and Santa Cruz. She eats her cactus taco, orders another while he barely touches his. Then she nibbles tortilla chips, glad he's insisted on the motorcycle. It feels good riding with her arms tightly wrapped around him.

When they arrive at the beach, it isn't that crowded, and, by the time they get settled on a blanket, it feels like a perfect setting. The sunset will be the crowning touch. *So why does he seem so pensive?* "Are you, okay?" she finally asks.

"Of course, I'm okay. Why'd you ask?"

"You just seem like you've got something on your mind," she says, covering her arms with the extra blanket. "What is it?"

He lies back, leans on his elbow. "It'll sound like I'm telling you what to do, and I don't want that."

"Whatever it is, tell me."

"I don't want you seeing Mignon anymore."

"I haven't been seeing Mignon. Haven't even heard from her in a while, since before we went to Texas. What brought this on, anyway?"

He rolls over on his stomach, looking toward the parking area.

She rolls over, too, lying next to him. "Remember that night you first came to stay with us, when you and I were drinking wine by the fire and you said you thought romance was dead for you. I said I couldn't believe that, because you're so young and still have all that ahead of you?"

He glances at her, barely nods.

"And you said I made mundane things seem romantic. It's like you could see another side of me I thought was over and helped me get back in touch with my wilder side I thought was dead. I guess this. . . thing with Mignon was just part of that. But you're the one that made me see the truth about Mike and brought me back to my art. And I love you for it." She grasps his hand. This is what she hadn't been able to articulate that night in the hotel room outside Dallas. "I love you."

He's not looking at her but listening. He sniffles and adjusts his sunglasses. "I love you, too," he says. "It's just. . . Mignon's not who she pretends to be. She's a faker and a liar and I don't want her taking advantage of you anymore than she already has."

Jessica pauses, not sure how to respond. "Where's this coming from? Who told you all this?"

She sees him glance at her through the side of his sunglasses. He rolls back over, sits and looks out at the water again. "Somebody who knows. Mignon's not even her real name."

"Who's this 'somebody'? How do you know they're telling the truth?"

"It's a longtime client of ours who found out her background. He knows who she works for when she's not working for us, and her boyfriend, and her ex-lover. He knows what she is and she's a liar. She's not above using you. Or letting other people use you."

She sits up, pulls the blanket tighter around her shoulders, suddenly feeling exposed. "Using me? How?"

"Like, blackmailing you. Squeezing you for money." He takes a deep breath. "Just don't ever be alone with her again. Don't do anything with her where there could be anyone hiding, taking a video." He turns to her. "Or pictures. Are there pictures of you and her together?"

Her heart's beating faster, their relaxing afternoon ending with a crash. "No."

"You— Did you text each other pictures?"

"Why're you asking me that?"

"Did you?"

"You know the answer, so why are you asking me?" While he figures out what to say, she gathers the blanket like a shawl, and starts walking toward where the waves break. Once again, this whole thing's taking a turn and she feels sick to her stomach. She can hear him walking toward her, footsteps falling lightly on the sand.

"Jess?" He puts a hand on her shoulder, but she doesn't turn around, so he walks in front of her. "I'm sorry I dropped this on you, but I just want you to be careful of her, that's all. I already realized I might have to share you. . ." Then, with a faint smile: "'Cause you're just too much woman for me, I guess. I want to be all you need and if I can't be, I'm the one that has to accept it, but. . . Don't see her anymore.

Anybody else. . ." She detects a crack in his voice as he says that. "Just not her." He takes off his sunglasses. "Please."

He looks like she feels. "I'm not seeing her anymore," she says. "And I'm not interested in anybody else." He takes her hand, walks with her out into the shallowest waves. "Does Mignon—or whatever her name is—still work there?"

"Not for much longer."

"What is her real name?"

"Margarite."

She gazes out at the blue horizon. It doesn't matter because she was sincere when she told him that was over. *Maybe his male pride is wounded. Or maybe he just feels wounded the way I had when Mike was lying to me* and then she found out Ambrose was lying about knowing him and being a Stanford grad student, but for totally different reasons. So, this is twice—no, *three* times—she's been lied to in a big way by people she trusted, and they all had different motives, though she's not sure what Mignon/Margarite's is. She hadn't known her well enough to really trust her anyway. Turns out Jessica hadn't known any of them well enough.

Ambrose squeezes her hand, guiding her a little further out, until the water comes up to almost their knees.

✳✳✳

Bennie hates being ambushed but, when her phone rang in the grocery store, she picked up, thinking it was Randy, but it was her mother, and those conversations always take so much out of her. It was almost enough to ruin her shopping trip, so she came home determined to not let it affect the rest of her day, only to discover Jessica called while she was out. She left a message with Randy that she's taking Beau to their parents' house to go swimming and wants to know if Bennie would like to meet her there for the afternoon, maybe an early dinner. And Randy's welcome to come, too, of course. If he wants.

"Well, I definitely don't feel like going today," Bennie announces, especially after listening to her mother rail against her marrying Randy. Then, if Bennie *insists* on getting married, to at least give them enough time to plan a decent wedding. Pamela probably figures the more elaborate celebration she can talk Bennie into, the longer it'll all take, and the more time she has to come up with a plan to stop it. Pamela already mentioned the possibility of her coming over while Jessica and Beau are there this afternoon. "You don't want to go, do you, Randy?" Bennie asks.

"Hell, no." Randy helps unload groceries. "Jessica said something else, too, that I was kind of wondering about."

"What?"

"That Beau wanted to go swimming last time she was here, after some camp-in, but she was too tired, and that you and Ambrose had stayed up practically all night. . . Was it that night?"

Bennie glances at him. "It wasn't all night."

"She said he spent the whole night."

"He just happened to stop by on the way home from work, and I was upset, so—"

"You told him everything?"

"No, but I couldn't exactly hide it either."

She has her back to him. He walks over, places his hands on her shoulders. "And it was all my fault." He draws closer. "It's just. . . I know Ambrose used to have this big crush on you, so—"

She turns to him. "What makes you say that?"

"He told me."

"He told you?"

"I asked. Only because. . . I had this feeling."

She steps away to place some lemons in the refrigerator. "For that matter, how did Jessica come to tell you he was here? It's not like there was anything going on, Randy."

"Well, what'd you do, cry on his shoulder and tell him what a goddamn idiot I was for letting you walk out?"

"Course not." She brushes a strand of hair out of her face and throws a bag of almond flour in the pantry.

"So, you talked all night. What'd you talk about?"

"Nothing," she says, voice strained.

"Did you and him go out somewhere?"

"There's no way I could've gone out that night."

"So, what'd you do?"

"You don't trust me?"

"I trust you. I just don't know if I trust him. I want to feel better about him since ya'll are such good friends."

"If you must know, he had some molly an old coworker had given him. He thought it might make me feel better, so we did it and watched movies and fell asleep. And then Jessica and Beau showed up first thing the next morning and that's all there was to it."

"Molly? Isn't that some kind of love drug? What'd you do while you were watching movies?"

"What kind of a question is that?"

"Did he try to kiss you?"

"No, Randy!"

"I'm sure he loved hearing we were over."

"He loves Jessica."

"Yeah, but he liked you first. A lot."

She goes into the bedroom, scoops some clothes out of the hamper, returns to the kitchen, and tosses them into the washer, barely sorting them, hands shaky.

He watches her, leaning against the kitchen counter. "Tripping on molly," he goes on. "Just you and him? No way he didn't make a move when he could claim, 'It isn't me, it's the drug.'"

"You're being silly." She tries to keep busy, starting the washer and walking over to the sink where sunlight pours in.

He watches her pluck a sickly leaf off the African violet on the windowsill. "That gutterpunk didn't try to get in your pants, did he?"

"Randy!"

"Feel you up?" He nears, and his eyes let her know he won't just let it drop. "Talk dirty to you? He didn't—"

"He didn't try to fuck me, is that what you want to know? You want a good reason to hate him, or hate me for something? Are you looking for a way out of our engagement?"

"No!"

"You already know I'm not a virgin, and neither are you, so yeah, he got me off, because he felt sorry for me, but he didn't fuck me!"

"What did he do?"

Her face burns as she realizes what she's done, because she'd walked in here all out of sorts from a conversation with her mother, coupled with Jessica's passive aggressive meddling on the other end.

"Did he go down on you?"

"Randy!" *This is a fucking nightmare.* "Nothing happened. Now please drop it."

He stares at her, stumped by this riddle for a few seconds before it hits, and he gets this look of shocked disbelief. "He fingered you?"

She feels exposed and ridiculous for handling this all wrong. Doesn't know exactly what Jessica was trying to do bringing this to Randy's attention, but, whatever it is. . . mission accomplished. Humiliation for betrayal.

Well-played.

***

She runs into the bathroom and shuts the door. He'd felt his dick getting hard thinking about Ambrose's dick getting hard over Bennie, which is pretty sick, but wallowing in the gutter of his thoughts brings back a shadow of the old him. The him who once fucked Brianna while watching Ambrose fuck Jessica on that sex video that's lost to the ages but lives on in memory.

Thinking about Ambrose doing any of those things to Bennie only pisses him off, but now he's the one doing those things to Bennie. *So there ya go, Randy: You won, you dumb fuck. Why didn't you just shut up?* If he could go back in time and take it all back, he would, but he can't, so he leans on the bathroom door, whining like the bitch that he is. "Bennie, I'm sorry. Come on out. We can talk about it, or not, whatever you want to do, okay?"

No answer.

He tries the door. Locked. "I didn't mean to get you all upset."

Nothing.

"Please come unlock the door."

"It is unlocked," he hears her say, tears in her voice.

"Oh." He tries the door again, and it opens after all, just one of those temperamental, antique knobs that look like a big diamond. That's what he used to pretend with the ones at Grandma Burke's house. Before he realized they were glass, he used to imagine selling one for a million dollars and buying everything he could ever want. Only now, everything he could ever want is hiding in the bathroom, crying. He feels like a horse's ass over his petty jealousy and whatever ego clap-trap made him do it. He walks into the sunny bathroom but she's nowhere to be seen. "Bennie? Where are you?"

He hears her sniffling, goes over to the big, claw-foot bathtub, pulls back the shower curtain and there she is, curled up on her side. He kneels down. "Please come on out of there."

"You're going to leave me," she sobs.

"I am not."

"Yes, you are," she insists. "You think I'm a cheater and that you have to get even with me. Now you'll look for ways to hurt me, and I just can't take it."

"No, I won't! Bennie, I never meant to make you feel that way."

"That night, I really thought it was over." She cries harder and the full brunt of what he's done hits him. "I was just heartbroken."

Watching her cry, helpless to make her stop, he matures a good five years, realizing this is his first real relationship, to end all others, and not the place for anymore childish games like the one he'd just been playing in the kitchen. He tries to get her to look at him, but she won't, striking real fear into his heart when he remembers that hellish night without her. "Come on, let me help you out of there."

"I don't want to get out."

"Please? That can't be too comfortable."

"I don't deserve comfort."

Jesus Christ. He sighs, stands up. "Okay, then. I'll get in there with you." He climbs in and lies down with her.

She looks over her shoulder at him, mascara running, positively devastated, but beautiful. "You don't have to do this," she sniffles.

"Do if I want to hold you." He gently puts his arms around her, far more aware of how fragile she is. "If you want to talk about that night or anything else, you can, and if you don't, that's fine, too. All I'll do's listen and keep my mouth shut." He kisses away a tear caught in a rivulet of mascara. "With all the stuff I've told you, you've never judged me, and I won't do it to you either. I promise. I don't want to lose you."

Holding her, he can feel her gradually relax. "Ambrose only came by 'cause he didn't want to go home alone that night. He didn't know what happened with us, or that I'd even be home. A guy he'd run up on at the coffee shop gave him the molly and, when he found out about. . . He thought it might make me feel better. It did for a while. He was upset, too."

"What was he upset about?"

"Jessica's been having an affair with this woman that works down at the dungeon. Her name's Mignon. She's a domme who was flirting with Jess that night at the gallery. Ambrose says he teased her about it on the way home, so he feels kind of responsible for it."

Working security at the gallery that night, Randy recalls Jessica talking to an attractive woman with bright red lips, in a black dress and matching hat. He happened to see her kiss Jessica on the neck and, when Jessica saw him looking, he'd looked away, figuring it must be some female thing, like an air kiss but hotter. *That had to be Mignon.* "I'll be damned," he breathes. *Maybe Ambrose has been in something of a tailspin trying to figure that out.* "So, Jessica's bisexual?"

"I don't know. I think after all those years of trying to be the perfect wife, she's just. . . experimenting. Guess time'll tell."

Where had he heard that recently? Bennie's dad had said that out on their patio before the Tahoe trip, about Jessica and Ambrose. Bennie melts closer and, now that some of the earlier storm has passed, it feels good here in this tub with her, mainly listening to her talk. She's stopped crying, and turned toward him. That ruined eye make-up makes her look tough and vulnerable at the same time.

She rubs his chest, fiddling with his shirt buttons. ". . .Anyway," she goes on, "after it—happened, I think I hurt his feelings."

"How?"

"I told him it was all a mistake and that I loved you." She reaches up, caressing the side of his face.

"You said that?" A pleasant feeling tinged with excitement envelops him. He notes she's wearing a short dress, ridden up on her thighs. The top two buttons are undone. "What'd he say?"

"I ran out after that and came in here. And when I went back in there, he was getting ready to leave. But it was after 3 in the morning, so I told him to stay. Then we just fell asleep on the floor." She strokes his chest, his arms.

"All that happened before I came over the next day?"

"Please don't ever say a word about it. Promise me you won't."

"I won't."

"I'm not usually the kind of girl that cries at the drop of a hat and runs out of a room. And now I've done it twice in a month. Maybe it's just PMS. You think?"

"Not on your period now, are you?"

"Mm. Not 'til next week."

"Not that it matters to me," he says, getting up on his knees to straddle her, unbutton her dress further. "You've been under a lot of pressure. I feel like that's my fault."

"Your fault?"

"Can't be easy for a nice girl like you falling for some reprobate like me."

"You think I'm nice?"

"Not everybody knows how wild you are, like I do." He helps her off with her panties.

She eyes the T-shirt he's still wearing. "Take that off," she says.

He inhales deep as he does it, the ever-present shyness about his body tempered by the way she looks at him: an amazing state of affairs he's still learning to accept.

"There's a new box of condoms in that drawer under the sink," she tells him. "Just sayin'."

"Good to know." He kneels between her legs, ignoring the pain in his knees, unsnaps her bra, and leans down to kiss her breasts. He licks and sucks her nipples as gently as he knows how, since she seems especially tender. He almost asks if she wants to go into the bedroom, but decides to just roll with it, working his way down, trying not think about Ambrose touching her there, making her come, when that's his job. She really belongs to him now—not in some possessive, toxic way—but in that her heart belongs to him. He kisses her there, caressing with his tongue, licking her deeply, hearing those soft, sweet moans, glimpsing her face to see her biting her lip like she's trying to be quiet about it. Maybe because it's the middle of the day, so bright in here, and all this tile. Afraid her voice might carry.

"Randy?" she says softly.

"Hm?"

"Come here."

He kisses the inside of her thighs, then moves up to look her in the eyes. All dreamy, glassy.

"Kiss me." Raising her chin slightly, reaching up, caressing his shoulders, it's like she wants him to kiss her on the mouth.

"Now?"

"Yes."

Hadn't really anticipated that, with her still all over his face, on his breath. He leans forward and kisses her.

She runs her fingers through his hair, pulling him closer, kissing him deeply, thoroughly. Her eyes meet his. "That's how I taste?" she whispers.

He nods.

"Like it?"

"I love it. You've got the prettiest, best tasting pussy I've ever had."

She smiles.

So good to see her smile again.

"Really?"

"Hell yeah. I'd eat your pussy anywhere, anytime."

"Anywhere?"

"On the Bay Ferry. . ." Another kiss. "Out at the park. On the Caltrain." A rush just thinking about it. "I'd get down and eat your pussy in the middle of Market Street."

She laughs. "That'd be quite a spectacle. Your former colleagues might arrest us both."

"They'd have to drag me away, kicking and screaming."

She laughs again and he gets up to grab a condom, slipping out of his jeans and boxers before rejoining her. He tears open the packet with his teeth and again kneels between her legs, knees numbing.

"Know what I'd do to you?" she asks.

"What's that?"

"I'd suck your dick in the middle of Ghirardelli Square on a Saturday afternoon."

"Aww. . ." He slides on the condom. Rock hard. "That's the sweetest thing any chick's ever said to me." He pulls her closer, rubbing against her, between her legs, trying to exercise a modicum of self-control, just to drive her a little crazy, knowing what she likes, remembering their first time.

"What're you waiting for?" she asks.

"For you to say what you want me to do."

"You know that."

"I want you to say it."

She slides closer and he backs up slightly, but she'd better say it soon, because he suspects he's no good at this new-age tantric game when all he wants in the world is right there at the tip. *Goddamn.*

"Say it, Bennie."

"Want you to fuck me," she says softly.

"Say it again."

"Fuck me." More breathless this time.

"And say my name."

"Fuck me, Randy."

He slips inside, partway. "Once more," he whispers, hearing the catch in her voice as he goes all in, mouthing it with her: "Fuck me, Randy."

✳✳✳

Ambrose lies on the sofa in Miss Dover's office, staring at the ceiling. Finally, he rolls over, drawing his knees to his chest. Jessica seemed genuine on the beach Saturday when she said it was over with Mignon, and he meant that he was going to tell Mignon her services were no longer needed. Mistress Lori from New Orleans and Le Belle Dame Sans Merci from Savannah, two of the visiting dommes Miss Dover booked before her departure to Europe, would be returning to their home bases in two weeks. They'd extended their stay to help out and explore the city. Momo's visiting her parents in Japan and doesn't even know about half the shit that's been going on here. If he does fire Mignon/Margarite, they'll be short-handed and still have no place to go at the end of the month because rent around here is fucking ridiculous.

They say keep your friends close, enemies closer.

No. I have to fire her.

Clients booked all the way 'til Christmas and a few beyond, and by then this place could be a Russian whorehouse. If they cancel all those reservations, Dover, Inc.'s as good as dead. Just like its founder. He cringes at the thought of Miss Dover lying lifeless in that Paris hotel room. She wouldn't have signed over this place on her own, not to that guy, not unless she was under duress. They might have drugged her, put a gun to her head. No telling what they did to get her to do what they wanted. Might've tortured her; that could've brought on a heart attack. According to Maxim, that brother of his would do just about anything, and there she was, alone and scared, at the mercy of thugs, who, if not official Russian mafia, are bootleg gangsters who'll do anything for a buck—or a ruble or euro. *A bunch of dirty bastards who deserve to get the shit beat out of them, only that isn't enough. Not nearly enough.*

Somebody has got to pay.

A knock.

He tenses, remembering with reassurance Miss Dover's pistol under the sofa pillow. "Who is it?" he calls out. The door is locked.

"It's Rajit. I have Terrence with me. We come in peace."

He stands and goes to open the door. It's good to see Rajit's familiar face. His former partner Terrence is with him; Rajit said he might be. "Hey, guys."

"A little paranoid, are we?" Rajit asks as they walk in.

"We are."

"And who could blame you, what with the criminal element sniffing around?"

"Plenty to be paranoid about these days," Terrence says, looking at Ambrose. "Hello, by the way. I'm Terrence Olivier. Rajit's told me a lot about you."

"Same here," Ambrose says as they shake hands. Terrence was there that day Rajit followed Jessica to the motel. So he knows Ambrose gets Rajit to do "extra" things for him sometimes, most likely saw Dimitri there in the parking lot, spying on Mignon. Rajit seems to trust him implicitly and Ambrose trusts Rajit. . . "Can I get y'all anything? Water, coffee? I think we're out of matcha. Shot of bourbon?"

"We're good," Rajit answers. "What's up?"

✳✳✳

The point is to make Alexei Rusovich and company pay for what they did to Miss Dover, and, if it helps Dover, Inc. to survive, so much the better. Ambrose told Rajit and Terrence what he wanted done, left it up to them to find the best way to do it, swore them to secrecy, and agreed to make it worth their while.

He already has faith in Rajit's abilities and, after getting to know Terrence better and finally hearing of the exploits that got them fired—only because Terrence was willing to talk about it while Rajit sat there with his arms folded—Ambrose somehow feels better about things. *They're young, hungry, up for a challenge, and thoroughly enjoy sticking it to the man.*

They're perfect for this.

And so, nervous as hell but confident in the righteousness of this mission, Ambrose stays at work late Thursday night, eating Chinese food. He sits at his desk with a new burner phone, his own phone, and Miss Dover's pearl-handled pistol next to packets of duck sauce, hot mustard, and napkins.

Rajit and Terrence have access to a remodeled building on Valencia Street, where a friend of Rajit's agents the sale of condos. How Rajit got hold of a key, key card, or code is something of a mystery but he and Terrence met the woman, acting like they were considering sharing a place there, so maybe distracted and stole the entry method from her. That's a possibility anyway.

He finishes the Kung Pao shrimp and tosses the container and chopsticks into the wastebasket before kicking his feet up on the desk. The wall portrait of Miss Dover gazes down upon him. He takes his feet off the desk and sits up straighter, consumed with curiosity. Rajit will text something when it's done, just to let him know it's over. Only it won't really be over; it'll be just starting.

Unable to sit still, Ambrose goes to the rooftop for a cigarette, taking the phones in one pocket, and the pistol in the other pocket of the blazer he'd been wearing all day.

Still the same shimmering city lights he's seen many times before under different sets of circumstances, and now he can feel the ground shifting again. He hears a text notification on the new phone. It's video of a computer screen with a window showing what looks like a download. He peers closer, straining to read the small type at the bottom of the window that says **transferring funds**. It's going quickly, not downloading but uploading to a new bank account. His heart beats faster as he realizes they are in this now. Deep. The only sound he can hear is suppressed laughter, maybe Terrence and Rajit realizing the same thing as they sit on the highly polished floor of an astronomically priced condo with their computers, wired on matcha coolers and Twizzlers, stealing a small fortune from a mid-level gangster-entrepreneur.

Ambrose goes back downstairs to the office, too stunned to think straight. All he can do is pace and needs more room to do it so walks down to the ballroom, turns on the lights that illuminate just the edges. He should just be sitting in the dark, waiting for word they got out of there okay, but if they don't, what does he do? Go try to rescue them? How? Maybe all he could do is bail them out if they get busted as trespassers. But what if they have to explain why they were there, how they got in, and why they were using the internet in an empty apartment? And worst of all, what if they get caught "drinking this guy's milkshake" as they'd put it, loosely quoting one of Terrence's favorite movies. That would be a whole other thing altogether. He wouldn't blame them for outing him as the instigator—not the mastermind because he's no tech genius, just a pissed off motherfucker with an axe to grind, using them to do his dirty work.

He walks the perimeter of the large room as if walking around a high school track, trying to burn off an incandescent case of nerves. It doesn't help much, so he grabs a whip from the nearest suite, then returns to the ballroom, turns on the glittered ball in the center of the ceiling. It turns slowly from the control panel in the corner. He leaves the phones with their ringers and notification sounds on high volume, on the wooden riser next to Miss Dover's chair, along with the gun and his jacket. No music tonight, just the sound of his footsteps as he listens out for news.

He walks out to the center of the floor, watching flecks of light travel in circles. It's been quite a while since he cracked the whip. Good a time as any to see if he's still got the touch. He swings it clockwise above his head, trying to get a feel for it again, before jerking it back in a lackluster snap. *Come on, boy, you can do better than that.*

He focuses on the lights crossing the floor all around him, swirls the whip and aims at one, trying for the satisfying *pop* he used to get out of a good leather whip. A little better, but not much. Not quick enough. He paces, taking deep breaths, stretching, trying to get rid of the tightness that comes from waiting and wondering. He swings the whip above his head, wrist getting looser and more supple as he warms up, then snaps it back in the opposite direction with that satisfying gun-shot *pop*, the little sonic boom that happens when the whip moves faster than the speed of sound. Good getting back into the groove of something he's actually learned to do well.

Finally, he gets his things together, slips the jacket back on, and walks back down the hallway with the whip. Just as he returns to the office, the text notification sounds on his personal phone. It's a text from Rajit: **going out for drinks. Care to join us?**

Ambrose texts back: **No thanks, turning in early tonight**.

Rajit's response: **Suit yourself. All work and no play bro** 😎

Ambrose replies, **Tomorrow lunch is on me**.

Rajit's answer is simply a thumbs up.

✳✳✳

Getting word that it it's a *fait accompli* was like a shot of some high-powered aphrodisiac and, whatever Jessica's doing, she'll have to take a break for a while. Rolling into the driveway after an exhilarating ride home, Ambrose can see the lights on up in her studio. So once inside, he throws off his jacket, hides the gun inside the safe in the study, looks in on Beau sleeping, then bounds up the stairs.

Jessica's standing there in front of a large canvas, gazing at a half-done painting. Her landscapes—redwoods, pines, the High Sierra—are growing brighter each time with a vibrance he's beginning to feel inside. The coffee machine is on in the corner, so she's pulling a late night anyway. Her hair is pinned up haphazardly, and she's wearing a loose linen dress with a paint-spattered smock. She turns to look at him as he walks toward her across the hardwood floor. "Hey," she says. "I thought I heard you outside." She glances at the clock. "I had no idea it was so late. Did you get a lot done?"

He walks up behind her, puts his arms around her waist and kisses her neck. There've been nights she might say, "This isn't the best time," but now she's not saying anything. It's clear she's been getting a lot done and at the halfway point: a place to step back and evaluate. She has to feel him hard against her. He reaches up, cups her breasts.

She places her paint-spattered hands over his, pressing down, squeezing. Her breasts are full, firm. She turns, kisses him deeply. He picks her up, carries her over to the desk in the corner that she uses to make sketches. There, he strips off her panties, tosses them aside, then unzips to plunge inside.

✳✳✳

Alexei gazes across the table at his date, a petite blonde with ice blue eyes. She smiles as he pours the last of a bottle of fine Bordeaux into her glass. He smiles back, watching her pick up her fork for another bite of lobster. From the corner of his eye, he catches sight of Dimitri approaching from the entrance, sliding his phone into the interior pocket of his coat. Alexei straightens in his chair to receive the already unwelcome news.

Dimitri leans down and whispers in his ear, negating the effects of the expensive wine and cancelling the rest of tonight's careful plans.

"When did this happen?" he asks.

"Within the last hour."

"No further information?"

"None as yet."

The convivial conversation, clink of silverware, and rattle of a cocktail shaker recede into the high-frequency hum heard when a firecracker is tossed too late and one must summon the courage to look and see if a finger is missing.

The shocking numbness makes it hard to tell.

ELEVEN

Bennie had never dreamed of a big wedding with lots of related events, and she'd never spent hours looking through wedding magazines, websites, and Pinterest boards like Jessica had before she married Mike. Jessica and Mike had a huge wedding with eight bridesmaids and eight groomsmen, and her mother had been on cloud nine with her high-profile role in the proceedings. Bennie had occasionally thought about what her wedding might be like, but only in the abstract, not because she'd ever come that close. Until now. And she doesn't care a lick about the wedding itself, just getting married to Randy. That's all that matters.

Watching TV on the sofa, Randy has his private detective licensing guide and study materials open on the coffee table. Their two wine glasses sit at one end, his sock feet propped up on the other. He always sits on the opposite end from where she used to be, but now she joins him there, appreciating this slightly altered perspective of the TV, this view of the kitchen, and the bay window that looks onto Columbus Avenue. She sits curled up next to him, enjoying the feel of his arm around her, his scent, his warmth. This is what she's always wanted, but could never get, not like this.

She's so relaxed, she jumps when there's a knock at the door. *Company now?* She gets up to look through the peephole.

"Who is it?" Randy asks.

"It's Rajit." She hasn't seen him lately and feels he's been avoiding Randy. Sometimes when they're coming into the apartment, she hears a door down the hall close and thought it might be his—that he was waiting for them to go inside before he headed to the elevator. Now, here he is, looking a bit stoned. She opens the door. "Hey."

"Hello. Terrence is making lentil soup and I forgot to get bay leaf while I was out. May I borrow some and I'll pay you back?"

"Sure," she says. "Come in."

He walks in and she closes the door behind him.

"I don't think you've had a chance to meet Randy." She glances toward Randy, introduces, "Randy, this is our neighbor, Rajit. I'll be right back."

Randy's looking over the back of the sofa. "Yeah, I've heard them talk about you. You're the Indian guy."

"Hello." Rajit nears the sofa, reaches to shake his hand. "I am an Indian guy, yes." He looks pointedly in Bennie's direction as she returns from the kitchen. "I wouldn't say I'm *the* Indian guy."

Her eyes meet Rajit's and she smiles as she hands him the small tin of bay leaf.

"It is a pleasure to meet you at last," he tells Randy.

"They tell me you're a computer whiz," Randy says. "I hope you use your powers for good instead of evil."

"I do my best," Rajit responds. "Congratulations to both of you on your engagement. When's the big day?"

"We don't know yet, but soon," Bennie tells him. "We'll keep you posted."

"How exciting. Well, thank you for sharing your spice. I'll return it forthwith."

"Keep it; I'll get some more later. Good luck with the soup."

"You're far too kind." He glances in Randy's direction. "Goodbye, Randy."

"'Bye, Raj."

Rajit smiles at Bennie, goes out and shuts the door.

"So that's Rajit," Randy says, almost to himself.

She settles back next to Randy on the sofa. "What about our big day? We need to figure that out, don't we?"

"You know how I feel. Anything's good with me," he says, intertwining his fingers with hers, looking at the ring. "But even getting ready for my sister's wedding took up almost a whole a year, so, if you want more time to plan something, I understand."

"No, let's speed it up," she says, pleased to see his eyes brighten.

"How speedy we talking?" he asks.

"How about next Friday morning at City Hall. 10AM. We'll get the license ahead of time. If the 10 o'clock slot's taken, I'll reserve the next one available."

∗∗∗

Ambrose spends the better part of the afternoon at Dover, Inc., wiping obscenities written in red-wine lipstick off the dressing room mirror, sweeping face powder off the floor, collecting mutilated vinyl suits, corsets, and other bits of edgy clothing from behind the sofa, the corners of the room, the blades of the ceiling fan, and the toilet. After he politely informed Mignon that they'd not require her services after the end of the month, she had politely left the office, gone to the dressing room, and trashed it before she left with a couple tote bags full of shoes, her favorite whips, and whatever else she could fit into her purse. She also poured some pungent, over-the-top perfume into the sofa and chairs, put lubricant on every door and fixture handle, and poked holes in the dry wall that spelled out **fuck you** with the heel of a stiletto. He'd propped open the door to the hallway to disperse the smell.

While he works, the talk he had with Jessica this morning keeps replaying in the shadows of his mind, about how she wants to go to an artists' retreat with Beau in Provence for three months. Without him. She didn't say the last part in so many words, but it was loud and clear. She said he can stay at the house and, when she comes back, they'll try to start over. *Try?* He was so shocked, he hadn't asked any follow-up questions, but now it all sinks in. He realizes she's struggling to come to terms with the whole Mignon affair, Mike and the divorce, any suspicions about himself and Bennie, hers and Beau's future, and who'll be allowed in it.

So the sex the other night when he came home had been a fluke: all-out horniness from the thrill of sweet revenge for him and birth of a new masterpiece for her. It wasn't about them drawing closer together, but what they achieved separately. *Victory fuck.*

He gets a rag from the cleaning caddy and starts wiping a gob of lubricant off the bathroom door handle.

"What stinks in here?"

He looks up, shocked to see Momo walking in, carrying her daughter, Suzie, on her hip the way he and Jessica often carry Beau. Momo is in a pastel blue dress covered in little white flowers and Suzie in a little white dress with red jacket. They're like a welcome fresh breeze. "Hey! What are you doing here?" he asks, running to give Momo a hug. "I thought you were in Japan!" He steps back, thrilled to see two friendly faces when he'd been expecting the absolute worst. Times like this he can feel the gap between what this place used to be and what it's become.

"Got back two days ago," she says, eyeing the obscenity punched into the wall. No wonder he didn't hear footsteps because the nearly two-inch-thick soles of Momo's white sneakers are truly stealth. "What has been going on here? It's like all hell's broken loose since I left." She turns to look at him. "And I can't believe she's dead."

"Yeah." He shoves his hands in his pockets. "You heard she sold the building, right?"

"Bennie told me."

"We're looking for a place, just haven't found one yet."

Momo circles the room, carrying Suzie.

"We're trying to keep going. It's just been a period of. . ."

"Transition."

"Exactly."

Momo circles back to face him. "And Miss Dover willed everything else to you."

"Crazy, huh?"

She gives him a sly smile. "Kind of. In a good way."

He reaches to gently grasp Suzie's hand, to admire her Hello Kitty watch. "I love this, Suzie. Get it for your birthday?"

"She did." Momo looks down at Suzie, squeezing her closer.

It's sweet to see, but then he has to ask. "You're really back, aren't you? I mean, you are coming back. The two replacements she hired are leaving, and the other girl—the one that did all this. . . I had to fire her."

She gazes at him, lightly twisting back and forth, like rocking Suzie in her arms. So innocent-looking, both of them, but Momo has an intense look in her eyes giving him a flicker of hope.

"Granted," he continues, "there's been a lot of—I don't know— drama, going on, but once we get set up and running full-speed again, you'd be our star."

She switches Suzie to the other hip, smiles.

"Please say yes."

Something about the way she's looking at him makes him want to get down on his hands and knees. This is why she'd be so good. He's willing to beg and that look makes him want to beg.

Then somehow, she breaks character, whichever one she'd slipped into, and laughs. "We'll talk. Let's go get a coffee."

✳✳✳

Bennie has an answer ready the next afternoon, when Jessica asks: "Have you guys decided on a date?"

They're sitting on the patio. Caitlin's on a rafting trip in Colorado, so she and Randy are there to babysit Beau while Jessica and Ambrose go to a gallery opening in San Jose. She'd had to talk Ambrose into going and, even as he sits there, dressed up, sipping a beer, he looks distracted, like he'd rather stay home.

"You know you can have the wedding here if you want to," Jessica offers. "Or over at Mom and Dad's. Are you sure you want to get married at City Hall?"

Bennie looks at Randy in the chair next to her. "We're sure."

Randy smiles.

"Congratulations again," Ambrose says, raising his beer bottle. There's another bottle sitting on the brick ledge by the rose bushes and Bennie wonders if that's an empty from earlier. "It's set in stone now, right? Done deal? This calls for a toast."

"Yes! Congratulations, of course." Jessica walks over, hugs Bennie, then turns to Randy, misty-eyed, between smiling. "Oh, Randy. I've never had a brother-in-law before."

"I'll try to be a good one," he says, standing.

Bennie feels her eyes cloud as he returns the hug, glancing at Bennie while Jessica's arms are wrapped firmly around his neck. Ambrose kills the rest of the beer, sets the bottle down, and takes a cigarette out of the pack before him on the table.

Jessica pulls back, delicately wiping her eyes so as not to smear her carefully applied make-up. "Oh, my gosh, I don't know if we have any champagne."

"There's some in the bar fridge," Ambrose says. "I'll get it."

"I'll get it," Jessica tells him. "But only one glass for you; you've already had a beer."

Bennie rises to help her. "And you'll be my maid of honor, right, Jess?"

"Of course, I will!"

Bennie follows her into the house with a backward glance at Randy and Ambrose. Randy winks at her. She winks back, feeling wonderful about their wedding plans already.

✳✳✳

Once the women go in the house, Randy leans back in the chair. Ambrose is quiet, lost in thought, or maybe just getting a buzz. Don't think about it, Randy tells himself. The night Ambrose and Bennie fooled around was a lost night when nothing made sense. Plus, Ambrose had his own drama going on with Jessica. *Must've ironed things out; they seem to be getting along. They look happy. Anyway, it's over and they're all adults here.*

"How you feel?" Ambrose asks, maybe just to break the silence. "'Bout everything."

"Good." Ambrose taps the end of the cigarette on the table.

Hard to tell what he's thinking. *No matter. Just float the idea. Be the bigger guy this once.* "Wanna be my best man?"

Ambrose looks up, shocked. "Seriously?"

"Sure."

"Hell, I'm honored." He finally lights the cigarette. "You'd rather me than your brother, or—"

"I haven't spoken to him in almost a year, and I can't think of anybody else to—that I'd rather ask. So will you?"

"I will." Then, "What does a best man do? For one thing, I'm supposed to throw you a bachelor party, right?"

"Don't do that. It's not like I have many friends and I don't want strippers, or— Maybe you and I could just get beer and pizza. Or not. You don't have to do anything, really; just show up and hand me the ring. If she has a maid of honor, guess I should have a best man."

"I want to do something for you, though. I don't have many friends either, but I could invite Rajit and Terrence, if you want somebody besides me to talk to."

"I only just met Rajit, and that other guy doesn't even know me." Randy sets down the beer. "Now that I think about it, there is one other thing you can do."

"What's that?"

"Since she's not supposed to see me beforehand, make sure I look presentable for the ceremony?" The sharp outfit Ambrose is wearing is a far cry from how he looked that night at the old pier. Nothing left of that ragged-ass gutterpunk. *He actually has taste.*

Ambrose looks pleased. "We can do that."

"Thanks."

"Sure thing."

Randy clinks bottles with him and settles back in the chair. Could be the alcohol or lush surroundings, but, watching through the window as Jessica sets slender-stemmed glasses on a tray and Bennie comes walking out with a bottle of champagne, he embraces the feeling of having people in his life who give a damn. It's been a long, lonely spell of walking in a desert strewn with sun-bleached bones of past mistakes, and coming into a green oasis where he feels fully human again.

✳✳✳

Dimitri sips vodka across from Alexei at the booth in the back of the tearoom, near the kitchen.

Alexei watches him from over a half-eaten bowl of okróshka soup, detecting that he may be getting drunk. "Tell, me; is it worth it?"

"Is what worth it?" Dimitri asks.

"Your obsession with Margarite, and her infatuation with that heiress. Jealousy is not a good look on you, my friend."

Dimitri remains stubbornly focused on the candle flickering in the middle of the table. "Your jealousy of Sergei and Ivan and that freak lover of his has animated your every move for the past ten years. And do not call me your friend."

Alexei nods slightly, taking a sip of coffee. "However, I do work with you on a more intimate level than anyone else in my organization. Some would call you my right-hand man these days. What would you call yourself?"

Dimitri shifts in the booth, gazes up at Alexei like he's just achieved checkmate. "Partner."

Alexei's expression remains unchanged. "How do you arrive at that title?"

"I've uncovered a piece of information worth a great deal to you, about who hacked your account."

"I should think you'd want to share that with me. After all, your paychecks are drawn on that account."

"If I've learned one thing from your mistakes, it's that I must make myself indispensable to you. I want it in writing. Call your brother and tell him to come here now and draw up a contract. A partnership between you and me."

"Partnership?"

"In your corporation, the businesses through which you launder your—other money. I can get back the money that was stolen from you in the hacking. And if I have a legitimate stake in your illegitimate empire, there is much more I'd be willing to do. But only if you make it well worth my while."

"Ah. I see." Alexei smiles, takes out his phone and glances at it. "Well, I've been unable to reach Maxim all day. He claims he no longer wishes to handle my business and legal affairs, citing health reasons."

"It'll be much worse for his health if he refuses to handle urgent matters."

Alexei pushes the soup bowl aside. "You're asking a great deal. How do I know any information you have to retrieve my funds is valid. . . and actionable?"

"Find Maxim and make him come here. Or I will."

✳✳✳

Randy paces the hallway. Ambrose helped him with his tie and pinned his boutonniere on straight. Got a haircut yesterday so it's all neat for once. Any nerves he feels are only because her folks are here and other people will be watching, too, because these ceremonies are open to the public, but no time for any foolishness because City Hall's on a tight schedule to get all these people hitched. He resists the impulse to loosen his tie. *Don't get the white collar dirty and don't mess with that knot; there are still pictures to take.* He gets out his phone.

Stupid to call now; it's been so long and no time for her to get here anyway. If he was going to do that, should've done it earlier. He wonders vaguely if Mr. and Mrs. Jenkins consider it odd that no one from his family's showing up, but, even if they do, they can keep it to themselves. The only one he's even considering calling is his mom. Ronnie, Jr., Alison, their spouses and broods wouldn't give a shit anyway. Only his mom. But she's written him off and would be a loose cannon at something like this. He sees Ambrose walking toward him and puts the phone away.

"Hey. Nervous?"

"Not a bit."

Ambrose nears, speaks quieter, "Did you want to call your mom or anything?"

"Too late now anyway."

"Could at least tell her you're getting married."

"Is your mom coming to the wedding when you and Jessica get married?"

Ambrose reaches up to straighten Randy's tie. "My mom thinks we're already married."

"What?"

"You're only allowed six guests, but there was room for one more."

Room for one more. That reminds Randy of a *Twilight Zone* episode, where Barbara Nichols plays a stripper hospitalized after a nervous breakdown. She keeps having the nightmare of being in a morgue. When she's released and goes to get on an airplane, the flight attendant tells her, "Room for one more, honey." The stripper refuses to get on the plane and then the plane explodes right after take-off.

So that's what he's doing: refusing to board that plane. There may be room for one more, but then the whole thing could go up in flames.

TWELVE

She's going. Standing in the driveway alone, Ambrose watches the car carrying Jessica and Beau turn the corner down at the end of Eucalyptus Lane. She never asked him to go, nor if he'd like to come over for a visit while she and Beau are there, even for a few days. He's never been out of the States before and this place sounds beautiful. They could go around sightseeing and looking at art and enjoying picnics in the countryside, but she never said she wanted him there at all. Said she'd miss him, but it wasn't too convincing. She's become like one of the twin marble sphinxes at the Stanford Mausoleum: stone-cold and impossible to read.

However, clearing out the old building isn't nearly as painful as Ambrose anticipated now that they've found a new building to go to. An *old* new building perhaps, a Victorian in Noe Valley that Bennie's friend had on the market, but still—a base of operations, space for five suites, three of which will be like a BDSM B&B, an attic that will become office space for Rajit and Terrence, housing all the security equipment, and a small room on the second floor for Ambrose's office. The ground floor has enough space for a small lobby and lounge, which Bennie can't wait to decorate or use the former storage room for her office.

He'd seen Mr. Bob one day at the smoke shop in Palo Alto and they walked to the diner on the corner for coffee. Ambrose hadn't told him everything, just that he'd inherited the business from the original owner, found a place that'd be perfect for what he wanted to do next, and Mr. Bob hinted that he'd come into extra money he was looking to invest, and knew a couple other guys, friends of his, that might kick in just for the hell of it. Not a bad ally: bored, rich man with time on his hands and money to burn. Mr. Bob brought up the possibility of a walk-in humidor just off the bar. There's a private patio out back with endless possibilities: could be a postage stamp of urban oasis with ultra-cool patio furniture, an outdoor fireplace, exotic greenery, room for a small band for intimate gatherings, whatever form those may take. Amazing how people are willing to jump on board once you get the ball rolling.

Their first investor and very silent partner is the shell corporation Rajit and Terrence set up with Alexei's money. Whatever hacker-voodoo magic they're using to make it all look legit has to hold. They've assured and reassured him that it will, and God help Ambrose, he believes them, even though the whole thing still seems like a dream. Every morning when he awakes alone in the house and remembers all this is really happening, he gets a strange, new sensation in the pit of his stomach: chemical cocktail of anxiety and anticipation that keeps him on edge, the only thing holding him back from black depression in the wake of Jessica's and Beau's departure. He sits on the patio in the mornings as the coffee kicks in, and euphoria grips him as ideas start flying for the new era of Dover, Inc.. Then he has to take a breath and remember: one step at a time.

Now that he's alone so much, he often thinks of Butch. Last time they talked on the phone, he asked if he'd ever gotten that numbness in his hands checked out and he said it was getting better, but Ambrose doesn't believe him. And if something really is wrong when Butch does get out, he may or may not be able to work full-time and will need financial help. Butch is the only one who ever tried to look out for him and now it'll be his turn to look out for Butch.

Even though Butch ran with some high-rollers for a while, and did pull off a few successful deals that put money in his pockets, that money's long gone. Butch doesn't consider himself a criminal genius by any stretch and not even all that smart; no one ever did, and even though he'd be the first to admit he's made a ton of mistakes, he's older, been around, able to see through the bullshit of a situation, just like that visiting day at the prison. Ambrose doesn't want Butch to ever know he's gotten involved with something that could land him in scalding-hot water if the unthinkable happens, so he, Rajit, and Terrence will have to keep the electronic Russian siphoning caper and any other shenanigans under wraps. And no need to pretend everything's fine on the next visit, because Butch'll take one look at Ambrose and know the score.

He'd better think of his and Butch's future because nobody else will. Jessica's under no obligation to him nor he to her, except to take care of the place while she's away and not bring any women back—not that he ever would. He flashes unwillingly on Bennie's and Randy's wedding, watching the groom kiss the bride, and how it had torn at him in some unspeakable way, adding another layer to the hardness developing around his heart: a light frost to protect it.

On the last day, he returns to the office to finish cleaning out and packing things. The moving van will be here tomorrow, and Bennie's coming to oversee that, but there are some things he wants to transport himself, such as the contents of Miss Dover's desk and cabinet, and any pictures. He'll take it all over in Jessica's car, the one she asked him to drive home from the country club that first time they went out together, and many times since. The days of living in her house, using her car—and, even though it's not the same thing but much more profound: going with her little boy to the park and reading him stories as if Beau were his stepson—might be over forever. Beau already has a dad who loves him, and it's just another wake-up call seeing how Jessica can take him away so easily, maybe forever if she decides there's no room for Ambrose in her life anymore.

He looks at the portrait of Miss Dover still on the wall. Yes, she'd sold the place out, but no telling how they threatened her into it. Anyway, if she hadn't so generously remembered him in her will, he wouldn't be making these new plans, nor have much direction at all. Maybe that's a case for keeping the name. Rajit and Terrence thought he should change it, and he hadn't taken it up with Bennie to get her opinion, but he's inclined to keep it Dover, Inc., in honor of her.

He reaches to take the portrait down just as the phone rings, giving him a start. It's Maxim, at the back entrance. He wants to take one last look at the place before his brother comes in and changes everything. When Ambrose opens the door for him, he's solemn, as if entering the home of one who's recently experienced a tragedy.

"How are you holding up, my boy?" Maxim asks.

"I'm all right. You?"

"Eh, well enough," he answers.

The tension recedes as Maxim walks around, maybe reliving moments of pleasure and exquisite pain from earlier times. Ambrose walks with him. *Good having someone here from Miss Dover's salad days.* Maxim looks at her portrait, light rising in his eyes. "Ah, the dear Dutchess," he breathes. "What will you take for this?"

Ambrose hadn't thought of selling it, but here's someone who would really appreciate it. "It's yours, Maxim."

Maxim looks at him in amazement. "But—are you sure?"

"I'm sure." Ambrose takes it down. "Want me to put it in your car?"

"I can do that," Maxim says. He takes it from Ambrose, holding it out in front of him. "Beautiful." He continues gazing at it, then leans it against the desk. "I want you to know, I've severed business ties with my brother. I've been experiencing heart palpitations and can no longer endure such a high-stress environment."

"Well, you've got to look after yourself." Then, "Guess he can't wait to move in?"

"Eh, yes. . . However, he has been at somewhat loose ends. One of his accounts has been hacked. A disgruntled former employee, perhaps. Apparently, whoever it is covered their tracks quite well." He looks at Ambrose. "I must tell you; your name was mentioned as a possibility, but I assured them you would have nothing to do with such a scheme. Would you, my boy?"

Ambrose flashes on Rajit and Terrence high-fiving in that vacant condo, the gleeful exchange of texts on burner phones, the motorcycle ride to Palo Alto at lightning speed, the epic sex that followed but wasn't enough to keep Jessica from leaving for France to find herself. "Hell, no. I wouldn't even know where to start."

Maxim looks relieved, for the most part. "Of course not. Nor would I. Oh, I almost forgot—" He takes out a small silver case and hands Ambrose a business card. "I'm still dabbling in real estate. And I will handle certain types of legal cases on a very limited basis." He grasps Ambrose's hand in a firm shake. "Please be careful."

"I will. You, too."

"I'll see myself out. Goodbye now."

"'Bye." He watches as Maxim picks up the portrait. There's a finality in seeing it walk out of here with him. Ambrose goes over and watches as he starts down the hallway toward the back door.

***

Maxim carefully places the portrait in the back of his late-model Saab, gets in and snaps the seatbelt, a sense of wistful melancholy descending as he starts the engine and drives for the last time toward the corrugated steel door. He reaches out the window, presses the garage button to exit. The door rises and he drives out a few feet, stopping when he sees a familiar vehicle parallel-parked across the street behind a delivery truck: a black BMW. He sees Dimitri clad in black, getting out of the car and walking toward the front of the building. Dimitri reaches into his coat pocket, as if adjusting something, then straightens the coat, facing forward with adamantine resolve.

Gasping, Maxim throws the car in reverse and hits the gas, making it back into the parking garage with a fraction of a second to spare before the steel door closes. He skids to a stop, jumps out and runs toward the back door.

***

Ambrose locates the bottle of bourbon in a box of odds and ends that had been in the cabinet when he hears pounding at the back door. He rushes down the hallway, glimpses the security cam, and lets Maxim in.

"He's coming!" Maxim cries. "He's coming in the front way!"

"Who?"

"Dimitri is here! Alexei's bodyguard." Maxim gasps for breath, casting around in his coat pockets for something.

"Are you all right? You don't really think he's here to—"

"He's like an assassin! An assassin, I tell you!"

Followed by Maxim, Ambrose rushes back toward the office, grabs the brown leather satchel he's using in lieu of a backpack these days, and takes out Miss Dover's pearl-handled pistol.

"Is the front door locked?" Maxim asks.

"The front door to this suite's locked," Ambrose says, fumbling to undo the safety.

"But that is a glass door!"

"He wouldn't shoot his way through that, would he? Somebody might call the cops."

"That does not scare him." Maxim takes out a small pill bottle, hands shaking. "I want to believe you, but if you are behind that hacking job, shoot to kill, my boy, because he will do the same." He tosses a tiny white pill into his mouth and swallows, eyes watering, face turning red.

Ambrose walks into the hallway, starting cautiously toward the frosted glass doors to the reception area. The lights are on, but he'd turned them on earlier. Maxim could be overreacting, but he knows these people, and so did Miss Dover who's dead because of these crazy bastards. This makes the confrontation with Lang all those months ago look like a minor tussle on a fifth-grade playground.

Holding the gun in his right hand, Ambrose places his left on the stainless-steel handle to the reception area and opens the door to meet his destiny.

✳✳✳

Another name change because the Queen is dead. Long live the Queen. She looks down at her business card. Phoebe Grace is the new owner of Aquarius Rising, based in Paris, with offices in London as well. The new atelier in Rue Cambon will soon be abuzz with activity, and the sunny room with its chandelier, antique crown molding, and newly finished hardwood floors will be the nerve center of an international, cutting-edge design firm.

Miss Dover may have had misgivings about accepting help like this when she'd worked so hard to be ultra-independent, but this new woman, risen from the ashes of the old, has no target on her back like the one who came over here and died like a rock star in a Paris hotel room. She has a clean slate, and what falls away like shattered ice is not her concern, save one shard that won't melt because it's made of glass.

She stands and walks over to the window, catching a glimpse of herself in an antique mirror edged with gilded acanthus leaves on the wall opposite. This woman's hair is long and straight, subversively sedate, and she wears a Chanel pantsuit and eyeglasses with Dior frames. The flamboyant Miss Dover might not approve, but Phoebe Grace thinks she looks fabulous, and so does Sergei Dobrev and his army of guardian angels whose vigilance is to thank for saving her from the vindictive bastards who were tailing Miss Dover from the streets of San Francisco to Paris, and who will never know that she didn't succumb to a night of hard partying and one too many amyl-nitrates, and that the money from the sale of her building didn't all go to charity, though a generous percentage of it did.

Even though Alexei Rusovich's hatred knows no bounds, it was Maxim's loyalty and disregard for his own safety that caused him to tip off Sergei, and Sergei took it from there. She looks out the window, where instead of the Transamerica Pyramid, the Eiffel Tower is the iconic landmark rising above the urban landscape. There are buildings back in The City now taller than the Transamerica building, but when she was new in town and quite lost, she walked there from a coffee shop in North Beach and saw a city worker in blue coveralls emptying trash cans, a handsome black man wearing a rainbow bracelet and a red scarf. She'd asked him how to get to Castro Street, and he told her which bus to take, and she will never forget that day.

She turns away from the window, thinking now of the only nagging, unfinished business left. Sergei and Alexei can hug it out any way they see fit; she doesn't even want to know. Phoebe Grace is unconcerned with macho posturing and gangsterism, floating above such matters like a butterfly over the dumpster behind Cafe Le Chat Noir. But Ambrose. . .

She walks in front of her wide, antique desk, pacing slowly with her arms folded. The boy had been doing his best to hold things together despite all the strange goings-on. She heard how he'd spoken at her funeral from Sergei who'd heard it from Maxim who was at the park that day. Hard to imagine Ambrose volunteering to get up and sing her praises in front of a crowd of mostly strangers. The Ambrose she'd known before would've hung back, listening and saying nothing, but this is a sign he's getting bolder. She feels a stirring, that nurturing instinct he awakens in her. *He must be growing up. And he doesn't deserve to be left alone, empty-handed. At least this gives him a chance to keep it going if he wants, and leadership experience he might someday take elsewhere. Besides, if the thing with the rich girlfriend falls through altogether, he'll need something to cling to, to keep him out of trouble. If he can just stay out of trouble.*

She catches herself smiling faintly, wondering who will be there now to slap him hard across the face when he needs it.

✳✳✳

Provence is beautiful: weather perfect, sunlight golden, and she loves her new workspace. Beau and Caitlin are out exploring in the garden and there are croissants and blueberry jam on a rustic, ceramic hand-painted platter in the sitting area, coffee steeping in a French press. She's barely been able to drag herself out of bed for the last few days. She pads into the sitting area next to a bright window in a small, book-lined room looking on the woods to the back of the property. She tears off a bit of croissant with her fingertips and eats it, hoping that might quell the strong wave of nausea. She runs to the toilet and vomits, pulls the chain to flush, and sinks onto the mosaic tile, her back against the cool enamel of the antique bathtub. Could be something she ate, but what?

She wants to enjoy herself now that she's here. Ambrose is waiting for her, and she has faith that he will be when she gets back. If he's not, it was never meant to be, and that's what she wants to know: Is it? Maybe it's counterintuitive to find out all the way over here, but in the fullness of time, the truth will be revealed, curiosity satisfied. Like whether there's anything going on between him and Bennie, if there ever was, no matter what they'd both say, and whether he'd blow up Bennie's and Randy's marriage and her relationship with her sister. . . And then there's this jealousy that she has no right to feel after the Mignon affair. So many things to work through. And time and space to do it, if she can just get over whatever's making her throw up.

As she manages to stand, she remembers that all the pain she's experienced in the past several months is a part of her transformation, a major realignment of her life that started that night in the dining room when Ambrose admired her painting, and then when she took him upstairs and told him the meaning of *et in Arcadia ego* carved on the base of the alabaster skull in her old studio. Maybe the death in her own Arcadia had been all the lies surrounding her in that "perfect" little island on Eucalyptus Lane, and now that the lies have been exposed, she can finally go forward. Only not now. Not feeling like she's going to throw up again.

As the next wave of nausea hits, another thought occurs to her. That this feeling isn't altogether unfamiliar. It's happened for the last two mornings. And she's been craving bubble gum ice cream. Hasn't had such a strong craving since she was pregnant with Beau. But it can't be that. *We always use a condom.*

She leans down to vomit into the toilet again and, as she pulls the chain to flush the rest of last night's light dinner, remembers the only time they didn't was that night he came home late and found her upstairs in her studio. She'd been really in the mood that night, and was thrilled that he'd wanted her so badly. Badly enough that she didn't even remind him. Or think about it. And she was supposed to have started her period by now but thought maybe she was off with all the stress of preparation and the flight and change in schedule. She instinctively places her hand on her stomach.

She'll go to the pharmacy and get a test once this wave passes.

The things that happened after he opened that door had all run into a blur, but, as the sun climbs higher in the sky the next day, he finds himself in a patio chair at a bar in Truckee. There's a shot of bourbon in front of him, the pearl-handled pistol in his khakis, hidden under an over-priced jacket he'd purchased at a sporting goods shop down the street. He stares into space, mind's eye still focused on the homicidal Russian falling to the floor, just hours earlier. But he'd shot the guy, so he must be homicidal, too.

When he opened the door to the reception area, the guy raised his nine-millimeter and Ambrose squeezed the trigger of his .38 (it's his now, after all). Maxim had peered around the frosted glass door in the deafening silence that followed. Ambrose stood trembling, looking down at the guy all dressed in black, neat hole through the middle of his forehead, blood seeping onto the floor under his head, making a cabernet stain on the dove-grey rug. Maxim approached, still red-faced but beginning to regain his composure, gazing down at the one he had referred to as Dimitri. A triumphant grin spread across his face, and he patted Ambrose on the back. "Well done, my boy!"

"He's dead, isn't he?" Not since Butch taught him to aim and squeeze, knocking beer cans off a wrecked Dakota pick-up in their parents' backyard, had Ambrose fired a gun, and here he was staring at this guy that, moments earlier, had Maxim in tears. "What do we do?" Ambrose asked. "Shouldn't I call the police?"

"Why call anyone?"

"It was self-defense. . ." Ambrose looked at the body again. *Wasn't it?* But what if this Dimitri-guy came in retaliation for him stealing that money. Plus, Alexei looks clean on paper and would have his ways of making Ambrose, Rajit, and Terrence look like crooks. Pressure built from his core as the dead man's blood continued flowing out onto the carpet. "Goddamn it," he finally uttered, trying to hold back tears of confusion and stress. "I don't fucking know what to do, Maxim."

"Get rid of him and the rug and never speak of this again."

"Won't somebody come looking for him? What about your brother?"

The grin left Maxim's face and he started digging around in his pockets for the pill bottle, looking faint, then: "I cannot take another nitroglycerin so soon. Did I not see you with a bottle of liquor earlier?"

Ambrose shoved the pistol into the back of his jeans waistband, flashing on how Juan, one of Lang's flunkies, had done that the night of the fake drug bust. That fateful meeting with the dirty cop, Randy, who took mercy on him. . . "Yeah," he said, taking a deep breath, rolling up his sleeves. Rajit and Terrence were at some tech conference in Santa Monica for three days, and, it being after 5PM, all the other places in this building were closed, so maybe nobody heard the shot. He locked the front door, sure it had been locked before, so how'd this weird bastard get in? *Alexei must have a key already, so this guy did, too, somehow, and came gunning.*

When he got Maxim situated in the office with a drink, he poured a shot for himself, then went to get a shower curtain out of the Charenton Suite for a makeshift shroud. Before he rolled the dead torpedo into it, he stood over him, contemplating going through the guy's pockets. The dead stare made it more difficult, but he steeled himself, got the guy's phone and wallet out of the inside coat pockets. He could shred the ID stuff, run over the phone a few times, and toss it in the trash or in the bay. . . He considered wresting the gun out of the stiffening right hand, but no telling what crimes had been committed with it, so he left it to be disposed of along with the body.

Maxim had said to roll him up in the rug, but, looking at this Dimitri, Ambrose realized he's not even that big of a guy. It's the coat with padded shoulders that made him look bigger, and the way he carried himself. Rolling him in the rug would make him that much larger and heavier, and the soaked rug would paint a crimson trail leading all the way to the dumpster. Plus, there's a sign adjacent to the dumpster that says it's under 24-hour surveillance. He doesn't know by whom. *The waste management company maybe? Could be bullshit, but still. Risky.*

He went to what had been the Tyrol Suite, got another shower curtain, rolled the body in that, then went through the boxes with bed clothes to wrap the corpse in a queen-size black sheet. He secured that with some thin chains that had been in the bottom drawer of one of the cabinets. He stared at the curious package, wrapped up as if for a BDSM burial-at-sea, dragged it to Jessica's car in the parking garage and, through sheer force of will, got it into the trunk. He managed to bag up the rug, then spent all night mopping and bleaching the reception area. Bennie might wonder what happened to the rug, but he'd come up with an explanation later. *Clock's ticking and movers will be arriving in a few short hours.* When the floor was as spotless as he could make it, he showered in the Charenton bathroom, quickly, since there was no shower curtain, and got into the extra clothes he had in the office, placing his other clothes into the trash bag with the rug.

Now in Truckee, he stands, stretches, paces over to the edge of the patio with his drink. If he were home right now, back on Eucalyptus Lane, he'd be sitting on the patio, gazing out at the guest house, remembering his arrival that first day and how he thought he had problems *then.*

After Maxim had a shot or two of straight bourbon to quell his panic, he again wished Ambrose luck. Maxim said they'd both need it as he pumped Ambrose's hand, kissed him on both cheeks. Then, he mumbled, "Dust off your passport, m' boy—just in case," and walked out. Before the whiff of bourbon on his breath had dissipated, Ambrose heard the back door shut, then the faint screech of tires on concrete. He was alone again. At least as far as he knew.

There was a time not long ago when he would be hyperventilating, curled up into a ball on the sofa. But after the visit to his parents in Texas, seeing their obliviousness that had sent him out on the road, and their matter-of-fact way of excusing and ignoring the very worst in themselves, he wonders if they're both just sociopaths. He'd never thought of himself as anything like them, but something happened on the road to Tahoe today. What little innocence he had left—and it wasn't much—is gone forever. Could be that he inherited their ability to detach, compartmentalize, along with a propensity for violence that he never knew he had in him.

Certainly never would've thought he had the brass balls to call up Randy and offer to bring him up to the lake for a belated bachelor's trip. It was like pulling teeth. And here comes Randy now, back to the table from a trip to the men's room, thinking they're just going to Bennie's parents' cabin for the night, to do a little fishing in the morning before they head back. Ambrose had said that since there'd be so much to do what with setting up the new place, he might not get another chance for a while, could use a short break. Bennie and Momo can order the movers around, so now's a window of opportunity. During the call, Ambrose got the impression Bennie didn't want Randy to come on this impromptu excursion, worried what they'd talk about. He'd first implied to Randy that Rajit and Terrence would be with him, too. But when he picked Randy up, he said they'd cancelled at the last minute.

Now that he and Randy are about to leave Truckee and head on over to the cabin, Ambrose feels a case of nerves coming on, just when he can afford it least. Should've figured out how to do this all on his own but dumping Dimitri off a pier seemed like something that could wash right back up to bite him on the ass. He'd thought about that lonely area where the fake drug deal went down all those months ago as a possibility, but the cops were watching that night. Yesterday, he'd struggled getting the body into the trunk by himself, so to be caught wrestling with it in public, just to hear the *whoop* of a siren and see blue lights flashing. . .

That day at the wedding in Napa, Randy said he owed Ambrose one. *Thank God he doesn't know what happened that night on molly at Bennie's; Bennie'd never tell him that, even married.* "Dirty deeds done dirt cheap," Randy said that day behind the coffee shop. Like Ambrose, he wants some money of his own. They both do, independent of the women in their lives. Yeah, Randy's studying for his detective license and Bennie's helping him work out some kind of business plan to someday make "Burke Security" a reality, but in the meantime, he's still that crooked cop who didn't turn Ambrose in, the filthy-minded, down-on-his-luck bastard Ambrose hired for the gallery opening, and he wouldn't have any of this but for Ambrose, including private access to a boat on a huge lake. Jessica rarely mentions the place and had never offered to bring Ambrose up here. For Bennie and Randy, though, this is their honeymoon love nest. *And Randy had said that day: "I owe you one."*

Goddamn right, Ambrose thinks. You at least owe me this.

Sitting behind the chateau, Jessica never expected to be planning her return trip this soon, but she left Palo Alto seeking insight into what her future might hold, and now has her answer. She'd even said it in front of Butch, so maybe that made it manifest. Even if such ideas are magical thinking, she must've wanted it to happen, or why would she have said it? Still hard to forget that frisson of doubt upon finding Ambrose and Bennie on the floor together, but she's come around to believing that was just her old insecurity rising to the surface. She must know she can trust him, but he has to know that while she's following her bliss, she won't decide he's not new and shiny enough. Even in the midst of her shock of what he told her about Mignon that day at the beach, he also said he'd let her have her freedom, whatever form it takes. Maybe that's all she needs to hear.

She turns to look at Beau, sleeping in the seat next to her, hugging a pillow. She smooths his hair, and he stirs. Beau has even missed him. She looks out at the deep green woods, almost too keyed up to read, but that's what she really needs to do: take her mind off it. There's no telling how Ambrose will react, and anticipating his answer will only make it harder, if it's not the one she wants. After all, she hurt him when she left him there all alone, with no idea what might happen.

So why should he say yes?

She sips from her cup of ginger tea, resolved to stop re-negotiating the past. And there's no need to run away anymore and keep hiding out at this retreat now that she knows what she wants and is willing to fight for it.

It's all right there, waiting.

***

"Why do you want to go park out by the boathouse?" Randy wants to know as they sit in the lakehouse living room. It's not like they're going fishing tonight. Almost sunset now that they're situated, and it's a nice walk from the house down to the lake; no need to take the car down there.

But Ambrose insists, says he has some beer in the trunk and wants to get it into a cooler and into the boat with some ice. They can take it with them for a nighttime boat ride and it'll still be cold tomorrow.

"I don't know," Randy says, starting to get tired as Ambrose picks up the car keys from the coffee table. "We can do that in the morning. Anyway, there's beer in the refrigerator and I can't get all fucked-up driving the boat."

"We don't have much time here," Ambrose reminds. "I've never been before. I really wanted to see the lake at night."

Randy flops down into one of the overstuffed chairs near the wide, stone fireplace. "I'm just learning how to drive the boat. I don't really know about doing it at night yet."

"Come on, Randy," Ambrose says pleadingly. "We came all this way. Where's your sense of adventure?"

That's back home with Bennie, but when Ambrose insisted that he drop everything for some ridiculous, half-ass male bonding mission, Randy reluctantly packed an overnight bag just to shut him up and get it over with. Bennie seemed really nervous that they were coming up here together, though she thought Rajit and Terrence would be along too. Ambrose said this was to make up for not doing anything special before the wedding, and he might not get another chance for a while. Randy reassured Bennie he'd never say anything about when Ambrose came by to console her and get her sky-high that night-from-hell. He told her to relax, do a little baking and make tonight a spa night.

Randy grabs the boat keys out of the top drawer of the roll-top desk and walks down the trail to the boat house while Ambrose moves the car. Maybe it's better now, but there was some vaguely unpleasant odor in that car on the way up here. *Maybe just more sensitive to mysterious smells now that I'm out of that dank apartment and living with clean-freak Bennie,* Randy figures, missing her already. The stars are just coming out and the air is cool and crisp. When Randy arrives, Ambrose is pacing next to the car, head down, rubbing the back of his neck.

As Randy approaches, he looks up. "Gonna open up the trunk? There's a built-in cooler in the back of the boat."

"A big one?" Ambrose asks.

"How big do you need?"

Ambrose takes a step closer, speaks quietly: "You're good at keeping secrets, right?"

Randy catches a chill from the fresh breeze off the water and Ambrose's tone. He senses there's a price to be paid for whatever answer he gives. "I have my moments."

"Remember that day behind the coffee shop, you gave me your card and said, if I ever needed anything, to call you?"

"Why you wanna bring that up?" Randy recalls the dizzying shock that day Ambrose caught him running down the arcade, grabbed him by the arm and slung him into the wall.

"I did call you," Ambrose goes on, "and that job led to good things, right?"

Randy bites the inside of his lip, determined not to let on that he knows about Ambrose and that Rajit-guy using that opportunity to invade his apartment and hack into his computer. Because, fucked up as it all was, it led to good things. . .

"I got a job for you now. Sorry I kinda brought you here under false pretenses, but I'll pay you $500."

"$500? I've got to know what it is first."

"Said before that you owe me one. This would square us and then some."

"What's the fucking job?"

"You can use 500 bucks, right?"

Randy turns away. Hadn't really wanted a drink before, but now could definitely use a belt.

Ambrose smells blood in the water. "You and I both know how that is," Ambrose continues. "Don't you want a little folding money of your own so you don't have to keep asking her?"

Randy feels caught and thrown against a wall all over again.

"C'mon, Randy. I'm your best man. We're practically family." Ambrose pops the trunk.

Even in the crisp evening air, there's that smell again, only stronger. Randy peers in at the large, misshapen bundle wrapped in silver chains. There's also a black garbage bag stuffed full of something. "What the fuck is that?" he asks, eying the one in chains.

"All you gotta do's help me toss it in the lake."

"You didn't answer my question."

"Less you know about it, the better." He sees the look Randy gives and shrugs. "It's some confidential stuff I found when I was cleaning out the building. I couldn't just throw it in a dumpster."

"What kind of confidential shit?"

"I really can't talk about it."

"You already asked me if I could keep a secret, but, if you can't tell me anything about it, maybe I don't need to haul it out on my wife's boat." Randy starts to turn away, but Ambrose grips his arm. Déjà vu, but this time Ambrose is holding out a roll of cash.

"Make it a thousand?" Ambrose negotiates. "Half now and half when we get back to the City."

"Where are you getting all this money?"

"This is everything we had in petty cash, and I'll get the rest out of my own checking account."

"What the fuck, Ambrose?"

Ambrose sighs, runs his fingers through his hair in frustration. "All you've got to do's help me load it in the boat and take me out on the lake."

✳✳✳

Randy barely says anything the whole time they were loading the boat, but Ambrose senses he knows. *He knows.* Steering the boat further from the shoreline as the moon rises, Randy only looks straight ahead.

Finally, about twenty minutes later, Randy shifts gears, slows, cuts the motor.

"Think this is far enough?" Ambrose asks.

"We've got to have gas to get back."

Ambrose turns, taking in the scenery before the sky turns to black, but the moon's glow is growing brighter. Randy gazes in the direction they just came. "What're you looking at?"

"I've got to remember how to get back."

"We're not lost, are we?"

Randy takes a deep breath. "Let's get this over with."

The two grim packages, Dimitri and the blood-soaked, triple-bagged rug from the reception area are in the back of the boat, under a couple of posh wool blankets, too big for the built-in cooler. Boathouse lights and others on the distant shore sparkle like the stars overhead. He wishes they really were just tooling around Lake Tahoe, going back for a couple beers before turning in, then coming out tomorrow to do a little fishing and enjoy a late lunch before driving back. But that's something normal people do, and he feels anything but normal as he climbs into the back, trying to remain steady, waves gently rocking them.

He picks up one end of the trash bag, tearing a small hole in it with his finger so it won't find a way to float. Would've done this before, but he didn't want blood to leak out. Maybe it's dried, but maybe not; there was so much of it. Nothing leaking now, just an odd, faint odor, nothing like the worsening smell from that other bag. Still, he wants to be sure it sinks, and wishes he'd poked a hole all the way through with a screwdriver or knife. He tears at the next bag inside the outer one.

"The fuck are you doing?" Randy asks.

"Nothing. It ought to sink, right?"

"...Yeah." Randy lifts the other end.

Ambrose feels the hand weights from Mignon's old dressing room shift inside the bag.

"All right," Randy says. "Ready?"

"Yep."

"One... Two... Three."

They push it over the side. It makes a splash and bobbles before sinking with a bubbly hiss. They turn to the other piece of cargo. Randy hesitates, then gets on the other side, trying to figure out how best to pick it up. He finally reaches down and manages to get a grip as Ambrose braces himself, lifting the other end of the unwieldy bundle, wondering if he should've weighed this one down. *It's heavy all right, but still.*

"Goddamn," Randy breathes.

Once they get it balanced on the edge, the boat tilts slightly. Ambrose glimpses Randy's face: In the waxing moonlight, he looks vaguely disgusted, like he knows what it is they're dumping.

"Sure you want to do this?" Randy asks.

"I'm sure."

"Push it over on three. Ready?"

"Ready."

"One. Two. Three."

They give it a shove and it falls with a greater splash. The boat stops tilting, relieved of the weight of one would-be hit man. Randy collapses onto the bench seat as Ambrose watches the spot where it fell, willing it all the way to the bottom to remain for the end of time. Silence except for waves lapping against the hull.

"Happy?" Randy asks.

"Glad it's done." Then, though it seems like a weird thing to say: "Thanks."

Randy looks up at him. "You're fucking welcome."

Ambrose sinks onto the edge of the seat, unsure what to say next. Finally, Randy stands and goes to the front. He pushes a gear shift forward and turns the key in the ignition. It sputters but doesn't start. He tries again with the same result.

Ambrose sits up straighter. "What's the matter?" The smell of gasoline wafts through the otherwise crystal-clear air. "I smell gas."

"It may be flooded."

"Flooded?"

"It did this once when me and Bennie were here." He reaches into the console and gets a flashlight.

"You can fix it, right?"

"There's a couple things I can try. Have to wait a few minutes to restart."

Ambrose's shoulders ache, nerves on fire. Beautiful as it is out here, he wants to be back on shore. "You only tried twice, maybe third time's the charm." He leans forward, reaching toward the key.

"Don't touch that," Randy snaps. "Keep your goddamn filthy hands to yourself!"

"All right." Ambrose sits back, takes out a cigarette, shaky. Kept it together so far, but things are fraying around the edges. It's not even that late, but he feels like it's 4AM, and he can't tell if it's tracers he's seeing or shooting stars. "Long's you know how to fix it."

"I just know what I saw her do when it happened. I don't know anything else." He looks pointedly at Ambrose. "I don't even want to know anything else."

"Still talking 'bout the boat?"

"You got me out here, got your way, got rid of your shit—whatever that was—and I never wanted to know about any of this."

"You don't." Ambrose starts to light the cigarette then wonders if it's safe to be smoking with gas fumes in the air, though they're getting fainter with the breeze. "None of this ever happened."

"What the fuck do you mean 'none of this ever happened'? If you hadn't dragged me up here, I'd be watching TV with Bennie instead of helping you do whatever *this* is!"

"Didn't put a gun to your head and I'm paying you a thousand bucks. Whatever happened to 'dirty deeds done dirt cheap'? Time was, I bet you'd do this for a hundred or less."

"But that was— It's different now. Anyway, what's dirty about it? You're admitting we just did something dirty?"

"I didn't—"

"You don't have to say it." He rests his forehead on the steering wheel. "Goddamn you. I'm trying to go straight."

So tired now, and out here on this lake that might as well be an ocean. All the nonstop work of scheming and manipulating have sapped whatever reserves Ambrose thought he had. He sighs, sliding lower in the seat, gazing up at the sky. "Hard going straight when you're broke, isn't it? I mean, you got a place to live, but nothing's yours. She gives you money just in case you need it. Don't want to take it, but you do, 'cause without it, you wouldn't have any. . ."

Randy sits up again, hands loosely resting on the wheel. "Well, you can have this money back. Not supposed to be a job anyway, just a favor. I'll soon be working for myself. I don't work for you."

"Keep it," Ambrose says, starting to fade. "Do you really want to have to ask Bennie for cigarette money? Again?"

"Do you really have to be such a cock-sucking asshole?" Randy demands.

Ambrose softly laughs. "How much longer before you can try cranking this thing?"

"Look, I said I didn't want to know, and I really don't, but. . . Who'd you kill, Ambrose?"

"I didn't kill anybody." His gaze shifts toward the sky again, hoping to see a real falling star, just to make a wish. "But if there's any heat from this, it's on me. I'll tell 'em I forced you out here, at gunpoint."

Randy smiles. "You don't even have a gun on you right now." Then, smile fading, "Do you?"

Ambrose draws the polished .38, opens and spins the chamber, then snaps it shut.

"I'll be goddamn. Where'd you get that?"

"Never you mind," Ambrose says. Dangerous being so tired. Then, just before he drifts off to the gentle rocking of the waves: "Anyway, it's done. Tomorrow morning I'll buy you a big breakfast."

✳✳✳

The next afternoon, when Randy arrives back at the apartment nearly dead on his feet, Bennie's on the sofa, laptop open on the table, coffee mug close at hand. She turns, smiles to see him. "Hey! I'm so glad you're back!" She runs over, embraces, and kisses him. He drops his overnight bag on the floor, holding her. "Did you have a good time?" she asks, then pulls back to look at him. "Everything okay?"

"Great."

"Catch any fish?"

"Not a goddamn one."

"Why am I not surprised?" She smiles, going to the refrigerator.

He shuffles over to collapse onto the sofa.

She brings him one of those craft beers with some crazy hipster artwork on the label. "So, what did you guys do?" She sits next to him as he takes a long swig with notes of fennel.

Something about the odd flavor of the beer reminds him that bad smell in the car was gone on the way back. "Went to a couple of casinos. Out to dinner."

"No strippers?"

He smiles. "No strippers."

"No. . . controversial things discussed?"

"Nope. Just boring, harmless bullshit."

She looks relieved. "Good." She gets back up to rummage around the pantry.

He rubs his eyes, hoping she won't notice the dark circles. *Never wanted to keep any secrets from her. . .*

"It'll be good if you and Ambrose can just be friends," she says. "And Rajit and Terrence of course."

"They ended up not going," he says. "Something came up. But don't worry, everything was fine."

"Oh. . ." She's making a snack over on the kitchen table. Getting out some nuts and chips. "Hey, by the way, did you and him do a little night fishing?"

"Nah." He turns to look at her. "Why?"

"Lake security called yesterday evening. We've known Lester and Buddy for a long time, and they have my number. Said there was a different car parked out by the boat house. When they described it, I knew it was Jessica's, so I told them it was you and some friends of ours."

"You told 'em it was me? And some friends?"

"Sure." She sets the snack tray on the coffee table and sits next to him. "Figured the only reason you'd take the car down there was if you had fishing stuff."

He takes another swig of beer, wincing at the licorice flavor and that she had to tell lake security anything.

"How'd it go, driving the boat?"

"It went fine," he says. "Piece of cake."

✳✳✳

Ambrose has a couple drinks after getting in from Tahoe, collapses face-first onto the bed, then wakes in the morning with a headache. He takes a couple aspirin, slips on a bathrobe, and turns up the heat before heading into the kitchen. Everything that's happened the last couple days feels like a dream but remembering the gun in the nightstand reminds him that it really did happen.

He sighs, leaning on the counter as coffee brews, the aroma dispelling clouds gathering in his brain but not the growing confusion. He folds his arms, staring at the shapes in the tile as shafts of sunlight begin streaming in.

Halfway through his first cup, he realizes that although Rajit's and Terrence's reasons for using their gonzo-cyber virtuosity to rage against the machine may be different than his own, they all took risks, stand to benefit from this new venture and could be in danger, too. He hears a note of panic in Rajit's voice when he calls to tell him to keep their doors locked when they get back from Santa Monica, not to answer any door unless they know beyond a shadow of a doubt who's there, and to watch their backs. "There are complications but not to worry," he tells him. "We'll deal with it." They're coming back to the city tomorrow, and he'll take them out to lunch, someplace out of the way where they can talk.

Thinking proactively helps to keep raw, debilitating fear at bay. He's determined not to slip back into his old patterns. *Fight, not flight— not anymore.* Just like he decided to finally face Lang, and go behind the coffee shop that day to see who left that quasi-threatening note, to be the first to pull the trigger yesterday instead of waiting for that poker-faced thug who had it coming, and whose boss had also better watch his goddamned step: That's the mindset he has to adopt, especially without Miss Dover around to slap sense into him. And she'd talked to him that day like she knew she wouldn't always be there, like she knew he'd cross this bridge one day. Kill your Buddha, they say. Maybe even the best and brightest, bad-ass, fabulous mentors eventually have to step, fall, or be shoved aside. Or just up and die.

As he refills his mug, he hears his phone ringing faintly in the bedroom. Heart pounding, he goes to answer it. Is this the way it'll be from now on, he wonders, walking through the living room. Panic every time the phone rings? Better just learn to handle it.

It's Jessica. The last person he expected.

"Hello?"

"Ambrose?"

Just hearing her say his name after all that's happened. . . "Hey! How're you doing?"

"I'm very well, thanks," then, "I have someone else here who wants to say hello." She must be holding the phone up to Beau because there's that carefree exclamation: "Am!"

"Hey, Beau." Ambrose sinks onto the bed, tears swelling in his eyes, melting his new resolve like high tide demolishing a sandcastle. "Gosh, I miss you. It's not the same around here without you and mommy. I miss you both."

"Miss you too," Beau says. "Boy night!"

"Yeah, we'll have a boy's night when you get home, that's for sure. I'll have everything ready. Tent, popcorn, your favorite movies. . ." He has to stop for a moment, conscious of the gap between that reality and this one in which he finds himself. "I can't wait."

Jessica comes back on the line. "We can't wait either," she says, then her voice shifts as if she's only speaking to him: "That's why we wanted to call and tell you to come over here and bring us home."

Joy and anxiety rise in his throat. "What?"

"We want you to come here for a visit, then we're going home."

"But— What about the retreat?"

"Great so far, and the place is beautiful, but something's come up that I need to talk to you about. I want us to talk in person. Can you meet me in Paris next week?"

He lies back on the bed, still holding the phone. Things are getting surreal now, and even the coffee can't hold back that floaty feeling you get when you have a fever or are on no sleep for more than 24 hours. *Her wanting to talk in person could be good or bad, but it won't be neutral. And Paris . . . Miss Dover's ghost is still there.* "Sure, I'll meet you in Paris," he hears himself say.

"Wonderful!" She sounds happy enough. "I'll book you a flight and call you back, okay?"

"Okay."

"'Bye!"

"Bye." He clicks the phone off, staring at the ceiling.

THIRTEEN

According to Sergei, Maxim has completely broken with Alexei, and is currently living in exile at Sergei's place in London. Apparently, Maxim told Sergei of his concern about a young man, one of her former employees, who may be in over his head with Alexei. Sergei wants to know, what does she know of this young man?

The freedom she'd sought—financial, creative and otherwise—is now hers, yet that shard of glass still tears at her heart. Much as she's always fancied herself a breaker of rules, creator of her own universe, she can't insulate herself from the guilt she feels that Ambrose has gotten caught up in all this. Never wanted to have any regret for the radical choice she'd made, having thought it over carefully and decided there was nothing back in the States she couldn't live without, but Ambrose was in her blind spot. She'd tried to leave him well-set, but anything to do with Alexei isn't Ambrose's fault; it's her trouble. If he's been contaminated by her fallout. . . As she catches sight of herself passing the mirror, there's a worried look on her face.

What kind of help can she offer from the grave? Sergei warned her not to get involved and gave Maxim strict instructions to stay out of it. Sergei liked Maxim, but Maxim's loyalty to his ice-cold brother had always been a sticking point. Now Sergei is willing to give him a chance, she senses against his own better judgement. Maybe he thinks he can use Maxim somehow. No matter, she thinks. Let them hug all that out.

But in the meantime, all she can think about is that Ambrose needs help, and she isn't really sure how to give it.

✳✳✳

The flight to Paris is a form of suspended animation. Over the Atlantic, no one can touch him. During that window of time, he stares ahead, trying not to think too hard about anything, least of all what'll transpire by the time he makes the return trip. Jessica sounds upbeat but wouldn't say what she wants to talk about in person, so he tries not to think about that either. Whatever it might be.

Still. The dead Russian.

He shifts uncomfortably in his first-class seat. He killed a man but it wasn't murder. *If it wasn't murder, why'd he hide it?* The man raised a gun at him, so Ambrose figures he was perfectly within his rights. And then there was Maxim freaking out, but that wasn't why Ambrose did it. It was him or me, Ambrose thinks for the thousandth time. Alexei found out about the cyber-shit and sent his hit man.

Nagging in the back of his mind, however, are the gaps in what he knows. He knows Miss Dover is dead. He knows Alexei is a crook who's glad she's dead. Maxim believes Alexei's behind it all and Maxim's flown the coop. He nearly had a heart attack over this guy showing up. But where's Mignon/Margarite in all this? Was the guy he killed the one Rajit and Terrence saw watching the cheap motel where Jessica and Mignon had their tryst? What was he doing there? In that text Mignon sent to Jessica that Ambrose shouldn't have read, Mignon said she thought someone was following her. Was he there to find Mignon? Maybe, as Rajit had said that day, this Russian was a jealous boyfriend?

If so, Ambrose wonders, had he and Maxim just gotten in the crossfire of some romantic fight between two of Alexei's operatives? Had Ambrose sacrificed his eternal soul unknowingly defending the honor of the bitch who seduced Jessica? And now he could not only end up alone, but alone in the gas chamber. Not to mention now Randy's in on this whole thing. In on the worst part anyway, and all because Ambrose wasn't smart enough to figure out something else. Only in desperation had he reached out to Randy. The only saving grace might be that if Randy wants to turn him in, he knows it would hurt Bennie. And Randy said that day by the fountain that he'd die before that.

Ambrose shifts around in his seat, uttering under his breath, "Fuck." He sighs, opens his eyes, and sees the elderly lady in the next seat gazing at him with a polite half-smile. "I'm sorry," he quietly tells her. "I really didn't mean to say that out loud."

She says something in French that he doesn't understand, but she doesn't seem the least bit offended. She leans her seat back, turns off the reading light. She says something in a pleasant tone, laughs, pulls her wrap snug around her shoulders and closes her eyes.

✳✳✳

Tea At The Savoy in London is a festive affair, even if Maxim is alone to enjoy it. He has a table near the gazebo, under the domed skylight, soothing piano music surrounding him as he refills his teacup with first bloom Darjeeling, and gazes at the shopping bags from his favorite store on Saville Row.

The drive back to his Presidio Heights flat the day Dimitri was killed had been a blur, as had the ransacking of said San Francisco flat, grabbing the things he needed most that would fit into his standard international carry-on. He'd nearly pulled out his back getting his passport from under the mattress and hadn't had a chance to clean out the refrigerator, but no matter. Survival was all he could think about, along with the high that would accompany arriving at the Prince Albert Hotel in South Kensington.

Since the break from Alexei and flight to London with his heart in his throat, head pounding, better things are in motion. He admires the delectable pastries on the three-tiered dessert stand gracing the table. That he's sitting in the lap of luxury, following such a harrowing departure, is not lost on him.

He takes a taxi back to Sergei's home in Chelsea, having decamped from the lovely but crowded Prince Albert just yesterday. It was overrun with tourists, and Maxim is most pleased to have this place more-or-less to himself. Sergei is in Monaco this month, to return in a couple weeks. After a most intense phone conversation wherein Maxim told him he was no longer representing Alexei in any of his dealings, and renouncing Alexei's most recent aberrant behavior, Sergei seemed receptive to further repairing his and Maxim's relationship, never having believed Maxim had been on board with Alexei's worst plans but allowed himself to be cowed by his older, far more forceful brother.

Maxim mentioned Ambrose in the conversation, because the boy had been foremost in his mind, and the guilt of leaving him there with dead Dimitri had caused great distress. Given Sergei's waning predilection for violence, Maxim didn't disclose the details of what happened, just that Alexei may go after those in the Duchess's orbit who dared resist him, and this young man resists.

For now, the only people ever here with Maxim in the pleasant three-story home are the cook, the cleaning lady, and Sergei's personal assistant, Lilly. She's the daughter of a local barrister, a comely lass who attends classes at London School of Economics, and spends the occasional evening playing darts at pubs. How much her father might be involved in Sergei's business dealings, Maxim doesn't know. She's been most kind to him since he's been here. Professional, efficient.

For the last week, he's re-established his morning routine of coffee from a French press along with two pieces of flax seed toast. This he enjoys in the private garden behind the house, under a white canvas umbrella. Lilly has her coffee here, too, always accompanied by some confection from the bakery around the corner. He enjoys watching her eat while she organizes Sergei's mail. Éclairs seem a favorite, along with the occasional Napoleon. Things with chocolate and cream. He finds himself studying her fascinating face as she indulges. Long eyelashes, bee-stung lips. . . He's started to notice more frequent eye contact between them, a growing attraction perhaps? Yes, he's quite older than her, but something in her eyes. . .

"What're your plans for today, Mr. Rusovich?" she asks with that lilting, cheery accent.

"Nothing special. Perhaps just a walk in the park."

"Lovely," she says, only, slipping from those lips, it comes out, *loovely*. "I'll be going out on some errands soon." She smiles at him over Sergei's stack of mail, sorting the unwieldy hodge-podge that appears under the letter slot each morning. "Mr. Dobrev's instructed me to make to you feel quite at home, so if there's anything you need or want me to get for you, don't hesitate to ask."

"You're doing more than enough, my dear. Please call me Maxim."

"Ah, very well. Maxim." Bite of éclair, licking those lips. Sip of coffee. That look.

Maxim shifts in his chair, watching as she picks up a midsize flat package.

"Hello? This one's addressed to me!" She looks at the sender's label. "From Paris!"

"One of your many admirers, no doubt."

"Oh, aren't you kind?" Peering at the label again. "Actually, looks as though it's from a new associate of Mr. Dobrev's. . ." She opens it and takes out a garment that's been carefully folded and tucked into cellophane wrap. "It can't be!" A black mini dress with leather straps crisscrossing the bodice, silver grommet accents, and a black skirt with tulle overlay. "Oh, my. . . It's just lovely." She stands, holds it up to herself. "Do you like it, Maxim?"

"Very much, my dear."

"Pretty, but a bit naughty, yeah?"

"Much like yourself, I suspect," Maxim ventures, pouring another cup from the French press.

"Aren't we cheeky this morning!" She laughs, draping the dress over an adjacent chair before sitting back down, reaching into the box to remove a small package in pink cellophane and ribbon, and a card. She reads. "Why it's from Phoebe herself!"

"Phoebe?"

"From one of her upcoming lines, along with a little something to go with my afternoon tea." Referring to the pink cellophane package: "Macarons from Ladurée. Mr. Dobrev put her onto these. He orders boxes of them as gifts and absolutely got her hooked. I'll share these with you, of course."

"I'd just as soon watch you eat them, my dear."

She glances at him. Those eyelashes.

"I wasn't aware Sergei was now in the fashion industry. Most exciting."

She sips her coffee. "Oh, he's mainly advising on a few points of business, I believe. I served as a virtual assistant of sorts until she got an office setup." She looks at the dress, reaching out to fondle the tulle at the hem. "This is quite a nice thank-you."

"Indeed. Why don't you go try it on?"

She looks pleasantly surprised. "You mean now?"

"I would deem it an honor and a privilege to be the first to see you in such an exquisite frock."

"Well. . . All right!" She gets the dress, starts off. "You'll wait here, then?"

"Of course."

She goes into the house. Maxim sits back in sweet anticipation, amid ripples of excitement that she's trying on clothes for him. And such clothes. He drifts back in memory to a corset the Duchess wore. All those straps. Thinking of her makes him think of Ambrose and again of his own guilt. He looks over the stuff on the table for distraction. The card that came with the dress carries an abstract logo and the words **Aquarius Rising**. Personal note. *Nice touch.* He picks up one of the items in the bottom of the flat box. A photograph of a young man, possibly the designer himself, along with a most striking—and most familiar-looking—woman. She has one arm around his shoulders, the frame cuts off half her image but nevertheless. . . He stares closely. *It looks like the Duchess, but that can't be. Besides, the hair is different, and the Duchess didn't wear glasses.*

But the resemblance is uncanny. He holds the photo closer, straining his eyes. The woman in the photo has a small tattoo on the inside of her right wrist. He takes out his readers, which he often slips into his pocket prior to breakfast for perusing *The Times*. It's a tattoo of a dove holding an olive branch.

Maxim removes the glasses, sitting back in the chair as his heart starts pounding, pulse quickening. He reaches for the small pill bottle in his other pocket.

✳✳✳

Ambrose manages to somehow navigate Paris Charles de Gaulle Airport and get a taxi to the hotel where she'd reserved him a room with a balcony. Since he's only traveled by plane to Dallas, she sent him a list of what to do, like triple-check he had his passport and credit card, and what not do, like accept an offer of a taxi ride into Paris from any rando. He'd applied for a passport some time ago, just in case he'd need to meet with Miss Dover while she was abroad. . . Uneasily, he notices that the photo looks like a mug shot.

He arrives at the hotel, and though he'd been nervous about the language barrier, all goes well getting checked in. He converted some money before he left Palo Alto, so has a tip ready for the bellhop. "*Merci, Monsieur! Merci beaucoup.*" he says, along with something else Ambrose doesn't understand, then goes out and shuts the door.

Ambrose turns to look at the room. It's a suite. The bedroom is through the double doors and what he's standing in is more like a sitting room. Looks like a really nice small apartment, decorated mid-century modern. Jessica and Beau will be arriving tomorrow around lunch time, and she said to get some rest, go exploring if he wanted to. It all sounds good, but he finds himself wondering what's the catch. Maybe his own situation is the catch.

He walks through the double glass doors to the balcony. The morning view of Paris rooftops and the Eiffel Tower takes his breath away and tears sting his eyes. People always say, "Be in the moment," so for this brief, shining moment, he is.

✳✳✳

Rajit opens a cardboard box containing modems, cables, and peripherals needed to get things running in the new office, while Terrence sweeps it with an electronic bug- and camera-detector. "I really don't think that's necessary," Rajit comments as Terrence walks around with the device.

"Can't hurt," Terrence responds. "'Specially after he said, 'Trust no one.'"

Rajit doesn't argue.

"Any word from him, by the way?"

"He arrived safe and sound."

"Think he'll go to the place where. . . you know. *It* happened?"

"Where what happened?"

"Where that Dover woman died. Does he plan on doing any digging of his own, or—"

"I seriously doubt it. He's really only going to meet. . ."

"Meet who?"

"Jessica. I'm not sure whether to call her his girlfriend. They seem beyond that."

"I saw a picture of her. Pretty." Then, with a glance at Rajit: "So's Bennie for that matter. And sweet. She's really nice, isn't she?" He notes Rajit's pause unloading the box. "Guess she'll always be the one that got away."

Rajit turns to him, aggravated. "Please do me a favor and shut your goddamn mouth."

Terrence laughs.

The new phone on the floor rings. "Answer the phone."

"Not my job."

"I am the boss in Ambrose's absence, so kindly answer the fucking phone."

Terrence goes to answer it, sitting cross-legged on the dull hardwood floor. "Dover, Inc.. Hello. . . He's out of town, can I take a message?"

Rajit tosses him a Post-It pad and pen.

He picks them up, still listening to the caller. "I don't really think I can give out that information. . ."

Rajit turns.

Terrence looks at him steadily through those glasses. "Sure. Could you spell that last name for me, please?"

Rajit sits by the phone, watching Terrence take down the name and number. He grabs the Post-It as soon as he's done.

"Sure thing, Mr. Rusovich. I will pass that information along. . . Yes. . . You're welcome, sir." Terrence clicks off the phone, looks up.

"Which Mr. Rusovich?" Rajit asks.

"Maxim. Says it's urgent."

✳✳✳

Ambrose goes to Montparnasse, the area on the Left Bank, that Miss Dover always talked about. He has dinner at a place called Café Degas: flank steak, French fries, and haricot vert with red wine and a crêpe calvados, which he learns is a pear crepe made with apple and pear brandy for dessert. This part of the city is much like he'd imagined Paris. As evening falls, he strolls sidewalks, past quaint shops, bakeries, cafés, through open squares under tiny, white lights strung through trees. He still carries a mild buzz from the wine. He keeps thinking about Miss Dover. Even those thoughts could've softened into fond memories with the coming of night and intensifying glow of lights in windows, flickering candles on tables where small groups gather for dinner and lively conversation, mostly in French, though he catches a few snippets of English here and there. Romantic couples sit lost in each other's gaze and he wonders if he and Jessica will enjoy that kind of closeness this time tomorrow night. Still, that frantic call from Rajit he received while walking to the Metro rings in his ears. "Call Maxim right away," he'd said. "It's urgent."

Ambrose gets to the foot of the Eiffel Tower at moonrise, walking back and forth in front of it a couple times, taking in the size and complexity of its real-life presence. He fights back sentimental tears before sitting down on a bench in a nearby park and allowing himself to cry, thinking back to that fateful day in Golden Gate Park when he finally broke down, called Bennie, and asked for help. He's come so far. From that hellhole existence in Texas, to the California dreamscape on Eucalyptus Lane, to being right here in Paris. And tomorrow Jessica and Beau will be here. He dares himself to believe again that they can be a real family. If only. . .

He tries to swallow the lump in his throat, but he can't. He walks on back to the hotel to return Maxim's call, with the feeling that if Maxim says it's urgent, the news isn't good.

✳✳✳

Champagne on ice back at the tearoom—not just for finally attaining what should have been Alexei's all along, but for regaining what he lost here, 20 years ago, when he and a few of his most trusted men excavated a space to house their future security. Little did he know that little square of prime real estate would be sealed like the pyramids when those who stole it from him added another layer of concrete to the blacktop and enclosed the garage more securely with a key swipe entrance. Now, however, this garage is a glorious cloak of invisibility so Lev can at last do this vital work, right under a skylight in the steel roof, no less.

If Dimitri were here, he'd be watching, too. Alexei's concern about Dimitri's disappearance is tempered with relief, after that wrong-headed effort at horning in as a partner. *The unmitigated gall of that humorless idiot. He was probably bluffing about knowing who drained that account, and even if he wasn't, the price he demanded was far too high. If he ever returns, he'll discover that in a most impactful way.*

In the back of his mind, irony of ironies, Alexei has to wonder if this is how Sergei felt when he unsuccessfully pulled some of his own presumptuous stunts. *Perhaps.* But still, Alexei had paid his dues longer, worked harder, and taken far more risks for Sergei than Dimitri ever did for him. And in the wake of all this upheaval, Margarite has left to try her luck in L.A. until things settle down. She confessed that Dimitri scared her and said that if something breaks for her down in SoCal, she'll stay there. Apparently, she's over that infatuation with the blonde artist/housewife as well, though he believes her leaving has more to do with being found out and fired than any real prospects or initiative on her part. And he had plans for her, too. Very big plans. *But no matter. More than likely, she'll come crawling back.*

Watching the sweaty flesh of Lev's upper arms jiggle with each pulse of the jackhammer, Alexei reflects on Maxim's sudden departure, whether his and Dimitri's could be somehow related. Dimitri had gone to find Maxim, and whether he ever made contact is unlikely, but unknown. Maxim's meddling will not be missed, and neither will the Dover woman, if that's what one could call her. The one who magically signed on the dotted line before passing, that decadent lifestyle finally claiming her. His contacts in France lost track of her. They may have bungled any attempt to cause an "unfortunate accident" anyway. Fate beat them to it. He would have had to stay right on top of them and he has other things demanding his attention. *Anyway, one shouldn't speak badly of the dead, so, good. She's dead.*

Alexei sighs, folds his arms, and begins pacing a wide circle around the opening created by Lev's patient, methodical approach. Alexei had been willing to provide some help with this, but Lev assured that would not be necessary.

For the best. The thought had once crossed Alexei's mind that, like with the construction of the pyramids and the burials of pharaohs with their treasures, if more muscle had been required, he might've had to kill any additional workers and leave them buried to ensure their silence, a messy and most unpleasant business. But one does what one must do. Lev is the only one who knows his place, and the only one Alexei can still somewhat trust.

After the top layer of concrete is removed to a wheelbarrow, and the last piece of blacktop that's blocking access to the metal square below crumbles, Lev puts the jackhammer aside. Alexei, having removed his jacket, rolled up his sleeves, and loosened his tie, sweats from the heat and watching Lev sweat so profusely. He hands Lev a crowbar. When the 4x4 metal square is removed, Alexei hands him a flashlight. Lev drops into the vault below to assess the condition of pharaoh's treasure.

"Well?" Alexei asks. "Tell me what you see."

"Everything perfectly intact," Lev answers. Grinning, he hands up a metal ammo box.

Alexei sets the box on the edge of the gaping hole, kneels and opens it. He takes out an item the size of a box of dryer sheets, wrapped in leaves, stamped with a gold logo. He pauses momentarily, swiping the sweat from his forehead with his other wrist, before finally tearing into the neat package.

"And?" Lev asks. "Success?"

Alexei tosses away the leaf wrapping to reveal a solid brick of rich, brown Afghan opium. "Success."

✳✳✳

The brief conversation with Maxim isn't what Ambrose expected, and he's not exactly sure what it *is* about. Maxim sounds kind of fucked-up, all nervous, claiming he can't just come out and say it because Ambrose wouldn't believe it. "It's something you'll have to see for yourself." Maxim says he's done some checking, calling the address on Lilly's package (*Lilly?*), pretending to be a buyer for a department store, an old friend of Phoebe Grace's and—because he knew of her love of Ladurée Macarons—the person he spoke to allowed that she stopped at the Rue Bonaparte location each morning to bring a dozen to the office, and that everyone dropped what they were doing to come claim their favorite flavor.

Ambrose tries to get clarification, asking, "Who the hell's Phoebe?"

Maxim simply says, "Be at the Ladurée Shop in 21 Rue Bonaparte at 9AM tomorrow, and all will be revealed."

Then Ambrose hears a female voice in the background.

"Please don't forget. 9AM. Talk later." Maxim hangs up.

Maxim makes no sense, but piques Ambrose's curiosity enough to get up, eat an early breakfast, and make his way to the macaron shop just to see what will happen. Jessica and Beau will be arriving at the hotel around lunch time. He buys a box of macarons to take back to the room, and another to have shipped back to Bennie and Randy, along with a book containing some recipes Bennie might like. He hasn't seen Randy since dropping him off after their night on the lake. A box of French macarons won't make up for dragging him from home under false pretenses to dispose of a body. *But maybe it's a start. That and the thousand bucks.*

Ambrose walks around near the macaron shop, swinging the bakery bag by the handle, smoking a cigarette. The sun shines brighter as anticipation grows for seeing Jessica and Beau. He's feeling better today, looking forward to being close to them again. He glances at his watch. *Whatever mystery this is should be solved within the next five minutes or so.* He surveys the street corner. Everything looks normal enough. No sign of anything happening that will "reveal all" as Maxim claimed.

As he turns, he sees a black Bentley pulling up by the curb: driver in the front, one passenger in the back. The back window goes down and a worker from the shop hands it to the passenger. Ambrose tosses the cigarette and walks closer. It's a woman with long, straight hair and glasses. . . *Could be a celebrity in that she looks familiar.* She smiles at the clerk, pressing a tip into her hand. The window goes up as the car creeps forward, giving a cyclist the right of way. Ambrose's gaze connects with the woman. For a moment, he feels the world turning slowly on its axis. Staring into each other's eyes, shock registers on both their faces: hers through the car window and his reflected in the glass. She excitedly tells the driver to go. Ambrose regains himself enough to run after the car, down the block, before it turns a corner and, winded as he is, he can only get there soon enough to see it turn the corner. Then it's gone.

He stands there catching his breath, experiencing a gamut of emotions, from relief and joy to anger and bewilderment. *It was her.* She knew him, recognized him, then took off as quickly as she could. *It was Miss Dover, though what she calls herself now. . . What was that Maxim had said? Phoebe Grace? No, it was her.* She didn't stop to ask why he was in Paris or tell him how she's alive when everyone thinks she's dead. *Maybe she thought I'd come looking for her. She clearly doesn't want to be found.*

Ambrose takes out his phone to call Rajit. Voicemail. "Hey Rajit," he says after the tone. "Just want to let y'all know we'll be changing the name of the place." He stares down the street into the urban oblivion where Miss Dover—or whatever her name is— disappeared. "I don't know what it's going to be, but it won't be Dover, Inc. anymore."

✳✳✳

Jessica and Beau leave after her morning sickness subsides, arriving at Aix-en-Provence Airport around 10:15 and landing in Paris by 12:30, just in time for a nice lunch. Tonight, she wants to have dinner in; there's plenty of time to go out the rest of the week, and what she wants to tell him won't wait much longer. She's already called and made arrangements for something special.

As the driver unloads her luggage and the bellman loads a cart to meet her upstairs, she and Beau go to the elevator. Jessica hadn't expected to feel this nervous seeing Ambrose for the first time after this "break." Using her key to walk into the room, carrying Beau on her hip, she almost calls out to Ambrose, then sees him on the balcony. His back is to the door, both hands on the railing to look out at the city.

"Hey," she says, setting Beau on the floor.

Ambrose turns to see Beau running toward him.

"Am!" Beau exclaims.

"Hey, Beau!" He scoops up Beau and hugs him. He really has missed Beau.

Seeing the expression on his face only makes Jessica want to tell him that much sooner so she doesn't know if she can wait until tonight. "God, I've missed you."

"We missed you, too," Beau says.

Ambrose looks at Jessica. "Did you?"

"We did," she confesses, moving to hug them both. "We both missed you so much."

"Seems like a year's passed."

"I know. Enough time to for me to—*us* to think, right?"

"Right." He sets Beau down on the floor and Beau promptly runs into the bedroom, checking out the place.

The bellman arrives and Ambrose tips him generously.

Jessica notices the box of macarons on the table. "Oh, I love these! How'd you know?"

". . .Little bird told me."

She slips her arms around his waist. "And who is this smart little bird that knows those macarons are our favorite?"

He pauses, like reaching for words, then: "Really just a lucky guess." He wraps his arms around her. "I'm so glad you called me."

"Me, too."

He pulls back to look at her. "What is it you want to talk to me about?" He looks nervous about what it might be, and she's getting more nervous about what he might say.

All thoughts of waiting go out the window. Glancing back at Beau tearing into his *Star Wars* backpack on the coffee table, Jessica grasps Ambrose's hand and pulls him back out onto the balcony. "I could've said it on the phone, but I just had to tell you in person."

"Tell me what?"

"I'm pregnant," she says, smiling. "I just found out the other day."

"Pregnant?" he echoes.

"Yes," she laughs, drawing her arms around his neck.

He looks shocked, but she goes on.

"And I couldn't be happier. I know before I left things were. . . I don't know. Off? With us. But I haven't been able to think about anything except you and—" She stops, looks him in the eyes. "Will you marry me?"

He seems to go weak, leaning against the balcony railing.

She still has her arms around him, awaiting his answer, searching his face for signs beyond the initial shock.

"Yes," he breathes, looking deeply into her eyes for the first time since their longest separation. "I'll marry you." He wraps his arms around her tighter, holding her body close to his.

She won't be taking moments like this for granted anymore.

Maybe he won't either.

And nothing will ever be the same again.

MORE FROM
OUTCAST PRESS

Percocet Summer by Paige Johnson encompasses the rush of the solstice, odd obsessions, and other crushables (people and pills and moods). From Florida sweat to Georgia peach sweetness, NYC high-rollers to skidding-by wannabes, these 35+ illustrated poems cover all the shady crevices of a summer well-wasted.

We're talking the lows of eating disorders and intervention, to the throes of psychedelia and romance. Gas station syringes and cotton candy softness. This collection blurs dirty realism and noir like a Lana Del Rey love song.

MORE FROM

NEVADA MCPHERSON

Poser, the first novel in the Eucalyptus Lane series, offers a class-conscious, peeping tom gaze into Silicon Valley's bedrooms and back-alleys, where dreams come true and unlikely, life-altering connections are made—for better or worse. Ambrose, a failed Bay Area drug dealer, has run afoul of his wicked connection too many times. He hides out in Palo Alto by posing as a Stanford grad student.

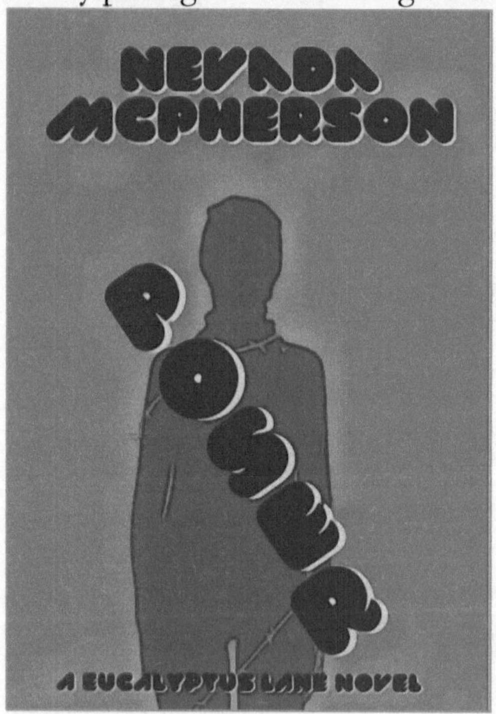

There, Ambrose settles into upscale suburban life and finds himself falling for Jessica, a lonely housewife/artist. Jessica's husband is a tech tycoon whose path crossed with Ambrose on a drug-fueled club night. When Ambrose's cover is blown, secrets spill and lies shatter on a posh, limestone patio deep in the heart of this California dreamscape.

ABOUT THE AUTHOR

Twitter: @ **NevadaMcPherso3**

Instagram: **@NevadaWrites**

Nevada McPherson lives in Milledgeville, Georgia, where she enjoys going for walks, taking pictures, and painting when she isn't keeping her husband Bill and Chihuahua Mitzi out of trouble. A graduate of LSU's MFA Creative Writing Program, McPherson has written several award-winning screenplays, nonfiction pieces, and graphic novels.

The latter includes *Uptowners*, a noir family drama set in New Orleans, its London-based sequel, *Queensgate*, and *Piano Lessons*, which is a gay teen romance set in the 1950s rural south. *Poser* was her debut novel. She also writes on film, books, and pop culture at the Backstage Blog on her website:

www.nevada-mcpherson.com